Advance praise for *The Han Agent*

"Amy Rogers's latest medical thriller, *The Han Agent*, is as exciting as it is frighteningly realistic. It could be tomorrow's headline. Here is a story fraught with tension, sudden explosive action, and threaded through with scientific accuracy and speculation that will leave you stunned. Read it...if only to prepare yourself for what might soon become true."

—James Rollins, #1 *New York Times* bestselling author of Sigma Force

"In a stunning 'what-if' author-scientist Amy Rogers resurrects the idea of Unit 731, Japan's notorious wartime biological weapons division, weaving together a diabolical tale of science, genocide, and modern-day bio-terror. Sobering, suspenseful, and absolutely chilling."

—Barry Lancet, award-winning author of *The Spy Across the Table* and *Tokyo Kill*

"In this gripping thriller, World War II-era history, ultranationalism, and biological genocide intertwine. *The Han Agent* is a surefire genre hit, fast-paced and full of elements of mystery and adventure.

—*Foreword Reviews* magazine

"*The Han Agent* will get your heart pounding and your blood boiling. Putting huge swaths of humanity in its crosshairs, this pressure cooker of a thriller portrays with chilling realism how individuals can use specialized scientific knowledge for good or evil."

—J.E. Fishman, bestselling author of *Primacy* and the Bomb Squad NYC series

"In this tense thriller, the scientific questions beget intrigue and terror."

—Toni Dwiggins, author of *Badwater* and *Quicksilver* (Forensic Geology series)

D0792429

PRAISE FOR PREVIOUS NOVELS BY AMY ROGERS

"Rogers artfully blends science and suspense in this top-notch thriller. Fans of Michael Palmer and Robin Cook novels will love this book."

—Brian Andrews, author of *Beijing Red* and *Tier One*

"...takes readers on a wild ride across the frontiers of science. It's a fun, frightening and memorable novel."

—Mark Alpert, *Scientific American* editor and author of *Extinction*

"The science is a consistent presence, easy to understand, enriching the story. A smart, tightly written, scary science thriller." —*Kirkus Reviews*

"This is the best science thriller I've read this year. Maybe ever." —BookTrib

"A great example of lab lit in what I think of as the Crichtonesque School of epic science disaster writing." —LabLit.com

"Compellingly written, technically literate."

—LA Starks, author of *The Pythogoras Conspiracy*

THE HAN AGENT

ALSO BY AMY ROGERS:

PETROPLAGUE

REVERSION

THE HAN
AGENT

AMY ROGERS

SCIENCETHRILLERS MEDIA

ScienceThrillers Media

Publisher@ScienceThrillersMedia.com
www.ScienceThrillersMedia.com

Publisher's Cataloging-In-Publication Data
(Prepared by The Donohue Group, Inc.)

Names: Rogers, Amy, 1969-
Title: The Han Agent / Amy Rogers.
Description: First edition. | Sacramento, CA : ScienceThrillers Media, 2017. | Series: [Microes] ; [1]
Identifiers: ISBN 978-1-940419-15-2 (trade paperback) | ISBN 978-1-940419-18-3 (hardcover) | ISBN 978-1-940419-17-6 (large print) | ISBN 978-1-940419-16-9 (ebook)
Subjects: LCSH: Women scientists--Japan--Fiction. | Japanese American women--Japan--Fiction. | Avian influenza--Asia--Fiction. | Biological weapons--Japan--Fiction. | Genocide--China--Fiction. | Genetic engineering--Fiction. | LCGFT: Thrillers (Fiction) | Medical fiction. | Science fiction.
Classification: LCC PS3618.O44 H36 2017 (print)| LCC PS3618.O44 (ebook) | DDC 813/.6--dc23
Library of Congress Control Number: 2017906108

FIC031040 FICTION/Thrillers/Medical
FIC028020 FICTION/Science Fiction/Hard Science Fiction
FIC028110 FICTION/Science Fiction/Genetic Engineering

Cover design by Xavier Comas, The Cover Kitchen www.coverkitchen.com

TO JASON

Han *(hän)*: The Han Chinese, Han people or simply Han (漢族; pinyin: Hànzú) are an ethnic group native to East Asia. They constitute approximately 92% of the population of China, 95% of Taiwan (Han Taiwanese), 76% of Singapore, 23% of Malaysia and about 18% of the global population. Han Chinese are the world's largest ethnic group with over 1.3 billion people. —*Wikipedia, The Free Encyclopedia*

Prologue

The logs were piled in rows four deep. They were stacked for burning in the stifling heat of the walled courtyard.

Smoke from the army's demolition work beyond the walls irritated his eyes. Major Masaji Ishii lit a cigarette anyway. Foul air at Pingfan was nothing new. After all these years, he barely noticed the stench. Excrement from the latrines. Singed fur from the incinerators. Formaldehyde from preserved tissues. Bacterial culture media, like sweet rotten meat. Bleach.

He kicked one of the logs and thought, what a terrible waste.

Unfortunately he had no choice. Three days ago, the Americans had attacked the home islands of Japan. Rumors said they had obliterated an entire city in one strike. Some kind of new explosive. A uranium bomb.

Masaji glared at the soldiers under his command as they flung more *maruta* onto the piles. Uranium, he grumbled. In the race to find the ultimate weapon and win the war, how did the American physicists beat the Japanese physicians?

He'd doubted the claims about the American bomb, but he could not ignore the urgent reports coming from the northern edge of Manchukuo. The Japanese Imperial Army had occupied the ethnically Chinese puppet state since 1931. Today, army scouts warned that the once-invincible military force was in full retreat.

Masaji knew what that meant.

The Soviets were coming.

And no matter what, the Soviets could not learn what Unit 731 had done at Pingfan.

A massive five-story building known as Ro block surrounded the barren grounds and concealed his soldiers' work. These remaining members of the deceptively named Kwantung Army Epidemic Prevention and Water Purification Unit, Number 731, wiped sweat from their brows as they dragged the last of the *maruta* from two small, windowless structures that cowered in the shadow of Ro block. Masaji moved into that shadow, pining for the dry wind that blew incessantly across the Manchurian plains on the other side. But inside Ro block, no person or thing was free, not even the wind.

His pencil hovered over his notebook, ready to document the exact number of *maruta* destroyed. For seven years he'd kept meticulous records of all the logs delivered to Pingfan—where the raw materials came from, the data they got from the logs, how the logs were disposed of when utterly used up. He was proud of the efficiencies he'd engineered in utilizing this scarce resource. With careful planning, they'd been able to recycle some of the *maruta* through multiple experiments. It was a shame to throw them away now, unspent, but his wise brother, General Shiro Ishii, had ordered the entire complex destroyed.

An explosion rocked the ground and crumbs of mortar fell from the walls of Ro block. Masaji Ishii realized he had lost count. Two hundred ten *maruta*? Two hundred eleven?

"Get the oil," he shouted.

His soldiers grunted and rolled barrels toward an enormous pit dug in the center of the courtyard. He spat out the butt of his cigarette and ground it with his heel in frustration. Time was running out. The high standards he'd consistently set for himself and for the scientists around him were collapsing like the buildings on the periphery of Pingfan. He had to estimate the *maruta* tally. His final data entries would be imprecise. The tip of his pencil angrily carved the page.

A subordinate approached, saluted and bowed. "Sir. Blocks Seven and Eight are empty."

Masaji searched the man's face and saw the usual combination of deep respect and fear. Like many of his fellow soldiers in Unit 731, this man was from the Ishiis' home village. The villagers shared a tribal loyalty not only to the Emperor, but also to the privileged Ishii family. Masaji's brother had stuffed the garrison with men like this, men he could trust. Now, at the end of things, this foresight was paying off. Because the Ishii brothers demanded it, for the rest of their lives the villagers would remain silent about what really happened at Pingfan.

Masaji nodded. "The Soviets have crossed the border."

"Our army will hold them," the soldier said.

"They will not," Masaji replied, expressing no emotion about this simple tactical truth. "First the Chinese jackals, then the Soviets, will come here. It's only a question of when."

The soldier stood rigid and said nothing more.

Masaji put steel in his words. "When they come, they must not find anything. This is our secret of secrets."

"Yes, sir. I understand."

"See that the task is completed swiftly. Other matters require my attention."

The soldier saluted, bowed, and turned, barking commands at the others who were now tossing the *maruta* into the pit with the oil.

Masaji walked briskly toward a fortified door leading into Ro block. On his way, he passed near the end of the stack of *maruta*.

One of the logs flexed an arm and groaned.

The major slackened his pace enough to draw his pistol and fire once into the *maruta's* skull.

No mistakes. No evidence.

The Soviets must find nothing but ashes.

Masaji emerged on the windowless outer side of Ro block, where the small military city of Pingfan sprawled across the desolate flats, ringed by earthen walls and barbed wire. In accordance with his brother's orders, the city was being razed. Only a few dozen buildings remained standing, including his private home, where his wife and four children—three of them born in Manchukuo—awaited evacuation.

A thick cloud of dust obscured the hot afternoon sun. Through the haze, Masaji surveyed the dismantling of his family's great achievement. Pingfan was his brother Shiro's brainchild, the crown jewel in Unit 731's extensive biological warfare research program in occupied China. Thousands of

Japanese scientists, physicians, soldiers and their families had lived here. Behind Pingfan's secrecy and security walls, Japanese women tended gardens. Japanese children went to school. There was a swimming pool, a bar, and other amenities that had made it a reasonably pleasant place to work during wartime.

Pleasant for the Japanese residents, that is.

He headed for home. His first priority was to get the documents loaded and on their way. Then he and his family would leave Pingfan together.

A murky rivulet seeped from the edge of Ro block. Glancing toward the source, he saw a column of pitch-black smoke rising from the hidden courtyard. The *maruta* were burning. He could smell it now, too. Ro block was empty.

His eye caught movement near the ground. Something broad and low writhed over the bare dirt like a living blanket. The blanket spread with a scrabbling, scratching sound and swept toward him. He leaped over the rivulet and turned to get out of the way.

Rats.

Escaped from one of Pingfan's austere research laboratories, the rodents were desperately seeking cover. Hundreds of them flowed past, a seething river of fur and long, bald tails. They splashed through the polluted stream, leaving a thousand paw-shaped puddles in their wake.

He swore aloud. He had no fear of the common rat, but these were no ordinary wild rats. They were infested with fleas that carried bubonic plague. General Ishii had ordered the rats released into a nearby Chinese city, not inside Pingfan. Someone had made a mistake.

The herd of rats disappeared into a pile of rubble. He resumed walking. He would waste no worry on the plague-carrying fleas. He and his family would soon be far away, and Unit 731's field trials in Ningbo and other Chinese cities had proved the plague-infested rats weren't as dangerous as hoped. The Black Death killed people, but it lacked the potency and immediacy of, say, a uranium bomb.

The American bomb, he thought. Was it true? Compared to that, the Ishiis' project had failed completely.

Unit 731's goal was to create a living weapon using microorganisms, a germ weapon that would slay Japan's enemies and allow the island nation to conquer and rule all of East Asia and the Pacific. The military had given his brilliant brother Shiro everything he asked for. Money. Secrecy. Exemption from any human laws. The Kempeitai secret police had supplied them with test subjects from the local Chinese population and prisoners of war, mostly Russians. Masaji and the unit's many other scientists had answered questions none had dared to even ask before. Questions about shrapnel wounds and burns and amputation. Questions about infectious disease and how to turn bacteria into weapons.

And yet a grand weapon, something like the Americans', remained beyond their grasp. If they only had more time…

Tires crunched gravel behind him. An armored truck passed him and came to a stop at his house, just ahead. The truck dwarfed the small Type 95 *Kurogane* scout car already parked there. Trucks like this one delivered *maruta*, rounded up from the streets and prisons of Harbin. Fittingly, the logs had been transformed into paper. Through Unit 731's effort, the *maruta* were now data, priceless information recorded in notebooks packed inside hundreds of crates. Data on everything from anthrax bombs to frostbite. It would take only one truck to haul away the distilled essence of thousands of *maruta*.

The driver climbed out of the truck. Like Masaji Ishii, he wore the insignia of a major in the army medical corps.

The colleagues bowed to each other.

"Kamei-*san*, you are no truck driver," Masaji said.

"We each do our duty," Kamei said. "Kitano-*san* took his share of the documents on the South Manchuria Railway to Korea."

"They will find their way to the home islands."

"Or he will burn them."

Masaji fingered the smooth, rounded cyanide capsule in his pocket. The elite group of couriers would not allow a single page to fall into the hands of the Soviets or the Chinese. Each would keep his secrets until he died, whether by his own hand or the hand of another.

"Are the records complete?" Kamei asked.

"Yes." He raised the final notebook he'd brought from Ro block. "Here, and in the boxes inside. Everything we learned is written down. Every experiment. Raw data. Observations. Analysis. Even today I did my duty." He gripped the notebook. "When the time is right, with this information we can resume the work."

Inside the house, a baby started to cry.

Kamei gripped Masaji's arm. "Unit 731 will endure. We will keep the data. We will find our weapon in biology, not physics."

A low droning sound drew both men's eyes skyward. An aircraft. Approaching Pingfan.

Kamei's expression darkened. Masaji squinted into the dry wind. "It is time to go."

He knew the Imperial Japanese Army Air Service was no longer flying over Manchukuo.

A curtain in the window shifted and a child's face appeared in the corner. Masaji leaped up two steps and threw open the door, scattering loose papers across a tatami mat floor. His wife knelt, holding an infant. His other children emerged from behind stacks of wooden crates. Despite the summer heat, they each held a heavy winter coat.

That, and the clothes they wore, was all they could take with them. The *Kurogane* was designed to fit three men. His family of six would flee to the coast in it.

His wife silenced the baby by offering a finger to suck. She looked at him, awaiting instructions, her face a mask of deceptive calm. His five-year-old daughter Harumi coughed. It was odd that he even noticed. The frail girl coughed constantly, rendering him almost as deaf to the sound as she was. Of course, her deafness was physical, a consequence of one of her many bouts with sickness.

"Carry the boxes out," he said. "All of you. Give Harumi the baby."

Wordlessly they set down their coats and pushed boxes toward the door. His thirteen-year-old son Akihiro carried one on his own. Masaji stepped into the sooty air and helped Kamei arrange the truck's existing cargo to make room for the additional documents from his house. They both paused when a distant explosion rumbled over them.

"Demolition," Masaji assured him.

The men loaded the crates of documents into the truck, one by one. Only two boxes remained, on the ground, when Masaji heard aircraft again. He looked up.

He counted five planes, flying in formation, aiming toward Pingfan.

"Quickly," he said.

The high-pitched squeal of falling ordnance reached his ears. Explosions followed, the first ones seemingly remote. Then like the footfalls of a monstrous runner, the blasts stepped closer and closer. His heart pounded as he lifted a crate toward Kamei in the open back of the truck. A concussive wave knocked him off balance. The crate fell. Instinctively he rolled to the ground, to the far side of the vehicle. A bomb detonated and he curled up against the truck's huge tire and covered his head. He felt the opposite side of the truck lift as if hit by a giant fist, tilting against him, threatening to tip over and crush him. But it did not. Then the aerial bombers faded away to the north, taking the explosions with them. He rose to his feet.

Loose papers drifted like leaves in the swirling eddies of disturbed air. He lunged into the truck—had they lost the data?

No. Only the last crate was destroyed. The armored walls of the truck had protected the rest.

He examined himself and found no serious injury. He looked around and discovered the *Kurogane* had not fared as well. His family's escape car was a crumpled and smoking heap, sprinkled with the shattered glass of windows from his house.

The ringing in his ears faded and he realized the sounds of battle had not ended. Shouts of men and machine gun fire and motorcycles…

"They're coming," he said to Kamei. "Chinese, Soviets, Americans. Whoever. You must get this vehicle out of here."

Kamei gave a half-bow and scrambled into the driver's seat. Masaji slammed the rear door and locked it tight. He sprinted to the driver's window and leaned in Kamei's face. "You know what to do?"

"I will get through or I will die trying."

"If necessary, destroy the cargo first. The enemy *must not* get our work."

"*Hai*, Ishii-*san*."

Kamei threw the truck into reverse, spinning the wheels and scattering shredded paper as he sped away. Masaji covered his face with his sleeve and staggered back into the house.

The five members of his family were there. Only Harumi was standing, biting her thin lower lip. Her scrawny fingers clung to a shabby doll. The other children clumped together against the windowless back wall with their mother, the baby screaming in her arms.

"Get up. We go."

His eldest son Akihiro ran to the door but stopped short when he saw the ruined car.

"Not that way," Masaji said. "Out the back." He yanked a bundle out of one of the children's arms. "Leave the coats. Leave everything."

His wife met his gaze for only an instant, but it was enough. She knew.

He hoped she also understood.

It wasn't supposed to turn out this way. They were ahead of schedule. They thought they had days yet to evacuate Pingfan. How could the enemy be here already?

He herded them to the other side of the house and paused to grab his sword. They emerged outdoors into the reek and noise.

"We make for Building Six," he said. Building Six was in the opposite direction of the fighting, and he'd seen cars there just yesterday.

He led them across the dusty plain, past rubble from the Japanese demolition crews and fresh destruction from the aerial bombardment. He spied rats, but they were the least of his concerns. Harumi stumbled and wheezed. Akihiro lifted her to her feet. The baby wailed. Fortunately they had no need for stealth. The noisy barrage of enemy fire drowned out all other sounds. Whoever the enemy was, they were getting closer.

The Ishii family scrambled through a gate in a wall. They'd reached Building Six.

He scanned the empty courtyard and fell to his knees. The cars were gone.

His wife and children huddled against the wall to catch their breath. Not one of them had yet dared to speak.

Another earth-shaking blast, no further away than his house. Perhaps it *was* his house.

The major knew his duty. But now that it came to it, his resolution faltered.

He clung to the knowledge that he'd achieved the most important thing. The Unit's records were safe, traveling to Japan. In the life of the Empire, his life did not matter. His duty, and the duty of his family, was to serve. To never reveal their story to the enemy.

He had personally done vivisections of Chinese women, men, and children. He knew how a sharp knife parted the soft skin of a baby's belly. If the Chinese were coming, he had no reason to expect mercy.

His wife's body tumbled to the side as the 8mm bullet he fired from his Nambu pistol ripped through her skull. He wanted to beg her forgiveness, but reminded himself pardon was not necessary because he was doing the right thing.

The children, too stunned to move, were easy targets.

His heart crumpled in his chest. If only he had cyanide pills for everyone…

No, he'd seen cyanide deaths. A bullet was better.

Koneko. Eiko. Akiko. The semiautomatic worked fast. Their bodies piled up, like logs.

Then Akihiro, his eldest son, stood and spread his arms in front of little Harumi.

Masaji quailed. Akihiro had always been protective of his feeble sister.

His gun hand shook. "It is our duty," he said.

"Please," Akihiro said.

A typhoon of feelings unmanned him. He hesitated.

Then the wall exploded. Flying bricks pelted him. Overwhelming pain in his face and ribs erased his psychic anguish. He found himself on his back, crushed and in agony, looking at the sky through one barely functioning eye. He could not move his right arm and each breath was a knife in his torso.

Akihiro kneeled over him. His son's eyes were impossibly wide. He pointed his father's pistol at his father's head.

Masaji channeled all his will into the focus of his one eye.

"Duty," he pleaded.

The boy pulled the trigger.

1

Shoulders aching from too many hours with her arms reaching into the isolation chamber, Amika Nakamura resisted the urge to scratch her nose. Violating biosafety level two precautions in the laboratory wouldn't kill her, but her research was at a critical phase and the last thing she needed was to get sick.

Cell incubators warmed the small, windowless room that smelled of yeast. The room was dark except for the garish fluorescent light that illuminated her workspace. An air filtration system ran constantly, filling her ears with a low roar that cut her off from the outside world. She wriggled her nose under the surgical mask to try to relieve the itch.

On a stainless steel counter inside the isolation cabinet in front of her sat a row of clear plastic petri dishes, each holding a quarter inch of urine-colored liquid. For the bird cells clinging to the bottom of those dishes, yellow was the color of death.

Time for resurrection.

With gloved hands she vacuumed the contaminated liquid away and replaced it with clean, pink fluid. She could almost imagine the cells sighing with relief as their little plastic prison went from fetid to fresh. Years ago, the ancestors of those cells had come from a real bird. That bird was long gone, and the cells were now a cancer growing in a dish. They lived a pampered, immortal life—at the cost of their freedom and identity.

Amika knew women who would make that kind of trade. She wasn't one of them.

The room's air pressure changed, making her ears pop. Someone had opened the door.

She glanced over her shoulder and saw her principal investigator (and employer) Professor Herberger, accompanied by a man she barely knew but recognized as Herberger's boss, the dean of the college.

Her muscles stiffened. Was the jig up?

The rumble of the air system was loud, but not that loud. She pretended not to hear them speak.

"Dr. Nakamura," the dean's stern voice repeated at higher volume, "put down the pipette."

She almost laughed. He said it like she was holding a gun.

Then again, considering what they probably suspected she was doing, comparing it to a lethal weapon wasn't a big leap.

She laid the small tool on the counter and turned slowly to face them. Her accusers. A couple of old men. Paunchy bellies. Six-figure salaries. Tenured. Two scientists who never put their hands on an actual experiment anymore. The dean had been out of the lab, working in administration for so long he'd have to go to a museum to find equipment he knew how to operate. These old men didn't understand how hard it was to launch a career in science these days. For anyone, but especially for a woman. They didn't understand how the competition was so fierce, you had to find a way to stand out. They were comfortable with the status quo and uncomfortable with risk.

I take bigger risks than they've taken in the last year just walking home on University Avenue after another fourteen-hour day at the lab. This project was a gamble they couldn't possibly understand.

I don't ever want to be like them. Except for the tenured part.

"Yes?" she said, putting as much peeve in her voice as she thought she could get away with without being openly insolent.

Professor Herberger spoke. "Amika, we need to talk. Shut down the bio-safety cabinet, would you please?"

Pompous cowards. With exaggerated care she covered the dishes and returned them to an incubator. Then she sprayed disinfectant and wiped down the workspace. How long could she drag this out? Dr. Herberger and the dean wouldn't dare to interrupt while she was following biosafety protocols.

Not if they thought a deadly flu virus was involved.

She wondered how long they would stand there, her professor resting his arm on a shoulder-tall tank of compressed gas, the dean rocking back and forth in his leather dress shoes. She fantasized about keeping her gloved hands inside the cabinet forever, doing the work that needed to be done, the work that would make her famous. Influenza virus—the flu—was her passion. The desire to understand its secrets had propelled her through her PhD years and into this post-doctoral fellowship at Cal. Answers to some of her most important questions about this life form were tantalizingly close.

The dean again. "Dr. Nakamura, I'm going to have to ask you to shut down now."

The surgical mask flattened against her nose and mouth as she took a deep breath to subdue her anger. Her younger brother Shuu Nakamura, a US Army veteran, had taught her you could lose some battles but still win a war. This confrontation with the administration at the University of California was her battle. She had time yet to win her war. She was only twenty-seven years old. On average, winners of the Nobel Prize in physiology or medicine were forty-five years old when they did their prize-winning work.

"Yes sir," she said and turned off the airflow. A heavy silence settled in its absence. She stripped off her latex gloves with a snap and tossed her face mask and paper gown into the trash.

"Let's go to my office, shall we?" Dr. Herberger said.

He closed the door to the cell culture room behind them as they left. Amika had a sinking feeling she would not be allowed to pass through that door again.

When they reached his office, Herberger stood next to a tall, black swivel chair behind a desk covered with documents and drab technical journals. "Have a seat," he said, gesturing to one of two small chairs on the other side.

Amika complied. The dean, in a typically male display of status, rolled the second chair away from her and over to the professor's side. Herberger's office wasn't much larger than his desk, and the dean rattled the cheap Venetian blinds on the window as he squeezed in. Diplomas and a photo of Herberger with the surgeon general scowled at Amika from the walls.

Her rage-fueled, righteous indignation cooled as fear took over. These men had all the power. She might be smarter, bolder, a better scientist than they, but she owned nothing of the currency of their realm. No independent grant money, no committee appointments, no endowed chair. Surely Dr. Herberger had access to dozens, maybe hundreds, of applications from junior scientists like her, all clamoring for a job at the fabled UC campus. From her boss's point of view, she was utterly replaceable.

Dr. Herberger sat and rested his elbows on his desk. "Do you know why we're here, Amika?"

She couldn't help herself. "To congratulate me on being invited to speak at the Global Virus conference?"

Neither of them cracked a smile. She sensed her dreams slipping away.

"I'm surprised, Dr. Nakamura," the dean said. "By all accounts you're an intelligent young woman. Did you really think you could submit banned research to a prestigious conference and the university wouldn't notice?"

Well, the university wasn't clever enough to discover that I was actually doing the research, right under their noses.

She chose a guarded response, defending her work. "The 1918 influenza killed tens of millions of people. It's not a question of if, but when it will happen again. We need to be able to recognize a potential pandemic flu virus in the wild and prepare—"

Dr. Herberger held up his hand to cut her off. "This isn't about the validity of your work. It's about following the rules." He lifted a sheet of paper and pointed at the heading from the White House Office of Science and Technology Policy. "We're under a moratorium for gain-of-function research."

"This university depends on millions of dollars in federal funding," the dean continued. "Your reckless work on influenza jeopardizes that."

"It's not only the money," Dr. Herberger added. "Mutating the virus to make it more infectious is *dangerous.*"

If there was one thing she couldn't stand, it was hypocrisy. "Six months ago you thought it was a brilliant idea. You agreed that it could teach us the difference between harmless mutations and ones that pose a threat to human health."

Her accusers exchanged a glance. The dean said, "Sometimes we get a little carried away by our ideas, don't we? Look, we're not here to argue about whether something important could be learned from your work. The point is, there are risks and I think it's wise for us to pause until we've had time to examine whether we can do it safely. And right now, the federal government says we must."

She wanted to say, *I can do it safely.* The elephant in the room was the *reason* the Feds called a halt to this type of research on disease-causing viruses and bacteria. There'd been some incidents of astonishing carelessness. Somebody at the National Institutes of Health had recently stumbled on a cornucopia of deadly germs in an old freezer, 327 vials in all, including small-pox, for cripe's sake. They'd been stashed and forgotten. Then the Centers for Disease Control had screwed up with anthrax, shipping live bacteria to labs that thought they were getting inactivated material. Thank God nobody died, but the lesson was clear: you couldn't trust scientists to manage their stuff.

So even though Amika was meticulous to a fault, and felt she was perfectly capable of keeping her viruses contained and properly labeled, those clowns at NIH and CDC had ruined things for everyone. Because of them, she was supposed to abandon her important work on flu.

But she hadn't abandoned it. And she'd made some breakthroughs in understanding the genetic differences between run-of-the-mill seasonal influenza and new flu viruses that could wipe out several percent of the world's population. This knowledge was valuable to humanity, and frankly, it was valuable to her career. She had decided to submit her work to the prestigious Global Virus meeting, in hopes they'd invite her to give a lecture.

I got invited for a lecture, all right. I'm getting it now.

"You broke the rules, Amika," Dr. Herberger said.

"The rules are wrong," she growled.

The men communicated silently yet again. She was ready to argue—nothing left to lose—but they apparently had this whole thing choreographed in advance. Discussion was not part of the dance. The dean dredged a legal-sized manila envelope out of a messenger bag and laid its contents on the desk. The paper was covered with text. Several red tabs labeled "Sign Here" stuck out from one side.

"This terminates your employment at the University of California," the dean said. "It applies to all campuses, not just Berkeley."

His words were like a gut punch. The genius of her work meant nothing. They were actually going to *fire* her. From the whole UC system. Her connections at UCSF, where she went to graduate school, were worthless. Speech failed as she forced herself to keep breathing. No tears, she vowed. No tears.

"It also mandates your cooperation in identifying and destroying any samples of genetically modified influenza virus in your possession," he continued. "Because your data on virulence could be misused, the University demands that you delete all gene sequence files derived from the prohibited research. You further agree not to store, transmit, or publish your data in any form."

Wait a minute. Asking her to destroy her data was pointless. You can't suppress genetic information. It comes from the natural world. The DNA was out there, just waiting for somebody to decode it. Even if she didn't publish her results, there was about a one hundred percent chance that another, less repressed scientist would do it in the near future. And she would get no credit for the discovery. This was punitive. They had no right to do that.

Galvanized, she wondered what would happen if she refused to sign the papers.

The dean must have read her mind. "Obviously we can't force you to sign. Should you refuse, however, the University will take legal action against you." His expression softened. "You made a mistake. Don't make it any harder on yourself."

A mistake? He was the one making a mistake.

"I'm sorry," Dr. Herberger said.

He wasn't sorry. She would make him sorry someday when she accepted her Nobel Prize, and people were talking about how stupid he was to let her go. She shook her head to hide the blinking of her eyes.

Do not touch your face. Do not let them see you cry.

The papers lay there, the red type violent against the bland backdrop of legalese printed in a small font. The air felt hot and thick. How was she going to tell Shuu that his big sister, who'd bailed him out of trouble more times than anyone could count, wasn't so perfect after all?

They're wrong.

Her lip started to quiver. Any verbal rebuttal died in her throat. With as much dignity as she could muster, she snatched the documents and marched out of the room. The second the office door closed behind her, she ran. Away, down the empty corridor. Thankfully no one saw her like this, distraught and weak as she slipped into the women's restroom.

She splashed water on her face. *This will not be the end.* She recalled that Marie Curie, winner of not one but two Nobel Prizes, was forbidden to attend university in her home country of Poland. *She left. If I must, I will too. I will find a way.*

2

MAY 24 (SIX MONTHS LATER)
SENKAKU ISLANDS
EAST CHINA SEA
(southern tip of the Japanese archipelago, near Taiwan)

Salty spray cooled her skin as Amika Nakamura stood at the rail of the *Kumamoto*. Brilliant sun heated the deck of the Japan Coast Guard's patrol vessel, evaporating the light rainfall from earlier that morning. She closed her eyes and breathed deeply of the misty sea air. Having grown up in arid Los Angeles, she loved the exotic feel of humidity here in the tropics of Asia. The ship rose and fell softly on gentle waves and the wind ruffled but failed to tangle her short-cropped hair.

After the trip down from Tokyo where she now lived, and a pre-dawn departure from the port on the island of Ishigaki, Amika was a long way from Berkeley, both literally and figuratively.

She felt something break the wind at her side and she opened her eyes. Hiroshi Naito, her traveling companion and the savior of her career, offered her a pair of binoculars.

"The captain let me borrow these," he said in Japanese. "Have a look. You can see the islands now."

In the distance, small, dark, formless masses of land interrupted what had been an empty seascape for the past several hours. With the binoculars, the tiny Senkaku Islands resolved into distinct specks.

"Shuu is waiting for us on the big one? In the middle?" she asked.

"Yes, that's Uotsuri-shima," Hiroshi said, "but I wouldn't call it big. It's only four square kilometers."

"It looks tall from here."

"A bit. The rocky peak is close to four hundred meters high."

She returned the glasses to him. "I guess the goats like it."

"They're breeding like crazy there." He smiled. "Must be a romantic place."

Her face burned. Was her boss flirting with her? Ever since he invited her on this wild excursion away from work, she'd been trying to tell if her presence was more than just a courtesy to her brother. She hoped he *was* flirting. Of course there was some risk but she'd be a fool not to start a relationship with this man if she could. Hiroshi Naito was rich, charming, and probably a mere ten years older than she. As heir to a family-owned Japanese drug company, he also had the power to determine her future as a scientist.

Job security plus a little fun? Why the hell not?

"I see why the islands' ecosystem is unique," she said. "They're totally isolated."

"Yet somehow the Senkaku mole and the Okinawa-kuro-oo-ari ant found their way here," he said.

"Like I did," she said. "It seems crazy that Shuu and I are working together on a project. Vaccines and guns are a strange combination."

She remembered the dark day six months ago when she was fired from her fellowship at the University of California and broke the news to her brother Shuu. He was living in Tokyo, so she could have kept it a secret, but that didn't seem right. Shuu had struggled after he left the US Army. About two years ago he'd announced he was going to get a fresh start—in Japan. She and he had learned to speak Japanese from their parents, but she was worried Shuu thought that moving to a new country would somehow solve all his problems.

Yet somehow, it did. Or at least it solved all the problems that had required her intervention in the past.

Then against all odds, Shuu had bailed *her* out when she needed help.

"As crazy as two Americans coming all the way out here to help protect a Japanese national treasure?" Hiroshi said.

"Japanese-Americans," she corrected him. "Our great-grandfather immigrated to California. He worked as a laborer, picking fruit in the Central Valley. Later my grandparents owned a strawberry farm."

Hiroshi turned his back to the ocean and stared up at the Japanese flag waving proudly from the ship's superstructure. White with a red circle representing the sun, the banner snapped in the breeze. "Did they consider themselves Americans, or Japanese during the war?"

She didn't have to ask which war he meant. "Americans, I suppose."

"Your president didn't agree."

He was referring to a piece of American history that many Americans themselves didn't know. In 1942 Franklin Roosevelt signed Executive Order 9066, depriving Japanese-Americans of their most basic civil rights. Even American-born US citizens who were as little as one-sixteenth Japanese were given about a week to sell or store all their belongings and shut down their farms and businesses. Then they were rounded up and sent to detention centers. Her grandparents never spoke openly about their experience in the internment camp at Tule Lake, but she'd studied history. Tule Lake, a godforsaken outpost in northeast California, was where they sent the troublemakers.

"No," she said. "They lost everything."

"They didn't lose their heritage. Your family still speaks Japanese. Language is a root connection to culture. Japan is your nation, too."

It is now. The scientific community in the US had cut her off. Japan was giving her another chance. She leaned in a little closer to Hiroshi than was necessary and said, "Let's go protect a national treasure." Though she found it a stretch to call a shovel-pawed underground rodent a "treasure," no matter how rare the Senkaku mole might be.

A Coast Guardsman wearing dungarees jogged toward them. Military culture in any country was foreign to her, and she couldn't tell if this man was a boss or a peon in the hierarchy. He bowed to Hiroshi and said the captain needed to speak to him at once.

Hiroshi touched her shoulder. "Excuse me. I will find you later."

Her arm tingled at the contact. *Please do.*

He walked away with the sailor, leaving Amika content to resume her watch on the uninhabited volcanic outcrops that were their destination.

She rested her forearms on the ship's railing and pondered her recent reversal of fortune. Not many people in the world studied viruses, and they generally knew each other. Getting expelled from the clique might have ended her career. But thanks to unexpected help from her brother Shuu, she was still in the business.

Shuu came to Tokyo with a unique combination of American military training and Japanese language skills. A private personal security firm had snapped him up, and he'd gone on to make a lot of well-connected friends. She wasn't surprised. When he wanted to, her brother could charm the fragrance off a rose.

He'd made the acquaintance of Hiroshi Naito, whose family traced its ancestry to a samurai clan of the shogun era. The Naitos were scientists and business people. They owned Koga Scientific, a major pharmaceutical conglomerate, and its philanthropic arm, the Koga Foundation. Shuu ingratiated himself with Hiroshi to the point that when his sister needed a job, the Koga Foundation awarded her a grant to continue her influenza research at their laboratories in Tokyo. Koga manufactured vaccines, including a variety of flu vaccines for both humans and animals. Her expertise was a good fit.

Thank you, little bro.

The cluster of Senkaku Islands was now close. The thrumming of the ship's engine changed tone and the air currents around her slowed. The water ahead looked darker, more colorful, and she could see coral reefs below the surface. Their project gear and provisions were stored in a hangar on the ship's helicopter flight deck, toward the stern. She headed that way to help load the Zodiac that would carry them to shore.

Movement out on the water caught her eye.

A boat, much smaller than the *Kumamoto*, sped around the southern tip of the main island. Another appeared, then a third, all racing toward the patrol vessel from the far side of Uotsuri-shima island. She squinted at the mini-flotilla. They didn't look like Japan Coast Guard; JCG ships were painted white. These ships were a mishmash of colors, dingy and grubby in appearance. One appeared to have nets draped from its rigging.

Fishing boats? Way out here?

A siren blared, painfully close to her head. Her hands flew to cover her ears. Aroused by the alarm, the *Kumamoto* came to life. Crewmen poured from below decks and descended from the upper levels. They moved with speed and purpose. Amika made it *her* purpose to get out of the way, as she seemed to be the only person on board who had no idea what was happening, or what to do.

The ragtag boats approached at high speed, bouncing over each other's wakes. This didn't look like normal behavior for fishermen. Movie images of

Somali pirates flashed through her brain. Was someone trying to hijack the *Kumamoto*? Ridiculous. This was an armed military vessel, not a container ship full of new cars. So who were these people?

Abruptly the siren stopped, leaving a ringing in her ears. She looked around for Hiroshi, hoping for guidance. She didn't want to do something stupid that would interfere with the crew—or get herself drowned. She could swim—had even done a couple of triathlons in California—but this was open ocean.

Life jacket. She had seen them stowed at the middle of the ship, near the lifeboat launch. Loitering there was probably a good idea in case of trouble. She scurried in that direction.

A voice bellowed from speakers on the *Kumamoto,* as loud as the siren had been, but less alarming. A man's words blasted across the water, words distorted by the lousy amplification.

Wait, that's not distortion. He's speaking Chinese. She couldn't understand a word of the language, but she could recognize it.

The watercraft didn't change direction or speed. Now she could see people on the decks. They were waving red flags.

Ah. The flag of the People's Republic of China.

She found the bin of life jackets and huddled against a bulkhead. The voice of the Japan Coast Guard repeated its message. The intonation sounded exactly the same. A recording? In Chinese? What the hell?

The metal wall behind her vibrated and hummed and she jumped in surprise. A whirring sound above her. She looked. Ten feet overhead, a massive gun turret rotated to face the starboard side of the ship.

I did not sign up for this! I'm just a scientist getting a ride to a remote work site. Where is—

"Amika!"

Hiroshi jogged toward her, his slim, muscular frame dodging uniformed sailors on the move.

She grabbed his arm. "What's going on?"

He peeled her off and aimed her toward a ladder about fifty feet forward. "Come this way."

She felt a flash of embarrassment at her ineptitude as she climbed the metal rungs up the wall. *Normally I'm good in a crisis. Really.* But the alien environment of this ship put her at a disadvantage.

He stayed close behind her, a human shield at her back. Because she half-expected bullets to fly, she was impressed by his gallantry.

They reached the upper deck alive.

"Is that the Chinese Navy?" she asked.

"Hardly. They're political agitators posing as fishermen."

"What do they want?"

"They want us to leave. China claims these islands belong to them."

They climbed one deck higher and she pondered this information. A territorial dispute? This seemed to be a rather important detail to mention when you invite someone on a trip. Sure it was her own fault she never read a newspaper, but neither Shuu nor Hiroshi warned her they were camping in a war zone.

Now was not the time to argue about it. "Are they going to attack us?"

"Harass, not attack," Hiroshi replied. "This ship can defend herself and they know it. This isn't the first run-in the *Kumamoto* has had with Chinese jackals."

Amika wasn't a native speaker of Japanese, but she was pretty sure he had just used an ethnic slur. She was a bit taken aback by that but at the moment she was more bothered by his admission that he knew there was trouble in this region—and had brought her out here anyway.

"Follow me," he said.

He led her to a sheltered spot behind some kind of tanks or metal storage pods. They were just below the ship's bridge, and at about the same level as the gun turrets. Below, men were no longer scrambling into position. They were stationed at their posts, waiting.

The verbal warning in Chinese played again.

On the decks of their fishing boats, the Chinese protesters shook their fists. They appeared to be shouting but the rumble of machinery on the *Kumamoto* extinguished the sound of their voices.

Hiroshi stepped out to the railing to get a clear view. She hesitated to join him for a moment but refused to be the cowering female. And she was definitely curious to see what happened next.

"Looks like they're going to ram us," she said, regretting that she hadn't grabbed a life jacket on her way up.

"Watch," Hiroshi said, a bemused look on his face.

Their adversaries crossed an invisible line in the sea. The recorded message cut off abruptly. The captain's voice boomed across the decks.

"Defense plan delta! Defense plan delta!"

A grinding noise, as of a giant gear turning, emanated from the bow of the ship. In contrast, lighter pinging sounds resonated from around the ship's hull. She felt a rush of adrenaline as she listened and looked. Some of the Chinese protesters were down on one knee, aiming what at this distance appeared to be rifles. Instinctively she scuttled back from the edge of the deck and took cover.

Hiroshi stayed where he was. "You should see this."

Something went *splat* against the bulkhead only a few feet from her head. Blood dripped from the spot where it hit. The blood wasn't hers. Her stomach lurched and she whirled toward Hiroshi.

"Cowards," he said.

3

Strangely for a man who had just been shot, Hiroshi's expression didn't change. Amika dashed to him and wrapped an arm around his chest to drag him to safety. Pinging sounds surrounded them. Another tiny missile hit the lifeboat hanging nearby. Another red splotch blossomed.

Hiroshi laughed and freed himself from her grip. "Paintballs."

She stared. There was no blood on her hands, or on his clothes, or hair, or skin. No one had been shot.

"Paint? You're kidding." But she saw that it was true and exhaled in relief. The dazzling white hull of the *Kumamoto* was speckled with red like a Caucasian kid with the measles. And although she'd never been in a firefight like her brother had, on a moment's reflection it was pretty clear she was not hearing the discharge of real guns.

The Japan Coast Guard retaliated. Pressurized water exploded from the turret where she'd been standing before. The thing was a water cannon, not a gun. The jet of water hit the Chinese boats, knocking down the shooters and flattening the Chinese flags to the deck. Protesters crumpled under the force of the spray and slipped on the torrent that swirled around their feet.

The *Kumamoto* blew her horn. Hiroshi shouted a taunt, an old-fashioned verse that sounded like something soldiers would chant to gird themselves for battle.

Her fear dissolved and she became a spectator. Instead of war, she was caught in the middle of a war game. Water guns and paintballs.

And I thought I was living in a grown-up world.

For ten minutes the ship's water cannon swept back and forth across the three boats, keeping them at bay. The *Kumamoto* held her position as the Chinese danced around the periphery of her range. She wondered how long they would keep this up. The *Kumamoto* wasn't going to run out of water. Would they be stuck here until nightfall?

The wait wasn't nearly that long. The protesters must have decided they'd made their point. Maybe they were out of paint. They turned and motored away to the west, and eventually disappeared around the far side of the island.

"Dogs run from water," Hiroshi said, clapping his hands. "Let's load the Zodiac."

"Load?" she said. "We're going to fetch Shuu and the others and go home, aren't we?"

He snorted. "Those Chinese jackals are finished. They won't bother us. We came here to do a job."

She didn't share his confidence. Admittedly, she knew nothing about this place, this dispute. But she'd just witnessed a lot of angry people retreat to the other side of the island where she was going to sleep in a tent for a few days. Those people had blown off some steam, and gotten wet. How could Hiroshi be so sure they were turning tail permanently?

"What if they land on the island?"

"The Senkaku Islands belong to Japan," Hiroshi replied. "Chinese landing on our territory would be an act of war."

"That's reassuring," she said sarcastically.

To her great surprise, Hiroshi faced her, put his hands on her shoulders, and earnestly looked into her eyes.

"Amika," he said, "don't worry. Your brother and I would never let anything happen to you."

Her heart fluttered. What an opportunity. Here she was alone with one of the most powerful men in Japan's biotechnology sector. He was an executive at Koga Scientific, the company his grandfather had founded, and he was on the board of the Koga Foundation, which was paying her salary.

He had money, of course. But she wasn't focused on that. She wanted an ally. She needed his influence and his connections to get her career back on track.

It didn't hurt that he was good looking, and taller than most Japanese men.

She reached between his outstretched arms and playfully touched his cheek.

"Okay," she said. "Let's go shoot some goats."

The Zodiac's outboard motor whined like a loud mosquito as they skimmed the water over broken lava rock and coral. Amika sat on a duffel bag surrounded by boxes of camp food. In her lap rested a large Styrofoam container marked with a bright orange biohazard symbol and the Koga company logo. Hiroshi chatted with the Coast Guardsman who piloted their water taxi. She dipped a finger over the side of the boat and caught the ocean's surface, sending a spray of warm water into the air. After nearly twenty-four hours of travel, Uotsuri-shima, the largest of the tiny Senkaku Islands, loomed minutes ahead. The sun set late this time of year, so they had plenty of daylight yet. She and Hiroshi only needed to pitch their personal tents; Shuu and another man employed by Koga Scientific had arrived two days previously and had the rest of the camp set up. Amika was ready for some food and a good night's sleep. She hoped the heat and humidity wouldn't keep her awake.

Might not want a tent.

Ahead, a man wearing a tight-fitting T-shirt that highlighted his muscular physique waved enthusiastically from the shore. Even though her little brother had been out of the army for a while, he pumped iron like his life depended on it. *I suppose in his line of work, his life actually might depend on his physical strength.* In Japan, private guards were not allowed to carry handguns. Shuu's extra muscle might make all the difference in an altercation.

She felt a burst of love and grinned and waved like a crazy woman. For the past five months, she and Shuu had both lived in Tokyo, closer to each other than in a decade, but she still didn't get to see him very often. She worked long hours trying to make a reputation for herself in the laboratory at Koga, and his hours were irregular while working security at events, many of them at night. Hiroshi's invitation to join him on this trip, ostensibly as a technical advisor on the Koga vaccine, was a gift to the Nakamura siblings.

A flat stretch of pebbled shoreline beckoned. Nearby she saw the ruins of a primitive fish flakes factory, abandoned long ago. For forty years, no one had lived on the rocky island. It was far away from everything, and although its mountain looked green and lush from the distance, the plant life was scrubby and the soil was poor. It was good enough, though, for the hundreds of non-native goats that thrived after the humans left. Too many goats were damaging the delicate ecosystem of the island and threatening Uotsuri-shima's rare endemic species. To manage the problem and protect the endangered island moles, the Japanese government had hired Koga Scientific to administer a contraceptive vaccine to the goat herd.

The sailor briefly gunned the engine and drove the Zodiac onto the beach. For the first time since she left the harbor at Ishigaki, there was no wind tearing at Amika's face. Her skin felt parched and raw, and the still air seemed to thicken.

With a radiant smile, Shuu reached out his strong hand and helped her step out of the inflatable boat on wobbly sea legs.

"Hey, 'Mika," he said. "You didn't let those Chinese jackals scare you off?"

Does that word mean something different from what I thought?

"It takes more than that. We had beer to deliver," she joked.

He gave her a high-five. "I'll unload the gear. You make us some *matcha*?"

Amika had no skill (or patience) with the ritual aspect of Japanese tea preparation, but Shuu loved the way she turned green tea powder into a steaming cup of bliss. Iced tea sounded more appealing in the heat, but the nearest freezer was on the *Kumamoto*.

"I'm on it," she said.

Shuu and the other man from Koga had made camp on a strip of land, part sand and part pebbles, between the surf and steep, worn cliffs that were impressively tall up close. As she neared the tents, an eddy of air drifted down the cliff carrying the pungent smell of goat. A rocky trail crawled up the cliff, passing a white frame tower crowned with a light beacon. The camp kitchen and dining area were open to the air under a tarp. Broken shells crunched under her feet. The area smelled of cooked fish.

She heated water over a propane stove and had the tea ready when the men walked up with boxes of provisions. The Zodiac fired up its motor and headed back to the ship, leaving the four of them alone.

Alone on a deserted island. She handed cups to the men. "Do you think we're okay here tonight?"

Hiroshi took a seat on a canvas chair next to a folding table. He looked at Shuu as if to say, your turn.

Shuu swallowed some tea. "I wouldn't be here if I thought there was a problem. This kind of thing, with the Chinese jackals, goes on all the time."

So her brother was aware of the troubles, too. Her temper flickered. "You knew about this? Before?"

"Of course. China's been pushing a claim on the Senkaku Islands for years."

What could she say?

Apparently I'm the only one whose knowledge of geopolitics is limited to playing the board game Risk.

"The Coast Guard maintains a presence," Hiroshi said. "This is Japanese territory. We will protect it."

She nodded and sipped her tea. Complaining that she'd been duped about the hazards of this trip would only highlight her ignorance. She wanted Hiroshi to think she was smart and capable, inside *and* outside the lab. And it was never a good idea to provoke Shuu. Best to let the matter drop.

Shuu set a pair of cases on the table and spoke to Hiroshi. "Still, they should've detained some of them. To set an example."

Hiroshi snorted. "Detain? By all rights the Coast Guard should sink them."

"Is that what you told Miyashita?"

"He agrees, but for now his hands are tied."

The name sounded familiar. "Who's Miyashita?" Amika asked.

"Captain of the *Kumamoto*," Shuu replied. "A mutual friend."

Another intriguing acquaintance for her brother. She looked at him with a motherly gaze. *I wonder if he has a Japanese girlfriend?* He hadn't mentioned it to her if he did. *I need to talk to him more.* Did he encounter rich women as often as he seemed to connect with rich or powerful men?

At the table, Shuu lifted the lids on the cases. Inside were a camo-colored pneumatic rifle and a collection of darts. The rifle was the reason her brother was here. Koga Scientific made the contraceptive vaccine, but they needed a shooter to deliver it to the goats.

Shuu raised the rifle to his shoulder and looked down the sight. "I tested the tranq and practiced putting on ear tags yesterday," he said. "If your vaccine is good to go, we're ready."

"The vaccine is perishable," Hiroshi said. "It's packed in enough dry ice to keep for two days, maybe three in these conditions. Is that enough time?"

"No problem. The island is tiny. Tracking the goats is easy." He laid the weapon back in the fitted foam of its case. "Might as well start now. We can sit around here after sunset."

Amika handed him the biohazard box from Koga. When he opened it, a puff of white smoke wafted from the dry ice inside.

Despite the labeling, she knew the tiny, frozen vials she had packed weren't really hazardous. They contained Koga's special zona pellucida vaccine, an injectable contraceptive for use in wildlife and livestock. It made female goats infertile for about a year.

I'm glad they're sterilizing rather than slaughtering the herd. With booster shots, the goats will age and die off naturally.

Shuu added vaccine to the tranquilizer and loaded the mixture into his darts. Amika finished her tea and went to set up her tent and change clothes in private. She emerged in running gear, ready to conquer the cliff trail.

She was already sweating when she reached the light beacon about a hundred feet up the trail. The Koga man who had come with Shuu was working on the tower, which was built near the base of the cliff to illuminate the small harbor. He was up on the scaffold, using a wrench to attach a piece of electronic equipment to the frame. A new Japanese flag fluttered just below the light. She greeted him and kept climbing.

Halfway to the top she passed Shuu and Hiroshi. Her brother carried the pneumatic rifle with the ease of a former infantryman.

"Stay away from the goats," he said. "Otherwise I might tranq you by accident."

"Would I get a year's worth of free birth control with that?" she said.

Deep into the night the seagulls stopped calling, leaving only the sound of waves sweeping the rocky beach. Amika thrashed in her one-person tent. The humidity was suffocating, and every few seconds the beacon on the cliff flashed an annoyingly bright light. She preferred to sleep outside, but Shuu had warned her the nighttime mosquitoes would eat her alive, even though they hadn't bothered her at dinner.

Sleepless, her mind went into overdrive. She fretted about her career and her dreams of scientific fame.

The American scientists just need time to cool off. Eventually they'll realize I was right. Or the whole thing will blow over. They won't blackball me from academia forever. Will they?

What if they did? Would Koga Scientific keep her long term? Equally important, could she do the kind of research she wanted to do in a corporate lab?

Probably not, unless she had special influence.

Hiroshi Naito could be that influence.

She thought about the conversations they had on the flight from Tokyo, searching for clues to her chances. Conversation with him had been surprisingly easy. He was intelligent and knowledgeable about the research at Koga. Not just a manager, not just the heir apparent, he was a scientist, interested in many of the same things that interested her. Then there was that moment on the ship.

I wonder if my being an American—

A violent flapping of wings startled her, as if a whole flock of resting seagulls had suddenly taken to the air. She sat up and listened to the darkness. The waves washed in slow rhythm, a blanket of sound smothering...

No, there was something else. The crunching of shell against rock. Again. Footsteps. The rustle of fabric.

Was someone else having trouble sleeping?

Why wasn't he using a flashlight?

She slipped on a pair of shoes.

Whispers. Human voices.

Her heart skipped a beat.

The voices were speaking Chinese.

For an instant she was paralyzed. Before she had the sense to call Shuu's name, chaos erupted.

Shouts and moving lights penetrated the thin nylon of the tent. She yanked a shirt over her head. Whoever they were, there were a lot of them. Voices were chanting, slogans or something. Many were yelling. They all sounded angry.

I need a weapon! Was there anything in the tent she could use to defend herself? At home she kept a heavy D-cell flashlight by her bed partly for this reason. Her lightweight camping headlamp was no substitute. She fumbled with her duffel bag in the dark, desperately feeling for anything sharp or hard.

Then a light rainfall splattered the tent, delivering the most horrible, sickening stench she'd ever smelled. Irregular flashes of light illuminated dark circles forming on the tent. The nylon was getting wet.

Someone was spraying the camp.

4

Could it be poison gas? Amika held her breath against the horrible smell.

I can't survive a chemical attack by not breathing.

The only way to save herself was to get out, get away from the tent. Or was the tent her only protection? Would this awful stuff burn her skin if she went outside? She grabbed a jacket to cover her arms and a small towel for her face.

Already her body screamed for air. Unwillingly she inhaled and the noxious vapors hit her nose and gut and brain and parts of her body she didn't know could respond to smell. Whatever it was, it was the most intense, indescribable stink, heavy of sewage mixed with comprehensive rot, a stink so powerful it was like a physical force.

And yet, she felt no pain. Her eyes weren't running. She choked on the foul odor but didn't cough. It wasn't tear gas or mustard gas.

Her stomach heaved. Whatever it was, the spray was going to make her vomit.

I am not going down hiding, alone, puking my guts out. No matter what happens, I'm going to fight.

She tore at the tent zipper and spilled out, gagging, to confront the unknown.

Snapshots of the scene seared her eyes with each flash of light from the beacon on the cliff. Two Zodiacs—not theirs—were dragged on the shore. Masked, black-clad human figures clustered on the lower rocks. In front of them stood a man wearing some kind of hazmat suit. He carried a tank connected by a hose to a very long sprayer wand. He was dousing the camp.

Chinese from the fishing boats that confronted us earlier?

The mob—twenty or thirty of them—stayed back, behind the leader with the sprayer.

The spray—was it an accelerant? Were they going to burn the camp?

"Amika!"

Shuu and Hiroshi and the other man were out of their tents, shouting obscenities. Amika turned away from the beach, ready to run. Drops of the foul liquid landed on her hair, her clothes, her skin. It didn't burn but now the extreme odor would go with her everywhere. The attackers fanned out from the beachhead. In another strobe of the beacon light, she saw they were carrying clubs and long-handled tools.

"Come on!" Shuu squeezed her arm and sprinted to the kitchen tent. Hiroshi headed toward the base of the cliff.

Follow the soldier or the scientist?

She chased after her brother. Shuu dashed under the tarp and snatched the tranquilizer gun case.

"Grab a knife!" he said.

"I'm way ahead of you." On her way past the cooking station she had snagged a kitchen knife and a broom, too, to use like a combat staff.

They ran out into a continuing sprinkle of stink. The mist drifted into her lungs. If it was poison, she was finished.

"Go," Shuu said. "Up the hill."

He slapped her back but she needed no encouragement. She clambered up the cliff and got out of the spray. Shuu followed close behind.

"They're going to destroy the camp," he said. "If they try to follow you, I'll fight them off."

Halfway to the beacon, he planted his feet and opened the gun case. She kept running to the others, who were waiting at the light tower.

"Let's go," she said. "Higher."

Hiroshi didn't move. "No. We stand our ground here."

"Are you kidding? We can hide on the other side of the ridge. Come on!" She took a step.

Hiroshi seized her wrist. "No. Stay here. The Japan Coast Guard will come. If we scatter they won't be able to protect us."

"Protect? It's too late for that."

He tightened his grip. "Wait. They will come."

Her first instinct was to put a knee in his groin and take off running, but that definitely would not be a good career move. Plus, Hiroshi wasn't stupid. He'd been right earlier, during the attack on the *Kumamoto*. Did he see or know something that made him so confident?

Below, the camp was overrun by Chinese. They slashed and cut the contaminated tents, leaving everything in ruin.

Shuu guarded the trail to the camp, dart gun in hand. The Japanese flag hung from the tower nearby, its white background gleaming in the moonlight.

She needed a reason *not* to flee. "You really think—"

Rather than answer, Hiroshi shoved her against the cliff wall and pressed his body against her, his arms spread wide to cover.

What the—

Three men in black came charging from the left. Somehow they'd bypassed Shuu's roadblock. They were headed for the beacon. The red flag of the People's Republic of China billowed from one man's hands. The others carried crowbars.

"Shuu!" she screamed.

He turned and saw that he'd been outmaneuvered. That the attackers were closing on his sister.

He raised the stock of the pneumatic rifle to his shoulder.

Amika knew he wouldn't miss.

Shuu fired and reloaded at light speed. Once. Twice. Three times.

The attackers cried out in succession as the darts embedded in their flesh and injected their load. One of them pulled the dart from his thigh and held it up to look at.

She counted the seconds. *How long does it take for the tranquilizer to work?*

The man's eyes squinted in anger and he roared in Chinese. He raised the dart, ready to stab Hiroshi with it.

No...

The man stumbled. Heartbeats later he and the others tumbled to the ground. Their crowbars clattered on the rocks. The Chinese flag fluttered down the cliff, glowing red in the eerie light.

The Chinese down on the campground saw what had happened. They raised a cry and mobbed together to assault the cliff. Shuu turned to face them, his at-ready stance daring them to make their way upward.

She wriggled away from Hiroshi. "Take this," she said, giving him the kitchen knife she carried, leaving her free to clench the broomstick with both hands. *Those bastards are not going to touch my baby brother.* "Let's go to him."

"No. Look," he said.

She followed his gaze to the sky and heard the helicopter a second before it cleared the ridge behind them, crossing from the other side of the island.

She froze. A helicopter could only have come from a ship. But whose ship?

The chopper beamed a spotlight at the beach. The blinding light skipped over rocks and tents until it found the Chinese invaders. Then it fixed on them while the aircraft came around.

Shuu whooped.

Ropes tumbled from the open door of the helicopter. Black figures slid down the ropes as smoothly as water droplets on a thread of spider's silk. They landed lightly, and with fluid movements drew weapons. Amid the rotor and engine noise, they were completely silent.

Amika let the broomstick drop from one hand and braced against the wind whipping from the helicopter. The terrible smell of the spray worsened as the vapors were blown upward.

A siren pierced the air, even louder than the helicopter. Another blazing light hit the beach, this time from the sea. She shielded her eyes and squinted.

The *Kumamoto,* in all its red paint-spotted glory, turned the lights on. The Japan Coast Guard had arrived.

"I told you they'd come," Hiroshi shouted over the din. "Special Security Team!"

Shuu leaped over the unmoving bodies of the men he'd tranquilized and joined her, Hiroshi, and the other Koga man at the beacon.

She hugged Shuu's free arm. "Are you okay?"

He nodded. Down on the beach, the Japanese team engaged the enemy.

"Should we go higher?" she asked.

"Wait," Shuu said.

The commandos and the Chinese hooligans were all dressed in black, but it was easy to tell them apart. The commandos' garb was thickened with body armor and helmets, yet they moved gracefully and in concert with each other. Their opponents looked sloppy, and bounced randomly like balls in an old *pachinko* machine. The situation was chaotic. In fear of stray bullets, she shrank back against the cliff.

Then for no apparent reason, the man wielding the sprayer dropped to the ground. Had she missed the sound of a gunshot amid the tumult? Were the commandos using silencers?

Tiny flashes of white-blue lightning ripped the darkness. A couple more Chinese went down.

Electricity. They're using Tasers, not guns.

Then it dawned on her that the Chinese weren't carrying firearms, either. Like the water cannon incident, this conflict was threatening but had a surreal, theatrical quality. As if everybody was play-acting a scene for hidden cameras.

What's my role?

"Help me," Shuu said.

She ran down the trail with him to where he'd left the rifle case. He picked it up and returned to the first of the prone Chinese that he'd shot. The man's head was twisted at an awkward angle. Blood pooled under his cheek, presumably from when his nose or forehead had hit the ground.

Shuu handed her a knife. "I need exposed skin on the shoulder."

"What for?"

He opened a small compartment in the rifle case and took out a loaded syringe with a needle attached. "Antidote. Shooters working with Immobilon always—*always*—keep the antidote ready."

"The tranquilizer's not just a sleeping drug?"

"It is for livestock. Can be fatal in humans."

She sliced a hole in the Chinese man's sleeve and peeled back the fabric. Shuu jabbed the needle into the shoulder muscle.

"Will he wake up?" she asked.

"We'll find out."

She glanced down at the beach, where some of the protestors were running for the Zodiacs and others were clashing hand-to-hand with the security forces.

I hope someone's ready to deal with him if he comes to.

Shuu quickly refilled the syringe, not bothering to change the needle. He probably didn't have a spare. She doubted there was a protocol for mass casualties with a dart gun.

They hastened to the next guy. Amika poked the tip of the knife into his clothes and parted the threads, exposing his deltoid. It didn't look like he was breathing.

"Empty," Shuu said. He threw the glass medicine bottle over the cliff in frustration. "I'll have to split the dose."

"Will that be enough?"

"How the hell should I know?" He emptied the syringe into the third fallen Chinese.

Hiroshi waved his arms. Two commandos broke from the melee and sprinted toward them. A Zodiac from the *Kumamoto* landed on the beach, with another close behind.

"That's our cue," Shuu said.

She leaned over the nearest body, trying to tell if the man was alive. The antidote wasn't having any visible effect.

Hiroshi took her hand. "Leave them. Let's go."

He'd been right again. She allowed him to lead her, following Shuu down the trail toward the edge of camp. Sand swirled in the air, lifted by the helicopter's spinning blades and trapped by the cliff. She tugged her shirt over her nose to block the dust but the fabric was contaminated by the spray and the stink was overwhelming. She was better off with sand in her lungs.

They met the two Japanese soldiers. One dropped to the rear of their line, Taser drawn. Shuu spoke to the other, yelling to be heard.

"Three of 'em on the ground up there." He gestured with his thumb. "Tranked."

The man nodded. "Let's get you out of here."

"The sooner the better," she said.

Under the protection of the escort, they ran along the dark perimeter of the camp, over the rubble of the old *bonito* flakes factory. Hiroshi shepherded her through the dim light, guiding her steps. The special forces squad had forced the Chinese who weren't incapacitated to the opposite side of the beach, where they were naturally fenced in by the cliffs. She imagined the stink over there was almost enough to knock them out.

The invaders' boats sat on the shoal, empty and under guard. As she dumped her contaminated jacket and climbed into a Coast Guard Zodiac, she looked back at the ravaged tents. Anger replaced fear. *My favorite travel pants, ruined. Thanks to these Chinese clowns everything I brought with me is now as toxic as runoff from Fukushima's nuclear power plant.*

It wasn't really the clothes that infuriated her. It was the reckless, dangerous foolishness of it all. This tiny rock, desolate except for a few feral goats and an obscure species of mole, in the middle of nowhere—two of the world's most powerful nations were fighting over it? Didn't people have enough problems already?

The Zodiac zipped over the calm, black water, the roar of the helicopter fading behind them. Ocean breeze replaced the wind from its spinning blades. In the chilly night air she scrunched to the floor of the boat to keep warm.

Hiroshi slid over to her side. "Are you okay?"

She nodded. Her heart rate was slowing toward normal until he squeezed down to the floor of the boat next to her. She felt a warmth much greater than that provided by his protective arm over her shoulders. Ahead, the huge Japan Coast Guard patrol vessel gleamed in the empty darkness, beckoning them forward. She noticed that there was no moon and pressed deeper into Hiroshi's embrace.

A hundred yards away from the beach they hadn't escaped the stench. The spray was with them, on their clothes and skin. When the sailor politely asked Shuu to move as far away as the small boat would allow, Shuu did the only thing he could to lessen the reek. He stripped to his underwear.

He was about to toss his clothes overboard when Hiroshi said, "Save them as evidence."

The rest of the men did the same. They bagged the garments. She didn't envy the forensics specialist who would have to open that.

"Amika?" Shuu said expectantly.

She wasn't wearing much, just sleeping shorts and a T-shirt, but the fabric carried plenty of odor. She wasn't prudish. She wanted to ditch her clothes— God, the stink was so bad—but didn't know if she'd be making some colossal social blunder.

As if there was an etiquette rule for a situation like this.

"It's okay," Shuu assured her, holding the bag open for her deposit.

Why not? Let Hiroshi know I look good in a swimsuit. She stripped to her underwear and bra, and discarded her ruined attire in the evidence bag.

A little less stinky, she curled up with Hiroshi again. The naked skin of her shoulders snuggled against his bare chest. *This would never happen in the lab. Maybe I owe those Chinese guys some gratitude after all.*

5

The *Kumamoto* rose above them, glittering and solid compared to the dark, bobbing Zodiac. A rope ladder dangled from the side of the ship and Amika realized she had to climb that thing in her panties. *Maybe I should've kept my clothes on after all.* As she shivered up the swaying ladder, practically naked, in the dark, she felt like she was starring in a teen slasher flick. She made sure her brother climbed up close after her. The sailor in the Zodiac didn't deserve a peep show of her crotch.

On deck someone handed her a Mylar blanket and hustled her to a shower. In a claustrophobic stainless steel stall, she scrubbed and scrubbed with coarse military soap. The small indoor space concentrated the stench. The ship rolled up and down and she quickly felt sick. She managed to lather-rinse-repeat three times before she was on the verge of throwing up.

As she dried herself with a rough towel and put on ill-fitting (but clean) orange Coast Guard coveralls, the stink lingered. It was embedded in her skin and hair beyond the reach of ordinary soap.

I won't be socializing with normal people for a while.

Pale pink rays of dawn streaked across the upper deck where she found Hiroshi and Shuu in their matching military-issue jumpsuits. Their faces were grave and they abruptly ended an intense conversation when she walked up.

"You're all right?" Hiroshi said.

"I stink," she said. "They got any tomato soup on this boat?"

Apparently her joke about a home remedy for skunk spray didn't translate into Japanese. "They will have breakfast for us soon," Hiroshi said. "The crew is busy."

He gestured toward the aft end of the ship. On the helicopter landing pad were about twenty scraggly figures in black clothes. They were sitting on their heels in rows. Coast Guardsmen and members of the Special Security Team surrounded them.

"Our attackers," Shuu said. "Now prisoners."

Amika looked down on the captives. *Damn fools. Gave me a helluva scare. Now see the mess you've gotten yourselves into.*

Paintballs and water cannons and chemical sprays and Tasers. Japan versus China. She'd never had a camping trip like this one.

And she'd never seen her brother shoot a man. "Any news on the guys you tranked?"

Shuu shook his head.

"The trip home will take twice as long," Hiroshi said. "Ishigaki, the port we left from, doesn't have facilities to process them. The captain informs me that we sail for Okinawa."

Keeping a polite distance because of the smell, sailors escorted Amika and the rest of the Koga group to a small recreation lounge on the ship. They were too stinky to be allowed to eat in the mess hall. Amika had a choice to sit on a molded plastic chair in an ugly shade of brown or a vinyl sofa ratty enough to be rejected by a college dorm. She chose a chair.

Even with the portholes open, the room smelled foul. Then again, maybe it was the food. They were eating rice and *natto*, a traditional Japanese dish of fermented soybeans notorious for its pungent odor. For once, natto didn't smell so bad.

She crossed her orange-suited legs and rested the bowl on her knee. "Why am I reminded of when you used to come home from soccer practice?"

Shuu shoveled rice into his mouth with his chopsticks. "You could never handle BO."

"After this, I'll be tougher," she said.

She looked at Hiroshi, who was devouring his breakfast and apparently paying no attention to her at all. *I'd pay a hundred bucks to know what he's thinking.* Did yesterday's events open the door to a relationship, or was that semi-naked snuggle in the Zodiac a one-off?

"They call it Skunk," a new voice announced.

Wearing the rank insignia of a commanding officer with the name Miyashita on his chest, the captain of the *Kumamoto* entered the room and closed the door. Shuu and Hiroshi rose and bowed. Amika followed their lead and did the same.

Despite having spent the whole night managing a combat situation and rounding up terrorists, Miyashita was impeccably groomed. He was shorter than Hiroshi, and twenty years older from the look of him. His dark blue uniform was crisp and kept his slightly protuberant belly squeezed in place.

"What is it?" Shuu said.

The captain took a seat. "That spray, or something like it, was invented by the Israelis. It's considered harmless, so they use it to break up protests. Looks better on TV than using tear gas."

"Can you buy it on the civilian market?" Hiroshi asked.

"Unlikely."

"Then those 'unarmed' jackals had to be military," Hiroshi said.

They didn't look military to me, but what do I know?

"More likely, they're civilians with government support," Shuu said. "Sending Red Army soldiers into Japanese territory would be one hell of a provocation."

Miyashita sat straight-backed on the edge of his chair. "I would prefer an open declaration to all this tiptoeing around. It would put an end to these charades."

Shuu grunted his agreement, but Amika was glad the war game hadn't been "real."

"That was no tiptoe." Hiroshi angrily set his bowl aside. "Last night was an outrage against Japanese sovereignty." Tapping his finger on the table to emphasize each syllable he said, "It must not go unanswered."

"Indeed," the captain said. "Your father has been briefed on what happened. No doubt the prime minister will be hearing from him soon." He looked at Shuu. "Other developments will also be driving events."

"What developments?" Shuu said.

Miyashita's face was expressionless. "I just received word. The Chinese jackals you tranquilized are dead."

Amika barely noticed the captain's use of the offensive term. *Dead? All three?* "But he gave them the antidote!" she blurted.

"They're dead. We airlifted them to a hospital but it was too late."

Shuu folded his hands on the table. Her heart went out to him. It was a terrible, terrible accident. It wasn't his fault. He was doing the best he could...

He avoided eye contact with his sister.

"Regrettable," Hiroshi said, "but they should have known something like this could happen. Beijing is playing with fire to encourage these people."

"We were victims of an unprovoked attack," Shuu said calmly.

"With a woman present," Hiroshi emphasized. "She's unharmed because of Shuu's decisive action. And because of the Coast Guard's swift response, of course."

Amika found this emphasis on "a woman" mildly offensive. The way she remembered it, she had defended herself as effectively as the *men* from Koga, but she supposed it was gallant of Hiroshi to be especially concerned about her well-being.

"We, in this room, understand the truth," Captain Miyashita said knowingly, "but others may see things differently. I predict there will be… consequences."

The pause in his speech was heavy with implication. The men stared at their hands in silence. Amika sensed much was being left unsaid. She tried to glean his meaning.

"You think my brother will be in trouble?"

The men looked at her with uniformly somber expressions.

"He acted in self-defense," she said. "He didn't even use a real gun."

"Japan is not the US," Miyashita said. "We Japanese do not keep guns. We do not have your country's many laws governing when it is permitted to use them."

Was he saying that Shuu might be accused of a crime?

"He tried to save those men! I helped him give the antidote."

"It'll be okay, Amika," Shuu said.

"No, it's not okay!" She had to make the captain understand how ridiculous his suggestion was. Her brother did the right thing. *He did it for me.*

"Miss Nakamura, you know his victims were unarmed," Miyashita said.

"Their group was carrying enough wrenches to bludgeon a horse!" She was too flustered to correct him about her title. *That's* Doctor *to you, pal.*

"You must understand, to some people this looks bad."

Hiroshi slid his chair closer and took her hand. The part of her brain devoted to relationships with the opposite sex barely noticed.

"Think about it, Amika," he said. "We know Shuu did what any of us would've done. But the media, they make everything so complicated—and oh, can you imagine what they'll say on Twitter?"

"The Chinese government will react very strongly," Miyashita said.

"They'll want your brother's head," Hiroshi said. "Tokyo will have to respond."

"That's totally unfair," she said. Was this a case for the rule of law, or the rule of expediency? Would her little brother become a pawn in a larger chess match between China and Japan?

Shuu stood up. "You can help me."

"That's right," Miyashita said.

"We need to win over the public," Hiroshi said. "Control the narrative. Keep people focused on the danger *you* faced. Make the conflict about you, not him."

"We must turn your attackers into demons," Miyashita said, "not worthy of people's misguided sympathy."

Shuu came and knelt down at her side. "You can do that for me."

Her breaths came quickly. Her rice bowl was gone and she couldn't remember what she had done with it. "How? What can I do?"

"There will be reporters when we arrive at Okinawa," Miyashita said. "They will want to hear your story."

"I'll talk to them."

Hiroshi and the captain exchanged a glance. He released her hand. "Amika, you're a scientist, and a good one, too. You've been trained to tell stories in a certain way."

"Logically," Miyashita said. "With facts."

"This kind of story is different," Hiroshi said. "The facts are, Shuu shot three men and they died. There won't be any argument about the facts."

"There's more to the facts than that," she said. "We were attacked—"

"Of course," Hiroshi interrupted. "But my point is, your story has to be about feelings, not facts."

She didn't know why but she started to wish the captain wasn't there.

"The truth is, you felt threatened," Miyashita said. "You felt your life was in danger."

"I suppose," she said.

"Your *brother* felt your life was in danger."

Shuu nodded vigorously.

"And that is how he behaved. To save his sister's life."

"That's the truth," Hiroshi said. "The facts, with the 'unarmed' protesters, don't necessarily tell this truth."

"You can tell them the truth," Shuu said, his eyes imploring. "The true truth."

True truth? What the hell is that? Everything had seemed much clearer a minute ago.

The captain rose and assumed a soldier's stiff pose squarely in front of her. He drilled into her with his stare. "Let's be frank. Did any of the jackals touch you?"

"No," she said.

"Were you physically harmed in any way?"

"No. Except the Skunk."

"Of course. But the liquid didn't hurt you, burn you, make you cough?"

"No."

"Did you see any guns during the attack?"

"No."

"Did you see or hear anything to make you think these people intended violence against your person instead of your camp equipment?"

"I guess not. But they were carrying—"

"It doesn't matter."

She was silent for a moment. "I see your point."

Hiroshi leaned closer. He put one hand on her thigh, the other on her shoulder. This time, she was acutely aware of his touch. "When you tell your story to the press, don't tell them what happened. Tell them what it *means*."

"For my sake," Shuu said.

"We can't allow the dead Chinese jackals to be the victims. We need a victim of our own," said Miyashita.

"Someone who can't be blamed," said Hiroshi.

"A woman," said Shuu. "Victimized. For being a woman."

As the men's request became clear, she wrestled with her discomfort. *I am not a victim.* Yet how could she refuse? She could embellish a little to keep her baby brother out of jail (or worse). She could add a grasping hand, a torn blouse, an attempted grope, or a forceful blow, into her story of what happened during the attack.

She nodded. Hiroshi squeezed her knee in approval.

Captain Miyashita bowed to her before leaving. "The *Kumamoto* is not a cruise liner, but if there is some comfort we can offer you, please ask."

He left. Hiroshi and Shuu returned to their chairs and spoke in hushed voices. Suddenly she felt terribly tired, so tired she lay down on one of the battered sofas. Up close it smelled like ancient cigarette smoke. Her cheek stuck to the vinyl. With her eyes closed, she rehearsed what she was going to say to the reporters. Then she fantasized about the hot bath she would take when they got to shore. She vowed to soak as long as it took to eliminate the Skunk.

But she doubted a bath would cleanse her of the grubby feeling the captain had given her.

6

MAY 28 (THREE DAYS LATER)
KOGA SCIENTIFIC RESEARCH LABORATORIES
TOKYO

The attention caught Amika unprepared. When the *Kumamoto* docked at Okinawa, military police had set up a cordon to keep the media at bay. There were dozens of journalists and video crews waiting for the ship. At first, Hiroshi Naito was the main attraction. Amika knew the Naito family was a powerful and wealthy dynasty in Japan, but she hadn't anticipated how an international incident involving the bachelor son would attract reporters like old Chinese ladies to a mahjongg set.

Maybe she was surprised because she was an American. American celebrities tended to be *nouveau*, young, trendy, entertainers. Rich, but also ephemeral. America worshipped meteors; Japan respected mountains.

The media's Senkaku Islands story began with Hiroshi, but focus soon shifted to her and Shuu. As she'd promised to do, she recited her tale of woe and juiced up the innuendo. The Nakamura siblings became the talk of Tokyo, and not necessarily in a good way. They gave a human face to the long-simmering Sino-Japanese conflict. To some, they were foreign agitators who were complicit in murder. To others, she was a helpless, pretty young Japanese thing whose gallant brother had rescued her from Chinese villains.

She knew it was all about the spin, and Japan was eating it up. So far Shuu was untouched.

Her personal and work phones rang constantly. Reporters and officials dropped in at her Koga lab, unannounced. Other people at Koga wanted to hear her story firsthand. Hiroshi arranged an exclusive interview for her with *Shufu*, a magazine that seemed like a Japanese version of *Good Housekeeping* or *Woman's Day*. Worn out, she was soon done with playing the victim. Her fifteen minutes of fame was turning out to be fourteen minutes too long.

In the solitude of the biocontainment lab she found peace. Her paper gown crinkled as she bent over to stretch the elastic of disposable booties over her shoes. She covered her whole head with a hood, trapping the humidity from her breath behind a clear plastic face shield. A faint odor of Skunk touched her nose as the protective gear concentrated the lingering vapors of that filth. The comfort of being isolated in her little cocoon was well worth it. Biosafety precautions were designed to keep hazards in the lab. They were equally good at keeping distractions out.

One distraction she would welcome: an appearance by Hiroshi. He'd visited the research building several times since they got back, and always came to see her. His demeanor was formal and professional, which she expected in the Japanese workplace, but the fact he was even there spoke volumes. Or so she hoped. Seducing Hiroshi Naito could be her best career move since earning her PhD.

The drama around her trip to the Senkakus, and her fears for her brother, consumed her attention but there were bigger problems in the world. She settled on a lab stool and disinfected her workspace. Dead birds were turning up all over Honshu, Japan's main island. The first ones had been found in Tokyo two months earlier. Other cities were struck soon after. The numbers weren't large. About a hundred dead birds, mostly pigeons and crows, had been surrendered to the authorities so far.

As an influenza expert, dead birds were her specialty.

Mysterious bird deaths in Asia screamed "virus," with a new bird flu at the top of the list of suspects. Japanese public health officials had confirmed this. Because Koga was in the business of making flu vaccines, including vaccines against avian influenza for both birds and people, Amika and her coworkers were part of the investigation.

She turned on the noisy air purification system in the small isolation room and felt the air move. Then she was alone with viruses from a bunch of dead birds. Wearing two layers of gloves that gleamed in the fluorescent light, she relaxed. This was exactly where she wanted to be. She felt safer with these dangerous germs than she did with people.

Whatever virus killed the birds probably came out of mainland China. New bird flu viruses spontaneously appeared from time to time, especially in Southeast Asia. Usually they stayed in birds and didn't pose a threat to humans. But when they jumped species, like they did in 1918, 1957, and 1968, global pandemics resulted.

Fear of a flu pandemic was a good reason for her and her fellow scientists to keep a close watch on the bird situation.

Things coming out of China are causing me a lot of trouble lately.

She pushed those thoughts aside. Her task was to sequence the genomes of the viruses in the specimens she'd been given from assorted bird corpses. With the DNA code, any decent virologist could tell whether Koga's existing vaccines were likely to be effective against the new flu, or whether a new vaccine was needed.

Amika was way better than decent.

The gain-of-function research that got her kicked out of the university gave her unique insight into the meaning of the virus DNA sequences. At Berkeley and now at Koga, she studied which genetic changes made a virus more dangerous. What subtle mutations would let a bird flu jump into humans? What gave it power to spread from person to person? If scientists could predict this very early in an outbreak, millions of lives might be saved.

She arranged her tubes of chemical reagents in the order she would use them, and unscrewed the cap on the first specimen.

Two hours later she rejoined civilization. After the windowless lab she squinted in the sunlit hallway of the Koga building. She paused to let the rays shine on her face. Outside it was hot and sticky amid Tokyo's concrete and pavement, but here on the air-conditioned fifth floor the sun's heat felt good. She pressed her forehead to the window so she could look straight down to the street. There, people in the neighborhood maintained a small shrine, or *hokora*, dedicated to a local Shinto nature spirit. Or maybe a Buddhist deity; she didn't really know. She did enjoy watching what the people brought as offering, usually fresh fruit or flowers, left on a small stone altar beneath a flared wooden roof, covered with green tiles. Little oases like this one were a soothing balm in the dense, overbuilt city.

She spent the rest of the afternoon at her workbench in the regular lab, where she had eight feet of countertop to do her experiments. The lab room was large enough to hold six similar workbenches, some for individuals, some shared by the group. By the cramped standards of Tokyo, it was practically a warehouse. One of her coworkers kept a small boom box on his desk always tuned on low volume to a J-pop radio station. She didn't mind the music in small doses but it was so banal she suspected that chronic exposure could lower her IQ.

If I'm ever in charge at Koga, I'll make a workplace ban on J-pop my top priority.

She sat down at her untidy desk to examine another DNA sequencing trace. The data weren't as accurate as she would've liked. What was the problem? Was it the polymerase reactions? The parameters she'd programmed into the sequencer?

"Dr. Amika Nakamura?"

A woman stood in the open doorway of the lab, wearing the light blue, short-sleeved dress shirt uniform of the Koga mailroom.

"Yes?" Amika said.

With both hands, the woman gave her an envelope plastered with labels. Amika couldn't understand most of the writing—unlike her speaking ability, her skill at reading *kanji*, the written pictogram language of Japanese, was limited to an elementary school vocabulary—but apparently this was a kind of certified mail. The woman checked her ID, asked her to sign for the letter, and left with a quick bow.

The return address was Tokyo, some government agency. She opened the envelope and skimmed the sheet inside.

She grabbed her phone and called Shuu.

"It's a fact-finding commission," he said. "They're calling everybody who was there to testify."

"I get it," she said. "I just don't like it. Will I be under oath?"

"What difference does it make?"

"It makes a lot of difference. We both know the story I've been telling the media exaggerates what really happened on Uotsuri-shima."

"Who gives a crap? The point is to protect me from a lynch mob."

"What mob?"

"The one in Tiananmen Square. In Beijing. Didn't you hear?"

"There's a protest about you in Tiananmen Square?"

"That's right. Your little bro is famous. China wants a piece of me."

That was Shuu all over. Always so cocksure. But her hands went cold with fear. "What do they want?"

"They say I'm a murderer," he gloated. "They'd like to put me on trial in one of their kangaroo courts. Too bad for them they don't have an extradition treaty with Japan."

Being ignorant of international law, she surmised this was a good thing for Shuu. "So they can't touch you?"

"Not unless the Japanese government decides I'm an embarrassment. Which is where you and Hiroshi come in."

She tried to make light. "If they ask, I'll have to tell them you've embarrassed me loads of times."

He didn't laugh. "You play the damsel in distress, so I look like a prince. Meanwhile Hiroshi works his family connections in the government to make sure everybody's on my side."

"And then they'll leave you alone?"

"Just lay it on thick," he said. "Tell them I saved you from those jackals. Leave no room for second-guessing. Hiroshi says some of the committee members are Chinese sympathizers so you better make it sound good."

He had it all figured out. Some things never changed.

"Shuu, what if they don't buy it? Those three men who died—"

"Had it coming. Any loyal Japanese will see that. As long as you do your job, I'll be fine."

"But what if—" *If I fail to convince them Shuu acted with honor? If he's arrested? Or...*

"You really want to know?" A violent edge came into his voice. "I'll tell you. Bad case scenario, Japan puts me on trial for the deaths. Worst case scenario, they put me on a plane to China and wash their hands."

So it *was* possible. Her baby brother could end up in a Communist prison.

That cleared up any misgivings she had about testifying. She would say whatever it took to make Shuu seem holier than the Pope.

After hanging up she went to the computer in her office to see what she'd been missing from the news. Her alarm grew as she pieced together reports from websites in English, Japanese, and Google-translated Chinese. Once she figured out that the Diaoyu Islands and the Senkaku Islands were the same thing (China insisted on using the contested islands' Chinese name to emphasize its territorial claim), "Diaoyu" became a handy tool to identify which stories came from the Chinese media, and were likely biased in that direction.

To her dismay, she found footage of crowds of several thousand people marching in the streets of Beijing and in Shenzhen and Hong Kong as well. The Chinese government normally suppressed public demonstrations, but the virulent anti-Japanese sentiment on display must have suited their purposes so they let it go. The marchers proclaimed their demands on banners, many of which were in English for a global audience. They wanted Japan to release the detainees. (*I didn't know they were still holding the Chinese protesters we brought back on the ship.*) They wanted the bodies of the men who died. And they wanted Tokyo to surrender Shuu Nakamura to face "justice" for the killings.

Lynch mob indeed.

"That doesn't look good." A woman's voice in the doorway interrupted her focus. "I think you need some *onigiri.*"

"Hi Manami," Amika said as an older Koga administrator came in and offered a snack. Manami's homemade *onigiri* rice balls were famous on the floor, so Amika gladly accepted. Manami sat down to watch a video with her.

"They make it sound like it was Japan's fault," Manami said.

"The Chinese reports keep using the words 'unarmed' and 'nonviolent' to describe the protest on the island," Amika said. "That's a lie."

"Communist censorship," Manami said. "They tell you what they want you to hear, not the truth."

Her words uncomfortably reminded Amika of her encounter with Captain Miyashita. *I guess I'm not the only one who knows how to embellish a story.* The Chinese press, manipulated by their government, ignored the fact that the Chinese protesters started the confrontation, and that they had indeed landed on foreign soil and attacked the Koga camp. They made it sound like the three dead men were on their way to serve lunch at an orphanage. None of the Chinese reports mentioned that her brother had tried to save them with the tranquilizer's antidote.

She swallowed a bite of the triangle-shaped block of sticky rice, wrapped in a fresh piece of dry seaweed that kept her hands clean. "I'll be gone next Friday," she told Manami. "There's a hearing about what happened on the island. My brother says they might make a decision about whether to prosecute him."

"Prosecute him for those dead Chinese jackals?" Manami said. "That's horrible!"

Manami, too? I must not understand that word correctly.

"I don't think it'll happen," Amika said.

"A few years ago, no one in Japan would've even considered it," Manami replied. "We've gotten soft."

"Huh."

"Now instead of standing up to them, everybody wants to keep China happy." She leaned forward and lowered her voice, as if revealing a secret. "We're too dependent on our exports to them."

Amkia didn't see what Japanese exports had to do with Shuu's case, but Manami liked to talk, so she let her.

"Don't you worry. Mr. Naito will quiet things down. He'll do whatever it takes to protect the company."

Screw the company. What about my brother? "You think Koga Scientific will get dragged into this?"

"It was a Koga expedition. And Koga was working with the Coast Guard." Manami sighed. "Here in Japan, company public relations departments are not used to managing scandal. We will do our best."

That struck Amika as disingenuous. Japan wasn't so squeaky clean. The Japanese were just good at keeping things quiet.

"As long as Shuu isn't the fall guy for the company," Amika said.

"Of course not," Manami said, but she looked away when she said it. Then she turned to Amika and smiled. "He's an American. The US will defend him."

That was even less reassuring. Amika knew Shuu's relationship with the US government was, well, complicated.

7

The old warrior wore a long cotton *yukata* robe, cinched at the waist with a sash. Sandaled feet followed the slate stepping stones from the *ryokan* country inn to the hot mineral springs. The rising sun was about to peek over the forest-covered mountains that surrounded the inn. This was the best time of day in summer, when the air was gentle and fragrant with iris blossoms. Thunderstorms were likely later. For now, only scattered clouds crossed the sky.

Meticulous gardens of stone, bamboo, and gnarled maple trees edged the path. Ahead, steam carrying a whiff of sulfur rose from the placid bathing pool. How wonderful the water was going to feel, water naturally heated by fires deep in the earth.

Fire built this blessed nation, the warrior thought. Japan's home islands germinated from the ocean as flaming lava rock, propelled by tectonic forces in the great Pacific Ring of Fire. Creation through destruction. Fuji, the sacred mountain visible in the distance, was still-living proof of this fiery origin.

It's time to light a spark.

The warrior folded the *yukata* into a basket and scrubbed naked, scarred skin until it tingled before lowering arthritic limbs into the milky, mineral-rich water. The trip from Tokyo in the first class Green Car on the *shinkansen* bullet train had been well worth the effort. The beauty and tranquility of this place put everything in perspective.

A flock of black-feathered Japanese thrush launched into the sky from nearby trees. The warrior offered a silent prayer of gratitude for them. They were soldiers in the war.

Birds are the beginning. And they will be the end.

Steam eased the tightness in the warrior's constricted lungs. The first rays of sunlight hit the snow-covered peak of Fuji-san. *A good omen.* This time of year the mountain was usually invisible, buried in clouds.

Though Fuji slept, the sleep was light. Gas-spewing fumaroles cracked the mountain's crust. Seismologists monitored the volcano, but none could predict when Fuji would erupt again. Fuji's sister Mount Ontake surprised everyone when a phreatic eruption—underground water instantaneously flashing into steam—killed fifty-six hikers on her slopes. When it came to natural disasters, serenity today was no guarantee against calamity tomorrow.

Do the Chinese jackals understand this?

The heat of the water was intense, loosening creaky old joints. Less tenacious bathers would have climbed out of the pool within a couple of minutes. But the warrior was resolute, in many things. Time and suffering were simply part of the journey. What mattered was the goal.

To put them in their place. And to make them pay.

How many thousands, or millions, of years did it take to build Fuji-san? This project had required the patience of mere decades.

One generation opens the road upon which another generation travels.

8

Amika stepped out of Harajuku Station too late in the morning to beat the heat. Within minutes, sweat plastered her running clothes against her skin. She had planned to get up earlier but she'd been too upset to sleep well the night before. Yesterday, a mob of Chinese nationalists had attacked the Japanese consulate in Qingdao. They demanded Japan get out of the "Diaoyu" Islands, and they wanted Shuu Nakamura handed over. Japanese companies in the area, and elsewhere in China, were getting jittery. Tomorrow's fact-finding commission hearing couldn't come soon enough.

High temperatures and suffocating humidity had rolled into Tokyo from the northwest, out of Manchuria, so Amika blamed China for the weather *and* her sleeplessness. She weaved through the crowd on the sidewalk in front of the train station which bore an out-of-place resemblance to a Swiss chalet. Harajuku was a magnet for cosplayers, mostly young people who dressed up as their favorite characters from Japanese *manga* comics and animation, and hung around the station. Because of the heat, there were fewer cosplayers and simpler costumes today. Wearing wigs and tights and cloaks was a health risk in this weather.

She stretched the muscles in her arms and sides as she walked around the corner and dove into the tree cover of Yoyogi Park. The park was one of central Tokyo's largest urban green spaces and she had a standard five-mile loop she liked to run. She'd stuffed a double-layered plastic bag from the lab, zippered and extra thick, into a running waist pack along with her phone. If she came across a dead bird she might as well pick it up and bring it in for analysis.

She dodged a few bicyclists and passed a couple of dog walkers on their way to the leash-free area. Her eyes lingered on a food cart selling cold *chukamen* noodles topped with fresh sprouts and rice vinegar sauce but she kept jogging until her glance fell on a magazine rack at the adjacent newsstand.

Where she saw herself on the cover of *Shufu*, the magazine she'd given an exclusive interview.

She stumbled to a halt and stared. The photo wasn't the main cover image. It was a smallish rectangle to the side of the layout, next to a sensational headline about China defiling the nation. She squinted to make sure. The picture was a slightly fuzzy close-up of a ladder hanging against a white ship's hull blotched with red. A naked woman was climbing the ladder.

"W-what?" Her hands clenched into fists. *That's me.*

She bought the magazine.

Any ambition to finish her run melted away. She sat down on a bench and turned the pages. *Shufu* magazine wrote for a wide audience and the *kanji* characters used in the writing were mostly common, so even with her mediocre *kanji* skills she was able to read much of the text. But she did examine the pictures first.

The picture from the cover was reproduced much larger in the body of the article. It was definitely an image of her boarding the *Kumamoto*.

Where the hell did they get this?

No attribution was given for the source. The perspective suggested the photo was taken by someone in the Zodiac.

It was bad enough that this singularly unflattering image of her was plastered all over Tokyo. What really pissed her off was that it had been photoshopped. Not to make her look good, but to give the impression that she was completely naked. That night she had cast off her Skunked clothing but was wearing a bra and panties when she climbed the ladder. The *Shufu* photo strategically placed little black marks on her upper and lower torso and blurred the edges as if they were censoring the X-rated parts.

As if they're protecting my privacy, when in truth I'm being exploited.

Why would they publish this? The photo wasn't pin-up material. This was a magazine for women.

She spotted another photo linked to the article. In the photo, a child, maybe four or five years old, with the help of his mother was hanging his bare bottom over a trash can in a Tokyo subway station. Other photos showed adults spitting on sidewalks. Amika tackled the text to try to understand the connection.

When she got to the point of the article, her blood ran cold.

Clearly she had misunderstood when she gave the interview. *Shufu* was no *Good Housekeeping*.

This was a jingoistic story that demonized Chinese people using sensational anecdotes. The editorial slant of the article was hotly nationalistic. According to the writer, the Senkaku Islands incident was an attack on Japanese sovereignty and should be viewed as an act of war. They claimed the Red Army had orchestrated it with the approval of Beijing. Not only were the actions of the Chinese military barbaric, but ordinary Chinese citizens were also vulgar as evidenced by the behavior of mainland tourists visiting Japan (hence the photo of public defecation).

But Amika herself was Exhibit A in their argument that China posed an immediate threat to the people, culture, and nation of Japan. Why? Because she was an ethnically Japanese woman who'd been raped by Chinese thugs.

Raped? She felt a gust of fury in her chest that was even hotter than the air. *That didn't happen.*

And yet, hadn't she left the door open to that interpretation? She tried to remember if she had exaggerated more than usual about the attack when she talked to the reporter from *Shufu*. Maybe, but she definitely had not made a rape accusation. This was a case of gross sensationalism.

Her hands trembled as she studied the Japanese characters used in the article. Was she translating it wrong? Did the characters she interpreted as "rape" have a subtly different meaning? With a little help from her smartphone, she decided the language *could* be interpreted more than one way, as if the writer was trying to head off a potential libel suit. But the story was dripping with innuendo. The doctored photo was part of the game.

She closed the magazine and slapped it on the bench. Anger and embarrassment wrestled for the top of her emotions. *How dare they!* She'd lived in the progressive culture of Northern California for years, so she was accustomed to a lot of openness and support for rape victims. *If that actually happened to me, I'm pretty sure I wouldn't keep it all hush-hush. I would tell the truth. Then I'd hire a hit man to castrate the guy.* The last thing she wanted was to be pitied and whispered about, as a victim so powerless she couldn't even come out and say what happened.

A pigeon landed at her feet and pecked for crumbs. Her left hamstring cramped from the abrupt end of her run. An elderly woman in an oversized straw hat shuffled by. Her hat tilted slightly as she scanned the cover of *Shufu* on the bench. There was no way the woman could recognize her from the cover but Amika's face grew hot. She rolled the magazine and wrung it in her lap.

I'll tell everyone it's a lie! I'll file a lawsuit against them! (Do people sue each other in Japan?)

But…

She unrolled the magazine with a sigh and stared at the cover. *My job is to create sympathy for Shuu.*

The *Shufu* article might be used to their advantage. It certainly gave her an aura of vulnerability. If she was too aggressive in her rebuttal, she would dispel that aura.

Embrace the lie. Be weak. Become a victim.

In her heart she realized this was what Captain Miyashita had proposed. It was what they all agreed was necessary to sway public opinion in Shuu's favor. Her frailty would be the ultimate defense for his actions.

She could play a role.

Just hope that it doesn't define your life in Japan forever.

FRIDAY, JUNE 6 (THE NEXT MORNING)

Amika looked at herself in the mirror and saw she was pale and frumpy with super-short hair that still managed to look slept in. She tried not to dwell on how easy it was to make herself ugly.

The drab, loose-fitting clothes she wore were the opposite of the neon activewear she preferred. She'd had to make a quick shopping trip to find the right "victim suit," an earth-toned mess of a full skirt and baggy shirt.

Remember, it's an act. It's not who you are.

Today was the day Shuu would get his life back. He and the whole team that went to the Senkakus would tell their story. Officials could get their questions answered. Her brother's innocence would be clear to all, the protests in China would peter out, and she could redirect her energy to studying the new bird flu.

At least, that was what she kept telling herself. In truth she was terrified that the outcome might be something very different.

In the subway she practiced meek postures. She slouched until she thought she'd get a back ache. At her final stop, she tried to shuffle and hang her head as she made her way off the train, but in the crush of bodies at rush hour she had to break character and show some spunk just to survive.

On the escalator out of the subway, she glided past a gigantic poster of a smiling mother and child with the Koga Foundation logo in one corner. The poster was a public service ad sponsored by her employer. The caption read, "Because I love my daughter." Then it exhorted people, young and old, to get a flu shot.

The ad campaign was good public policy. Dead birds were in the news, and people were spooked—for good reason. One goal of Amika's work was to figure out whether this new bird virus was a threat to humans. As of now, nobody knew. They did know that the best way to forestall an outbreak of bird flu in Japan was to vaccinate as many people as possible, against regular flu and against bird flu.

The campaign was also a good way for Koga to sell a lot of vaccine.

She stepped off the escalator into the sticky air. The smell of fried food came from a nearby McDonald's, reminding her of her daily walk to work back at Berkeley. She headed down a narrow street jammed on both sides with outdoor stalls selling everything from raw squid to fresh flowers and ceramic lucky cats to slippers. She wasn't hungry but when she was less than a block from her destination, she dropped a few yen into a vending machine for a can of iced coffee.

"Dr. Nakamura?"

She turned from the machine to see who was speaking. A young Japanese woman, about her same age, bowed to her. The woman's hair was cut in a shag, layered in multiple lengths, none of them longer than her chin. The style conveyed a spirit of effortless chic, unlike Amika's hair, which merely looked like she had made no effort. The woman's clothes suggested she was the kind of girl who could turn a thrift store budget into a fashion statement. Or maybe the sleeveless gray cardigan she wore cost two days' salary. Amika wasn't the type to know.

The young woman extended a business card with both hands. Amika bowed and tucked the can of coffee between her upper arm and side so she could accept with both hands. In observance of the Japanese custom (and with natural curiosity), she respectfully studied the card.

Jun Taniguchi
Asian Center for Investigative Journalism

Another reporter. I should have known.

"I'm on my way to a meeting," Amika said. "This isn't a good time." She put the card in the pocket of her dowdy outfit, opened the coffee can, and twisted to walk around the journalist.

"I know," Jun said, spinning to match her stride. "I'm going too."

"I thought the committee's proceedings were closed to the media."

Jun shrugged her shoulders. "Why did you go to the Senkakus?"

A red light sorely tempted Amika to violate the local norm and jaywalk to get away from this person. After *Shufu*, she was done with reporters. "That's really none of your business."

"Didn't you understand the risks?"

"I thought I was going camping on a deserted island," Amika said. "I didn't expect the *goats* to be dangerous." She tapped her foot. A little red figure warned her not to cross the street. *Will this light ever change?*

Jun stayed glued to her as the signal switched and the mass of pedestrians swept across the intersection. "Camping with restricted military hardware. Whose idea was that?"

"Nothing about that trip was my idea."

"Whose, then? That navigational equipment is the reason you were..."

The building where the meeting was to take place was a generic example of modern bureaucracy architecture, about twenty stories of boxy glass and steel. Amika reached the tile steps that led to the main doors. Jun touched her arm.

"Whoever provoked the Chinese by bringing the DGPS system to the island is partly responsible for what happened to you," she said, her face dripping with sympathy.

Amika tried to keep her expression neutral. *Play the victim.* "Nothing happened to me."

Jun's eyes widened. The sympathy in her face morphed into the hunger of a keen investigator. "You weren't raped," she concluded.

"I never said I was." Amika started up the stairs toward the building's entrance.

Jun forced herself into the revolving door with her. "What really happened?"

"No comment."

"You didn't know about the DGPS, did you?"

Amika had to stop for the lobby's security guard. *Stuck again.*

"I don't know what you're talking about." It was the most truthful thing she'd said all day.

Jun smiled, a tight, cold curling of her pretty lips. "You'll soon find out."

The guard examined Amika's passport and typed her name into a computer. She tried to ignore the pesky newshound but Jun leaned into her ear.

"The Naito family is ruthless. They've abused their power for generations."

The security man handed back her passport and bowed. "They're expecting you on the fifth floor, Doctor."

She thanked him and turned away. Jun wasn't finished. "The Naitos only watch out for themselves. If push comes to shove, they'll make your brother the scapegoat."

"Goodbye, Miss Taniguchi." Amika aimed for the bank of elevators.

The guard raised a hand at Jun. She started talking fast to him. Amika pressed the up button. Apparently there *was* a media ban.

"Call me. I can help!" Jun urged one more time.

Amika's stomach was churning and she realized she was wound up, carrying herself more like a predator than prey. *If this is that woman's idea of help, she has it all wrong.*

Victim. She let her shoulders droop.

Jun was still arguing with the guard when Amika entered the elevator and the doors closed.

9

Amika texted Shuu and Hiroshi from the elevator. They had agreed that she would not walk into the conference room alone. Leaning on a man for support would add to the image she was going for: a feeble, fragile female.

She swallowed her disgust. *Small sacrifice for Shuu.*

The elevator opened to a small lobby brightly lit from a window. Reproductions of famous Japanese woodblock prints hung on the walls—stylized images of a blue ocean wave, Mount Fuji, flowering trees. She caught a vaguely familiar scent that she associated with warm paper. An overheated photocopier nearby?

"Amika."

Hiroshi and Shuu appeared. Her heart skipped a beat when she saw her baby brother.

"I can't remember the last time I saw you in a suit and tie," she said.

The outfit made him handsome and respectable. His bearing was straight and strong, as if he were still wearing his army dress uniform. He had looked so good in that uniform.

When did she last see him dressed up like this? *The wedding. A long time ago.* Shuu was maybe five years old when their cousin invited him to be ring bearer. Amika was excited for him that day, and jealous, too. *Where are those photos? He was so dang cute.* At least in the pictures. In real life, well, maybe not so much, even then.

She kissed his cheek. "You look great."

"Thanks," he said. "And you—"

"Don't finish that thought, I don't want to hear it." In his ear she whispered, "I'm in costume, remember."

He squeezed her shoulders and turned her to Hiroshi. She'd seen her boss in business attire several times before but it still made an impact. The dark, custom-fitted suit on his tall frame exuded power.

This is a guy you want to have on your team. Or in your bed—

Hiroshi put his arm around her waist. "Are we clear?" he said in a low voice.

"Completely," she replied. Suddenly her heart swelled with emotion. She wanted this to be over. She wanted the cloud lifted from Shuu. She wanted the opportunity to hang out with Hiroshi Naito for pleasure, not business. She wanted to do science without distractions.

They walked toward the conference room. She hung her head a little for effect.

"Some woman came up to me outside," she said. "A reporter. With questions about the island."

People flowed past as they moved slowly down the hall. She resisted the urge to walk at her normal rapid pace.

"They're sharks," Hiroshi said. "They smell blood in the water. After today it'll quiet down."

"I hope so." She didn't want to repeat the nasty things Jun Taniguchi had said about Hiroshi's family, but she did wonder if he knew what the journalist was talking about. "She asked me about some military equipment we supposedly had with us. A GPS or something?"

She felt his body stiffen slightly.

"Was that what you used to track the goats?" she said.

He shot a look at her brother.

"Excuse me," he said. "I need to use the restroom before things get going. Would you?"

He transferred her hand to Shuu. She took her brother's arm and watched Hiroshi retreat down the hall.

"What was that about?" she said.

He shrugged. "Rich guys are weird. Don't ask."

"I'm a scientist. Asking questions is what I do."

"Not today," Shuu said. "Today we answer questions the *right* way. And we put this behind us."

He patted her arm. An attendant opened the conference room door for them.

Wallpaper mimicking shoji screens covered the walls, softening the austere room. About twenty people were already present, with padded chairs for another fifty. Seats for seven representatives waited on the dais at the front of the room. Nameplates indicated they would all be filled by men.

"Watch out for the guy second from the left," Shuu whispered. "He's a Communist."

The proceedings began promptly on the hour but dragged on. The committee had summoned a dozen witnesses, not just those who were on the island, but also Captain Miyashita and crewmen from the *Kumamoto*; a member of the strike team; someone from the government who'd hired Koga to go to the Senkakus. None of the Chinese attackers were present, even though they were still being held in Japanese custody. Amika assumed they would get their side of the story separately.

As far as she could tell, they were keeping the press out of the room. Jun Taniguchi certainly wasn't there.

Hiroshi was called early and got off easy. The representatives on the panel from the ruling party, the LDP, lobbed him simple factual questions. Why were you on Uotsuri-shima? Who gave you permission to go there? The Communist managed to hit him with one combination question/accusation: why didn't you cancel the mission after the attack on the *Kumamoto*? Amika had been wondering that herself. *If we had picked up Shuu and turned for home that day, we would've been spared a lot of anguish. And three men would be alive today.*

Hiroshi's response showed no regret. "Why should I cancel? The Senkaku Islands are part of the nation of Japan. Doesn't the central government's authority extend to all parts of our territory? Should Japan cede control of territory to China because some paint balls were fired?"

The LDP members nodded their approval of his answer and the committee chair subtly cut the Communist out of further questioning.

When they called Shuu, Amika expected them to be as deferential as they'd been to Hiroshi.

She was wrong.

After establishing his identity and role in the expedition, they let the opposition reps loose on him. Rather than asking him about the circumstances that forced him to shoot those unarmed men, the first question took her, and possibly her brother, by surprise.

"Do you know what this is?"

An aide took a saucer-shaped piece of technology about the size and shape of a ceiling dome light from the politician and walked it to Shuu. Shuu turned the device over in his hands and said nothing.

"Let me jog your memory," the politician said. "The US Army uses similar devices in Korea, where you were stationed during your enlistment."

Shuu nodded his recognition. "It's a differential GPS unit."

Amika sat up in her chair. That's what the reporter had asked about.

"What is the purpose of a unit like this?"

Shuu leaned over to the legal advisor at his side and they exchanged whispers. Shuu said to the questioner, "DGPS gives more accurate location readings so they're used for a lot of things. Primarily navigation."

"Did you install a military-grade DGPS unit on the island of Uotsuri-shima without permission?"

Another whisper. She forced herself to slouch and look detached as she tried to understand what was going on.

Shuu replied. "There are reefs around the Senkaku Islands. Some of them pose a hazard to ships. The Koga team brought a DGPS unit to Uotsuri-shima to make the region safer."

The Communist chimed in. "An open provocation! Militarization of the islands is forbidden."

"This was a civilian application," Shuu said.

"But one that could be easily misinterpreted. You brought a military navigational system to an uninhabited island a mere two hundred fifty miles from China. You didn't think Beijing would see this as a threat?"

How would the Chinese even know? I was right there and I didn't know about it. Whatever it is.

"No sir, we did not," Shuu said.

His interrogator huffed. "Your lack of foresight was costly. Three men are dead, and your sister paid a terrible price."

She felt her face turn the same color she saw blossoming in Shuu's. *Arrogant, self-serving bastard! To suggest that my brother was to blame for what happened. Ridiculous!*

Hiroshi touched her arm and shook his head slightly. *Calm yourself.* Her fight had to take a different form.

Shuu wilted, as if his regret caused him unbearable pain. "I had no idea." Dramatic pause. Deep breath. "I'm very very sorry."

The penitent. A good role for him. Puppy-dog eyes and exaggerated contrition had gotten him out of trouble more than once over the years. She'd seen it.

"If I could bring those men back, I would." He lifted his downcast gaze and looked straight at the committee. "But my team isn't responsible for the dangerous aggression of the Chinese. Those men chose to commit an act of cowardly violence against a young woman. My *sister*. I defended her honor, as any man would."

"That may be true, but murder is not a proportionate response," the politician said. "You might as well have used a bullet."

Shuu folded his hands. "I carried a twenty-two caliber cartridge-fired projector, not a gun. The projector carried a five-shot clip of tranquilizer darts loaded with a dose of Immobilon for goats. That's not a murderer's weapon. And I had permission for it. After I was forced to shoot those men, I gave them Narcan. The antidote. Right away. Just like I was trained to do in case of an accident. I don't know why it didn't work." Falter. Show remorse. "Amika—my sister—she helped me. We tried. Ask her."

The committee chairman turned his attention to her. "Is that correct, Dr. Nakamura?"

Mild confusion rippled through the room as heads turned. This wasn't the normal protocol, for them to address someone in the crowd. Her heart pounded at the unexpected question. Hiroshi leaned away from her, as if to avoid the figurative spotlight.

Do not screw this up.

"Could you please repeat the question, sir?" Amika said.

"Did you assist your brother in administering the antidote to the fallen men?"

"Yes." Her memory of those moments was clear, not muddied by exaggeration to the media. "It wasn't more than a couple of minutes after. We gave a full dose to the first man. We split a dose between the other two. Because that was all we had."

"You saw this yourself?"

"Yes. I pulled their sleeves out of the way so Shuu could do the injections."

The men on the dais gave each other knowing looks. Her knee bounced as she waited for the next question. Hiroshi stilled the movement with a touch under the table. She sat motionless as a premonition of trouble came over her.

They left Shuu where he was but summoned a dark-suited woman. Amika had noticed her enter the room mid-way through the proceedings. She took a seat at the front of the room.

The Communist opened the round. "Dr. Otani, did you perform the autopsies on the victims?"

"I did."

He waved a piece of paper and an aide showed it to the pathologist. "Is this your report?"

"Yes."

"Please summarize for the committee your findings in regard to the drugs in the victims' bodies."

"Victim number one exhibited a blood level of etorphine approximately forty-five percent higher than the average lethal dose for humans."

"Etorphine. That's a drug?"

"Yes. It's the active ingredient in the animal tranquilizer Immobilon. It's chemically similar to morphine."

"Very well. Please continue."

"Victim number two had an etorphine concentration approximately twenty-five percent higher than the lethal dose. Victim number three, twenty percent."

Tell us something we don't already know. The drug killed them.

"And what about the antidote that supposedly was given so diligently?"

"Naloxone, the reversal agent found in Narcan, was not present at detectable levels in any of the three victims."

The parts of Amika's brain that process speech started spilling neurotransmitters. *What did she just say?*

She wasn't the only one taken aback. Amid the shocked silence in the chamber, the committee chair asked for clarification. "There was no antidote in the bodies of the men?"

"Not enough to detect. I can't say the amount was zero, but our system is sensitive to even very small quantities."

Was the medical examiner testifying that we didn't give the antidote?

"Can you explain your findings, if the standard dose had been given?" the chairman said.

Surely there was an explanation. How much time elapsed between the shots and death? What's the half-life of Narcan? Is it metabolized by the liver? Could circulatory collapse have left it in the muscle of the men's arms and it never entered their blood? Did the examiner run good controls in her test? Amika could think of a hundred scientific explanations for the anomalous data.

"No, sir," the pathologist said.

Amika pushed her chair back to stand up. Hiroshi pressed her shoulder, holding her down.

"Don't," he whispered.

"Are you kidding me?" She squeezed her armrests. "Someone has to challenge that claim."

"Not you. Not like this."

"I might be the only scientist in the room."

The Communist leaned into his microphone. "You're saying they were murdered."

This time she did leap to her feet, and so did others: Captain Miyashita, the people from Koga, more people she didn't know. A commotion arose in the room as arguments broke out. Hiroshi scrambled to consult with his advisors. She briefly made eye contact with Shuu, who stayed where he was. His lips were tightly drawn and there was anger in his eyes. She mouthed the words, *it's okay*, in English.

But it wasn't okay.

Voices rose in the crowd. Some rebuked the Communist. Others demanded justice for the slain. The committee chair asked for order. He didn't get it. Doors opened and extra guards entered. They spread around the room; a couple of them closed in on Shuu.

For his protection, she presumed. The politician had definitely inflamed the Chinese sympathizers.

A gavel clanged. The chairman raised his voice. "The inquiry on the Senkaku Islands incident is now in recess. We will resume at one o'clock."

The room filled with conversation as the representatives gathered their papers and left through a door behind the dais. Amika clutched the back of her chair, looking around in a daze. None of this had gone as planned.

What happened to her story, her defense of her brother? The heat was all on Shuu. They'd actually used the word murder. And they were blaming him for goading the Chinese with some kind of military equipment. He didn't do that.

Did he?

Hiroshi was occupied with his people. She went to Shuu and hugged him. He felt like a robot and gave her a distracted, half-embrace.

"That was rough," he said.

"But you've seen worse, right?" She forced a smile and almost mentioned the time he got suspended from school for a prank, when he and his buddies spray painted a bench on campus. But that trivialized his current predicament. "There's an explanation for that doctor's findings. Koga's scientists will find it."

"Do you think they could test the needles and bottle we used?"

She pictured the darkness and chaos on Uotsuri-shima, so far away. In her mind's eye she saw Shuu throwing the empty medicine bottle aside in frustration, from a cliff, over a rocky shore.

"Not likely. And that wouldn't prove we did the injections anyway."

"You told them we did. They'll believe you, won't they?"

She rubbed her eyes. "Shuu, what was that about a GPS system?"

"A bunch of nothing." He balled his fists and Amika saw the muscles in his biceps twitch.

"Is it true, what they said?"

"It's true the team brought a DGPS to the island. Our guy installed it on the beacon the day you arrived. But it's not some kind of secret military tech. It's just a navigation aid. They're used in all kinds of civilian apps."

"Then why—"

Shuu slammed his palms on the table. "Because they're out to get me, okay?"

"Okay," she soothed. He was scared. So was she. But if he lost control... "Let's talk to Hiroshi."

They turned to go to the Koga team. The guards who were still standing near moved to block their way.

"What the hell is this?" Shuu said.

"Please wait, Mr. Nakamura," they said.

At that moment, several police officers, not mere building security, entered the room. They caught a signal from the men with Shuu and strode purposefully in his direction.

And as Amika watched in shock, they arrested him.

Shuu shoved the nearest guard and hollered curses, against the cops, against the government. He was sliding into a rage.

Amika knew what he was capable of, where his anger could lead. A danger to himself and others. She reached for his arm. "Don't—"

The cops pushed her aside and had her brother cuffed in seconds.

Hiroshi came running. "What's the meaning of this?"

Red-faced, Shuu strained against the handcuffs. "This is bullshit!"

So much for the penitent. At least the committee members weren't here to see it. Right now her brother looked like a killer.

The police herded him toward the exit. She followed. Wasn't Hiroshi going to do something?

He grabbed two of his lawyers and pointed them at the fracas around Shuu. "Go. Find out what's going on."

They hastily shoved laptops into cases and left with the police. She wanted to stick with Shuu, to calm him down. He was too hot to notice her at the moment but maybe in a few minutes she could talk to him.

"Stay here," one of the Koga lawyers said to her. "We'll handle this."

Then Hiroshi was at her side. "They won't let you near him," he said. "You can't help."

"I need to go with him."

He took her hand. "My people are the best. They'll figure out who's behind this. And we'll get it straightened out."

As long as Shuu doesn't assault somebody in the meantime.

"You need to stay here for the afternoon session," Hiroshi said. "That's the most important thing you can do for him."

Her chest tightened as tears tried to force their way into her eyes. What did she know about politics? Or Japanese law? Nothing. She knew her brother shouldn't be blamed for the tragedy on the island, yet she was starting to see that larger forces were at work. Things were happening behind the scenes. Hiroshi's father was a personal friend of the Japanese prime minister. That's why the committee handled Hiroshi with kid gloves. Her little brother was an outsider, a foreigner with a history of getting into trouble. If the powers-that-be decided a head had to roll, guess whose head it would be?

If Shuu was being set up to take the blame for an international scandal, the Naito family and their connections were his only hope.

That "helpless female" role she'd been rehearsing might be useful after all—with Hiroshi.

She pressed her cheek into his chest and clung limply to him. "You have to help him."

He stroked her hair. "I will."

You better. Because I don't think it was my brother's idea to bring that damn GPS to the island.

10

Amika gripped two bars of the wrought-iron fence that surrounded the American embassy in Tokyo, her anger making her even hotter than the sun-baked pavement. Unbidden, a string of Japanese-language racial epithets she'd heard came to mind as she stared daggers at the impassive African-American Marine standing guard at the gate.

He's just doing his job, she told herself. Today, and for the foreseeable future, that job included refusing admittance to one Amika Nakamura.

The American officials inside were the problem, not the guard. As far as she could tell, they refused to lift a finger to help her brother. Shuu Nakamura was an American citizen imprisoned in a foreign country on trumped-up political charges, and it appeared the embassy was doing *nothing* to secure his release—or to stop him being handed over to the Chinese. She wondered if they were prejudiced against him because of the Korean incident a few years ago. *He paid his debt. They shouldn't treat him differently!*

It's not like the Americans didn't know what was going on. The Senkaku skirmish, and the protests in China, were all over the news. Amika had bolted to the embassy the day Shuu was arrested and spoken to a low-ranking member of the staff. Because she was insistent (and she had to admit, alarmingly agitated), she got an appointment with a senior diplomat. He assured her the US was aware of Shuu's situation—and they would not discuss it with her.

She'd come back every day. The embassy's hospitality had decreased in proportion to her rising impatience. And now she'd managed to get herself banished from the grounds.

Video of a Chinese mob shouting her brother's name played in her head.

How can they sit at their desks in there and not do anything? Can't they see he's a pawn?

A pawn. She snorted and walked away from the fence, back toward the Metro station. Not only Japan and China were playing chess. The US was, too. She'd learned that in about a month, the United States and China were scheduled to meet for sensitive, high-level talks about a variety of strategic and economic matters. The Senkaku incident was a distraction. The State Department must have decided Shuu, with his bad conduct discharge from the army, wasn't worth it. Like Pontius Pilate, the diplomats were washing their hands.

Which meant Hiroshi Naito and his influential family were her only allies.

They say, don't put all your eggs in one basket. But what if it's the only basket you've got?

A train carried her back to the lab. She stood swaying amid the smell of sweaty bodies. The one good thing about her banishment from the embassy was she no longer needed to spend half of each day making her petition in person.

To pass the time on the train she glanced at her emails on her phone. She sighed but wasn't surprised to see none from her brother. Hiroshi had explained that since his arrest, Shuu was allowed very limited access to the internet. While he could write paper letters to her, his computer time was better spent managing his legal situation. Supposedly someone censored and then printed out the emails she sent to him. She wrote to him twice a day.

In her pocket, she fingered the one letter she'd received from him so far.

He has more important things to worry about than his anxious big sister.

The scant written communication made their brief phone calls all the more precious. The Koga lawyers talked to him regularly, but she'd gotten only a few minutes on the phone with him twice.

I just wish they would let me visit in person more often. Too many people were competing for Shuu's limited visitor time. She'd only been on the list to see him once so far.

She scrolled through the list of humdrum emails. *Delete. Delete.* A flash of irritation when she found yet another unsolicited message from that reporter Jun Taniguchi. Like all the other emails Jun had sent, this one would go unread.

Delete.

She exited the train at the station near the Koga building. On a billboard, smiling faces ranging in age from two to at least eighty expressed their satisfaction that they'd received Koga's flu vaccine. Her phone rang.

It was Hiroshi. Her stomach fluttered a little.

"I have a surprise for you," he said.

A hot, humid draft pushed against her as she emerged onto the street. "Shuu?" she said hopefully.

"No, still working on that. Guess again."

She suppressed her disappointment and allowed herself to be curious. A guessing game? With Hiroshi? *Playful* was not his style.

"Is it a good surprise?" she asked.

"You'll think so."

"Something with my research?"

"Yes!"

"You're giving me a raise?"

"That's not what you really want."

He was right about that. "What do I really want?" she said.

"Yes or no questions only," he said.

What I really want is freedom. Freedom to do the most important, the most interesting science without having to worry about institutional review boards and grant money and politics… Maybe he understood her better than she thought. "Koga is taking me off the DNA sequencing?"

"Yes."

"No more looking for flu virus in dead birds?"

"That's up to you."

She entered the lobby of the Koga building and flashed her ID. "You're going to let me choose a project?"

"You already chose it. I'm going to support you."

She took a sharp breath and ignored the elevator door opening before her. Could it be?

"Gain of function research?" she said.

"Your talents are wasted on routine sequencing. We need to get you deeper into the genome. Figure out its secrets."

Yes!

This was the work that got her kicked out of Berkeley. The work that really mattered. The work that could make her career. She'd been hoping for this chance ever since she moved to Japan. Despite the cloud of worry hanging over her, her feet tapped a happy dance.

"You won't regret it," she said. "I was close to getting answers to the big questions."

"Good. We need some answers. We're worried about the new bird flu. It's killing more and more birds. Koga wants to do something about it."

"You've got your vaccines."

"Yes, we have a vaccine for people and a vaccine for birds. The problem is, those vaccines have to be administered individually. That works for pet owners or zookeepers. It doesn't do anything for wild birds."

And they're the ones that pose a risk. They can infect poultry on farms, and they could be the source of a virus that jumps into humans. "What's your idea?"

"Koga wants to modify the vaccine for birds so that it spreads from one bird to another."

"A vaccine that propagates itself."

"Exactly. We could trap a few wild birds, vaccinate and release them, and then spread immunity to their whole flock," he said.

Hiroshi's proposal wasn't a totally new idea. Amika knew that the Sabin oral polio vaccine worked in a similar way.

"But you don't know how to do it," she said.

"Do you think you can show us what changes to make in the DNA sequence?"

"I know I can. I did something very similar at Berkeley."

Take that, UC. Those closed-minded jerks at her old lab would eat crow when she published a paper on her work. She could imagine the title now, in bold letters with her name at the bottom. If a University of California campus invited her to give a lecture, she would gleefully refuse.

"Excellent. I'll make sure you have whatever resources you need."

The call ended and Amika pressed the button again for the elevator. This was the best news she'd had in months. Years, even. Finally someone recognized her brilliance. The gesture was also a gift. Maybe it was Hiroshi's apology for the Senkaku Islands fiasco. Or a love offering better suited to her than flowers would be.

When she passed Manami's office on the way to her lab, she gave her administrator friend a big smile and wave. A cheerful music greeted her at her desk. Shuu had adopted the Asian hobby of keeping a singing cricket as a pet. When he was arrested, Amika assumed care of his pet insect in its tiny bamboo cage. The cricket vocalized at night and kept her awake, so she had brought it work.

Today, the cricket sang.

A pang of guilt pierced her. Shuu was in prison. She didn't deserve to be happy. And yet, he was safe (for now). Hiroshi and the Koga lawyers were committed to working things out (*I think*). All this would pass with time.

Influenza, on the other hand, was an implacable foe. Fighting it was her life's calling. Her genius was revealed not on a grand political stage, but on the stage of a microscope. She was a scientist, a *virologist*. For the first time since she'd left California, it was time to do what she did best.

Immersed in thoughts of hemagglutinin and neuraminidase, she was entirely unprepared when the first reporter called the next morning.

June 14 (the next day)

A digital timer counted the seconds as Amika measured and combined three chemical solutions for a crucial reaction. When the landline to her lab and her cellphone jangled at the same time, she glanced at the phone on her desk. No caller ID. No reason to interrupt her work. The call went to voicemail.

At once the cellphone rang again. Before she could silence it, another call came in, stacking up behind the first. Then a text message. From the corner of her eye she could see the sender was a reporter she'd met earlier, from *Asahi Shimbun*, Japan's national newspaper.

The insistent ring tone doused her spirit like a bucket of cold water. *This can't be good.*

She buried a plastic vial into a bucket of crushed ice and took off her gloves, then reached for her cellphone like it was a rattlesnake. Her core muscles tensed. In the next few seconds, she would go from a state of blissful ignorance, to knowing…something.

The phone vibrated its way toward the edge of the desk.

"Hello, this is Dr. Nakamura," she said.

Brief pleasantries exchanged, followed by a torrent of questions. She listened, asked one question of her own, and hung up on the reporter. Her hands trembled as she opened her laptop and got on the internet. Typing errors littered her search query.

The reporter had mentioned a specific website: home page for the Asian Center for Investigative Journalism.

As the site loaded, a headline screamed, "New autopsy data from Senkaku deaths: was it murder?"

The byline? Jun Taniguchi.

Amika pressed her fists into her thighs. *That woman. What did she do?*

The phones kept ringing. Suppressing the urge to throw her mobile across the room, she turned it off and lifted the landline from its cradle. Her heart pounded in the ensuing silence as she read the just-posted news article.

"Unnamed government sources…Secret official autopsy report leaked… Chinese victims of Senkaku Islands shooting…"

Taniguchi had no right to publish this. She's going to land her pretty little butt in jail.

Imagining Jun's suffering was cold comfort as she digested the information and the claims being made based on it.

In the report Jun reiterated the testimony Amika had already heard, that the three men had died of an overdose of animal tranquilizer. That point was not in dispute.

Jun's article went further with new data. Investigators had done a more thorough forensic analysis looking for the antidote Narcan in the victims' bodies. At the government hearing, they'd claimed the antidote was undetectable in the blood. Now they added that none was found locally at the site of injection in the victims' arms, either. They'd even tested for chemical breakdown products of the drug, in case it was metabolized into something else. Nothing.

That can't be. I helped Shuu inject the antidote.

She remembered how hastily Shuu had worked, trying to save those men's lives. Her brother had no experience as a medic. Was it possible he'd screwed up? Didn't fill the syringe correctly? Spilled the liquid? Or maybe the antidote hadn't been stored in the right conditions. Did Narcan decompose in the tropical heat?

Then her eyes skipped over phrases with the words *pharmacokinetic analysis…etorphine volume of distribution…95% confidence interval* and her heart stopped.

Impossible.

The article stated, "The amount of tranquilizer found in the victims' bodies vastly exceeds the amount predicted from a single dose intended for goats. The deadly quantities present in the tissues of the deceased indicate multiple injections of the standard dose (or the equivalent)."

Multiple darts?

I was there. Shuu fired only once at each man. Hell, he barely had the time to do even that. The floor of her stomach fell. *Dear God, did he grab the wrong bottle?*

Those moments on the cliff at Uotsuri-shima were soaked in chaos and fear. There had been darkness and wind and the terrible stench of Skunk. She pictured her brother stabbing the medicine vial, pulling the antidote into the syringe.

What if it wasn't the antidote?

She desperately needed to talk to him. She powered up her phone and, ignoring all the messages and alerts, called Hiroshi.

"You heard already?" Hiroshi said.

"People called me," Amika said. "Within minutes."

Hiroshi grunted. "Vultures."

"I have to talk to Shuu."

"What for? He can't explain it either."

"Maybe he remembers—"

"He doesn't," Hiroshi said decisively.

"Don't put words in my brother's—" Amika stopped. *How could he know that?* Then it dawned on her. "You've seen the report. You already knew, and talked to him about it."

"Of course I knew. The report was classified, but something that hot was bound to leak. The prime minister gave my father a copy so we could be prepared."

"So *are* you prepared? What are we going to do?"

He sighed. "My lawyers went over and over the situation with your brother. He swears he did everything by the book."

"But if he didn't realize he'd made a mistake, he wouldn't very well remember, would he?"

"Obviously. Without physical evidence, his defense team is up against a wall."

"What if he *did* mix up the bottles? It was an honest mistake."

Hiroshi's voice darkened. "There's a reason the PM wanted that autopsy report kept quiet. Beijing is itching for a confrontation over this. Inflammatory misinformation could have dire consequences for the region."

"Misinformation?"

He paused. "You say your brother might have made an honest mistake. I have reasons to believe the data in this report are neither honest nor mistaken. There are powerful forces who seek to undermine the Japanese nation. They want us to be guilty even if they have to manufacture crimes. They want us to hate ourselves, to be ashamed to be Japanese. They're using Taniguchi and her group as a tool."

A conspiracy to frame my brother?

Lights flashed on a sophisticated piece of equipment near Amika's workspace in the lab. Somebody's DNA amplification was finished and she was suddenly struck by the uselessness of all her expertise, education, and intelligence in this strange rabbit hole into which she and her brother had fallen. She cried out. "But what about Shuu?"

"I'm working on it. Can I count on you?"

"I'll do anything for him."

"The love of a woman is a powerful thing," Hiroshi said. "I won't let it go to waste."

The conversation ended and Amika slumped in her chair. What could she do? What would Hiroshi do?

His comment about a woman's love left her puzzled. Was there a double meaning? Did he think she loved him? She didn't, but the *perception* of love could be useful.

Hiroshi had insisted she not speak to the media until the team had a strategy for public relations and legal defense. A unified front, a single message, was key to winning the battle for public opinion. The energy she felt when she'd arrived at the lab burned away. Even the prospect of doing the gain of function experiments wasn't enough to restore her joy.

Unable to focus on work, she thought of Jun Taniguchi. Her despondency turned to anger.

That woman is going to get my brother shipped to China. She knew about the GPS unit before the committee meeting. She had government spies who gave her the autopsy report. What would she do next?

Know your enemy. What's actually in all those emails?

She opened her computer and searched her trash for messages from Taniguchi. The emails were brief and ominous.

One theme dominated: Don't trust Hiroshi Naito.

It was a brash demand, and Amika noted that it was not supported by any solid evidence. Taniguchi repeated a variety of harsh but vague warnings about Hiroshi being untrustworthy, about his father being ruthless, and the whole clan being amoral. She hinted darkly about "family history" and offered to fill Amika in if she would just give her a call.

Call her? After what she just did to Shuu? Over my dead body.

The emails pleaded with her.

"Talk to me. I can help."

"If you want to protect your brother, you need to get away from Naito. He has powerful connections but they have their own agendas. Call me. I know people you can trust."

Agendas indeed. What was Jun Taniguchi's agenda? Why did she have it in for Hiroshi? Was she a jilted girlfriend? Amika expected an eligible bachelor like him had plenty of those.

"There's a lot you don't know. Call me."

"If you have information that you're holding back to protect someone, you'd better think about protecting yourself. The truth will come out. My employer has resources. Let us help."

And finally, in the most recent email, Jun alluded to the pending storm:

"Major revelations about your brother's case coming today. I will be at this number waiting for your call."

You'll be waiting a long, long time.

Whether she was motivated by jealousy or ambition or a desire to bring down the rich and powerful, this self-described journalist was a shark. *She wants to use me to get to Hiroshi. If she truly wanted to help Shuu, she wouldn't have published that autopsy report. Maybe she even helped to make it up, like Hiroshi says. It'll be her fault if Shuu is handed over…*

The mere thought roiled her insides and she put her face in her hands. She saw Shuu's face, much younger, with the pudgy cheeks of a child. Their mom was asleep, or maybe passed out, and Shuu wanted *udon* for lunch. Amika knew how much he loved the hot soupy noodles. The fact she had never used the stove before was nothing in the face of his plea. To this day she wasn't sure how she'd managed to set the towel on fire. Her mother rushed in to the sound of the smoke alarm. Amika told her mom she was hungry. She was always willing to take the blame for her baby brother.

This time, she couldn't.

With great discipline, she avoided the internet and email. Shuu's cricket took up its song. She moved the bamboo cage to a counter near the warm coils behind a lab refrigerator. She'd heard that crickets sing faster at warmer temperatures. Here was a simple experiment to distract her while she washed some dishes and did other brainless housekeeping tasks in the lab. Her mind was too scattered and the day now too short to do any meaningful work. The secrets of the influenza virus would wait until tomorrow.

Gathering up biological waste in a bright orange bag to be sterilized in the lab's autoclave, Jun Taniguchi's voice nagged at her. Her own instincts detected nothing of the malevolence Jun accused Hiroshi of.

Trust your brother. Shuu chose to be friends with Hiroshi. He trusted Hiroshi, worked for Hiroshi, introduced me to Hiroshi. That counts for a lot.

Not to mention that being on Hiroshi's good side had some significant advantages to her.

For a while, the cricket chirped as steadily as the ticking of her timer. When the sound flagged, she refreshed the insect's drinking sponge, gave the cricket a morsel of cabbage, and returned the cage to her desk.

"I hope your master is getting service this good in *his* cage," she said aloud to the cricket.

"I'm sure his servers are not as beautiful," someone replied.

"Hiroshi," she said in surprise. Water running in the sink had concealed the sound of his entry.

Hiroshi picked up the delicate little cage and turned it around in his hand. "That's your brother's cricket?"

"Yes." She took off her soiled lab apron, feeling anything but beautiful. "Do you have news about Shuu?"

He set the cage down, reached forward and brushed her cheek.

"Always," he said. The hand dropped to his side and Amika felt warmth linger in her face. "But news is like waves on the sand. You see the water move up and down, and it blinds you to the *real* movement of the tide."

Her temper flared. "So you're not going to tell me anything?"

Again he gave her a searching look. Was her American bluntness too much for him?

"You are an expert, Doctor," he said. "The best influenza virologist in Japan. One of the best in the world."

You got that right.

"But we all have our areas of expertise," he continued. "Don't be too eager to play politics. Given your history, I'd say it's not one of your strengths."

The warmth in her cheeks flared hotter. "He's my brother, not yours."

"True, but you're not the only one with something at stake." He stepped away from her and prowled the aisle between the lab workbenches. "A lot of people care about Shuu's case, and they're working for his release. You're dissatisfied with the way I'm handling things. Would you like to meet some of these other people? Perhaps they will fill your head with the 'news' you crave."

"Who are they?"

"Friends of mine. Friends of Koga Scientific. Friends of Japan." He stood beside her and leaned against the counter. His eyes hinted at a grin. "I'm inviting you to a party."

She hadn't seen that coming. A *party* party? With rich, single Hiroshi Naito? Visions of glamorous, wealthy people and flashing dance lights and loud music glimmered in her guilty thoughts. "This doesn't seem like the right time for celebrating."

He chuckled. "Your brother's not dead. We're going to get him out. And he would want you to go. A lot of his friends will be there."

A date—an actual *date* with Hiroshi? "When is it?" she asked demurely.

"Day after tomorrow. It's a charity event. You'll need a dress."

"I don't—"

"I've taken care of it. There's a shop. They'll be expecting you."

"Oh. Okay." *That takes some nerve—* She took a breath. *Relax. He's being generous, not controlling.* Even if she had big bucks to spend on her wardrobe, her tastes ran more to Lycra and denim than formalwear. They both knew she didn't own anything suitable for a high-class event.

"Great. I'll text you the details." He kissed her hand and headed for the door. "I'm looking forward to it."

"Me too."

Shuu's cricket chirped. Amika finished her work in the sink with racing thoughts. Hiroshi had advised her against "politics." *Paternalistic jerk.* Nothing would keep her from using every resource she had to protect her brother. One of those tools was Hiroshi himself. *A formal date.* It was her most successful stratagem yet. Aid for Shuu, job security for her, all entwined with a good-looking and wealthy guy.

Watch out, Hiroshi. I've got my sights set on you.

11

The old warrior knelt on a *tatami* mat, misshapen knees hidden under the silk of a dark blue *kimono*. Soft natural light filtered through the rice paper lattice of *shoji* screens amid profound silence in the small, empty room where the tea ceremony would be performed. The old warrior's tired eyes rested on the lone piece of art hanging on one wall, a calligraphy scroll from the 18th century. Four characters were painted there.

Harmony. Respect. Purity. Tranquility.

The spirit of the tea ceremony.

The hostess entered the tea room with graceful, precisely choreographed movements. The old warrior watched respectfully as the hostess followed the ritual: wash the tea bowl, the scoop and the whisk; wipe them with fine silk cloth.

It was possible to have too much tranquility. The young people of Japan today were tranquil. Peaceful.

Passive. Emasculated. Instead of the tranquility of discipline, the tranquility of laziness.

They had their video games and cell phones and *manga* graphic novels. They *didn't* have babies. A fantasy life on screens and in books had replaced the real life of struggle and sex and sacrifice. With an atrociously low birth rate of 1.4 children per woman, the Japanese nation was tranquilly, slowly committing suicide. It had already begun. Japan's population peaked in 2009, and had declined every year since. If the trend continued unaltered, a thousand years hence there would be only five hundred pureblood Japanese left.

Extinction.

The tea hostess's pale, delicate hands moved like the neck of a swan, arranging the utensils in the prescribed order.

The young men of Japan, they go to China for business, or even vacation. As tourists, when they should go as conquerors. The thought was repugnant. They fed the beast with their buying and investment. As recently as 2010, Japan's economy was bigger than China's. Now it was dwarfed by the enemy.

If they knew what the Chinese jackals were capable of, of their barbarism, of the things they would do even to a child...

The hostess prepared the tea. Six scoops of *matcha*, the green tea powder, into the bowl. Hot water to cover the powder. Whisk.

A pleasing aroma filled the air.

The hostess offered the bowl to the old warrior, who bowed and raised the bowl to sip. *What a shapely bowl, a fine work of Japanese craftsmanship.* The bitter tea had a cleansing power that washed through the throat and belly, eliciting a cough.

When the tea ceremony was over, the hostess cleaned up and departed with the same elegance she'd displayed throughout. The old warrior rose painfully from the floor and exited through a different sliding screen door.

In the adjacent room, pine wood paneling covered the walls and floor. A planter box with bamboo stalks almost as tall as the ceiling formed a screen behind a wide computer monitor on an expansive wooden desk. When the door opened, a fan automatically puffed the scent of sandalwood into the air.

The old warrior sat at the desk and brought the computer to life. Oversized fonts chosen for aged eyesight detailed a packed events calendar.

In all these years I've never been idle. How can there be so much yet to do?

The old warrior blotted forehead sweat with a tissue and studied the "to do" list. There was an update on Koga's vaccine campaign, with current numbers and projections: *I will read the summary report later.* A meeting with lobbyists tasked with promoting Koga's favored nominee for executive director of Japan's Pharmaceuticals and Medical Devices Agency: *The lobbyists know what they're doing. That's what I pay them for.* A presentation by category 2 staff scientists on the Han genome sequencing project: *They*

*were supposed to close the final gaps in the euchromatin sequence and achieve
99.99% accuracy in the locus of interest. I should be there to listen to them.*

And then tomorrow there was the Koga Foundation benefit for the
Japanese Red Cross.

I hate parties.

Social networking was so much easier online. The old warrior had been
an early adopter of internet-based methods of communication, and believed
strongly in keeping up to date with technology of all kinds. After all, advances
in biotechnology had finally put the goal of the project within reach. A pipe
dream in the 1940s was now a straightforward scientific exercise for those
bold enough to do what was needed.

The men of Unit 731 were bold. We must be too.

The warrior turned to a rosewood table against the rear wall, where a
beautiful piece of the mineral jadeite rested in a custom-fitted wood base.
The shape of the greenish stone resembled a miniature mountain, and it was
an excellent example of *suiseki,* a viewing stone used for meditation. Behind
the stone, the grain of the wood paneling hid the outline of a small door. A
gentle push, and the door retracted upward, exposing a wall safe. A digital
keypad and fingerprint reader unlocked the safe.

A leather-bound volume, thick and large like a scrapbook, was the only
item in the safe. The old warrior hoisted it to the desk and reverently ran
fingers over the smooth, unmarked cover.

My precious inheritance.

The pages of the book had the yellowed appearance of age but not the
musty odor that clung to the original documents. These were high-resolution
reproductions of some of the handwritten records of Unit 731 smuggled out
of China in 1945. The old warrior knew the terrible price paid in Japanese
blood—family blood—to save these papers, which traveled by car, train,
boat, and air, divided into multiple shipments. Some made it directly to the
Japanese home islands. Others were sidetracked, delayed, or lost. Only a tiny
fraction of the material from Pingfan fell into enemy hands.

Shudder. *I was part of that fraction.*

Thousands of originals were stored in a climate-controlled archival facility
owned by Koga. The digitized pages preserved both the data and the history
of the papers' journey, written in stains, rips and decay. Even after the documents safely reached Japan, they had to be kept hidden. Many were buried

in the gardens of Japanese loyalists. War crimes trials were in progress, and the documents were evidence. The secret was kept. None of the officers or scientists from General Ishii's Unit 731 were prosecuted by the Americans. They survived to work another day, infiltrating the highest levels of postwar Japan's scientific establishment.

Finally the information in these precious records had borne fruit. The old warrior stroked the pages and felt peace. *We've come so far.* Most of the Unit's experiments failed. Thousands of prisoners were consumed, and plagues were released into Chinese cities, but Unit 731 never produced a practical biological weapon.

Until now. I became a scientist like him. I have kept my uncle's dream alive. On August fifteenth, the attack would begin with a tweet, not a bang.

12

JUNE 16

On the second day after Jun Taniguchi's group leaked the autopsy report, the furor in China was still growing.

Amika sat cross-legged on the only chair in her tiny studio apartment, eyes glued to the screen of her laptop. On screen, smoke spewed from the roof of a warehouse the size of a city block. According to the report, the warehouse was near Shanghai, China, but it was owned by a Japanese company. Rioters set it on fire in protest against Japanese aggression.

More specifically, her baby brother's aggression.

A translated video clip showed a government official talking. "Chinese scientists have confirmed that a one milliliter dart cannot produce the drug levels found in the victims. China demands that the perpetrator, Shuu Nakamura, stand trial in Beijing to determine if his actions were criminally reckless, or intentional, when he took the lives of those men."

Oh, Shuu.

Nervous energy pulsed through her. She wanted to *do* something, but what? Without political influence, without authority, she had no power to alter Shuu's fate. The three hundred fifty square feet of her apartment might as well have been a prison cell like his for the helplessness she felt.

Now a crowd paraded down a Beijing street, waving anti-Japan banners. They gathered along three rows of security fences in front of the Japanese embassy. Normally the Chinese government cracked down on unauthorized public assemblies. Today the blue-suited police force stood by, stone-faced with hands behind their backs, observing.

The government is behind the protests. Just like they were behind the Senkaku Islands attack. They're using civilians. Can't people see that?

A reporter like Jun Taniguchi should see the truth. How could that woman sleep at night, knowing she'd created so much conflict?

Amika left the computer to shower off the sweat from her earlier five-mile run. Her thoughts went to the evening ahead. The Koga Foundation—Hiroshi's family's foundation and the charitable arm of Koga Scientific—was hosting a benefit for the Japanese Red Cross. Members of the Naito family, including Hiroshi's father, would be at the gala, along with board members, public officials, and assorted friends and associates of the Naitos. This was big-league philanthropy.

As the water ran over her shoulders, her stomach churned and for the umpteenth time she considered backing out. *I'm a scientist, not a socialite.* What if her mediocre Japanese language skills embarrassed her in front of Hiroshi? What if his friends rejected her as a foreigner?

I can do this. Find allies for Shuu. Bind Hiroshi tighter to me.

Then there was the dress. Amika was happy wearing a T-shirt and jeans, but even she could appreciate the elegance and craftsmanship of the formal gown she would wear tonight.

She toweled herself dry and lifted the dress in front of a mirror. The fine silk felt cool and smooth in her hands. The designer Hiroshi had chosen was known for her modern designs based on traditional Japanese kimonos. The bare-shouldered garment highlighted Amika's toned upper body. Boldly colored in black, red, and gold, it fit her personality: forceful, not frilly. Skin-tight around the torso, the dress widened slightly to her feet, a spray of hand-stitched flowers wrapping her legs. She could walk, but long strides would be impossible in this.

Why do women handicap themselves with their clothing?

She set the dress aside and opened several new packages of cosmetics. Applying makeup was not part of her daily routine and unlike the products she used at the lab, these did not come with step-by-step instructions. In the end she wasn't sure if she had improved her appearance, but her skin was definitely paler in color, faintly *geisha*-like. Her hair, close-cut and rather masculine, was as far from *geisha* style as it could be, but there wasn't anything she could do about that tonight.

From her computer, a Chinese mob chanted her brother's name. She turned the machine off, slipped into the dress, and wrestled to close the zipper. The noise of the mob lingered in her head until she got a text message announcing the arrival of her car. She looked at the stranger in the mirror and readied herself. *This is it.*

The driver did not speak as the black Mercedes sedan Hiroshi had hired muscled its way through the crowded streets of central Tokyo. They were headed for the Bunkyo ward, known for its shrines, gardens, cemeteries, and universities. Amika had done some running in the area, which was unusually green and tranquil in parts.

"Turn down the air conditioning, will you please?" she said to the silent driver. It was unusual for her to feel cold and with the heat outside, she hadn't bothered to bring a wrap.

As they neared the venue, lush foliage edged the street. They passed a walk-up Shinto shrine nestled amid old trees, with two stone lions standing guard over the steps that led to a small wooden altar. The final few hundred yards of the trip on a forested driveway left the bustling city behind.

In a crowded metropolis like Tokyo, money could buy tranquility.

She extricated herself from the car and was leaning over, arranging the dress when someone touched the back of her neck.

"You look beautiful, Amika-chan," Hiroshi said.

She straightened, but not so quickly as to dislodge his hand. "Thank you. It's the dress."

"The dress is only fragrance on the flower." He lightly kissed her cheek. "Come, there are people who want to meet you."

An attendant opened the door for them and they entered a lobby buzzing with activity. Well-dressed guests stood in line to check in. Hiroshi waved to the greeters and ushered Amika past the lines. She felt the gentle pressure of his arm around her waist, guiding her. It soothed the nervousness she felt and reminded her of their strange encounter back on the Zodiac, after the attack. This was the first time since that night that she felt his full attention, a masculine protective possessiveness that she found both repellant and beguiling at the same time.

The setting changed the rules. As she speculated on who Hiroshi was going to be tonight, she wondered what role she ought to play. More Japanese, or more American woman? Does he want deferential or forceful? She would have to read the cues, something she wasn't terribly good at.

They entered an expansive hall where an elegant crowd balanced drinks and appetizer dishes in their hands. The women's long gowns all had at least a splash of red in them, and glittery red teardrop-shaped cutouts decorated the cocktail table centerpieces. Traditional Japanese foods were presented on linen-draped tables, impeccably arranged to please the eye. She had never seen *sashimi* served like this, whole gutted fish lying raw on platters, with the skin pulled back and the flesh cut into chunks to make it easy to grab with chopsticks.

"Would you like a cocktail?" Hiroshi asked.

"Yes. Surprise me," she said flirtatiously.

He looked her up and down, as if deciding what suited her. "*Ume chuhai,*" he said. "Do you know this drink?"

She wrinkled her nose. "Doesn't that come in a can?"

"Not here. They mix the best *shochu* liquor and sour plum. You'll love it."

He did not abandon her to get into the line at the bar. This was Hiroshi Naito. He had people. He whispered his request into the ear of a server going by. His hand stayed on her back until the drinks arrived. As she accepted and tasted the cocktail, simple pleasure started to replace her complex social calculations about her evening with Hiroshi.

"You're right," she said. "I do like it." She didn't know much about *shochu,* except that it was a traditional Japanese distilled spirit. This was her first taste.

She looked around the room. "I'm the youngest person here."

"In some cases, by sixty years," Naito agreed. "This is Japan. We're becoming a nation of old people."

"Old *rich* people, here."

"With the Koga Foundation, yes. My father's and grandfather's generations are well-represented on the board." He took a sip. "Be grateful. These old rich people are paying your salary. Ah, there's someone you know."

Holding her free hand, he led her toward a man in full military dress uniform. The finery of the man's dress was almost enough to neutralize the feeling of disgust she got when she recognized Captain Miyashita from the *Kumamoto.*

Behave yourself. Keep up appearances. Reluctantly she bowed to the Coast Guard officer.

"Miss Nakamura," he said.

"*Captain* Miyashita." She expressed her irritation in her tone. *Jackass still refuses to call me "doctor."*

"Is the prime minister coming tonight?" he asked.

"No," Hiroshi said, "but as a courtesy to my father he's sending his cabinet secretary. The minister of health might also make an appearance."

"It's the minister of defense I'd like to talk to," Miyashita grumbled. "My ship's been pulled back. They say the Japan Maritime Self-Defense Force is patrolling the Senkaku Islands now, instead of the Coast Guard. I don't believe it."

Hiroshi leaned in. "What have you heard?"

"They're holding back. With the situation in China, they're avoiding a confrontation. Nobody's there. Not the *Kumamoto*, not anybody."

"Pussies," Hiroshi said.

Warmongers, Amika thought. "Isn't that the law in Japan? To avoid war?"

Miyashita looked at her coldly. "Article Nine of the Japanese Constitution requires us to renounce war and forbids the use of force to settle international disputes. It does not mean we offer our arm for the Chinese jackals to bite."

"A vigorous self-defense is entirely permitted," Hiroshi agreed.

The assertive girl in Amika could not be silent. "Seems like the 'vigorous' part is what got my brother in trouble. You do remember my brother Shuu, don't you, Captain? At this very moment he's in prison. For a 'crime' he was forced to commit because you delivered that navigation system to the island."

"Installing the DGPS was a decision between Koga Scientific and Tokyo," Miyashita said. "The Coast Guard was only a courier."

"The men who died were going after the DGPS unit. So why is all the blame on Shuu? Nobody's calling out Koga. Or the government. Or the Coast Guard. Why aren't you—"

Hiroshi draped his arm around her waist and pulled her close. "Amika-chan, calm yourself. The captain is on our side."

I know. Plenty of people are on Shuu's side but none of them are really involved. All the consequences are on him. None of them *are in prison.*

"Yes of course he is," she said, taking a long swallow of her cocktail. She noticed Hiroshi's scent, a light cologne, so very different from the smell that night in the boat when she rested her head against his bare chest. "Do you have any thoughts on my brother's situation, Captain?"

"My thoughts? He should've killed more of them."

"That's not very helpful, sir."

"It's the truth."

Hiroshi must have noticed her body tense. "Now Captain, that's not the civilized behavior of an honorable man, or a great nation. Shuu Nakamura acted in self-defense."

"And so do we, if we keep China out of our waters. I'll tell you what I think, Miss Nakamura. The US better not forget that China is the enemy. The Americans and the Japanese must be united in the fight against Communism. Your brother is part of that fight, and the US is letting him down. They're letting all of us down by kowtowing to Beijing."

"Because of the summit?" Amika said.

"That's one excuse."

"I agree they should be doing more—a lot more," she said, remembering the doors closed to her at the American embassy, "but Japan should, too. Shuu was working on a government contract. And no matter what you say, the Japan Coast Guard is involved in this."

"Not as involved as I'd like it to be," he muttered.

"What do you propose?" Hiroshi asked.

Miyashita sneered. "We give Shuu Nakamura a medal and tell the Chinese jackals to go screw themselves."

This isn't getting us anywhere.

"I see you disapprove," the captain continued. "But you're not from here. This is a rough neighborhood. The People's Republic of China, North Korea. They only respond to one thing: strength. If you were one of us, you'd understand."

"Oh I understand. I understand that my brother is a pawn—"

Hiroshi interrupted. "Amika-chan, they're asking everyone to take a seat. Captain, I'll see you on August fifteenth." He touched her elbows and rotated her toward the banquet hall. "Our table is at the front."

She acquiesced. Miyashita was no more likable tonight than he was on the ship. *Is that the best ally I'm going to find among these people?*

"Sorry about that," Hiroshi said. "Miyashita is a patriot. He tends to be passionate in his views."

"He's no help to my brother."

"Don't be so sure about that." He stepped behind her and kneaded the taut muscles in her bare shoulders. "Try to relax. We're going to take care of your brother. Tonight, I'm here with a beautiful woman—a brilliant woman—and I'm going to show her off. Will you let me?"

The pleasure of the massage spread from her back to her neck and arms. The warmth of the *shochu* cocktail glowed in her belly. *This man is the ally who really matters. Focus on him.* "I'd like that," she said.

"Let me get you another drink."

The main banquet hall held more than fifty large round tables, richly decorated with place settings, programs and floral arrangements. A string quartet played European chamber music in one corner. A long head table fronted the room on an elevated platform. She spotted Hiroshi's father there.

"We're not sitting with your father?" She had hoped to use this opportunity to ingratiate herself with him. The senior Naito had the prime minister's ear, an advantage which could be crucial to Shuu's case.

"He's led the Koga Foundation's support for the Japanese Red Cross since its founding. Earlier, even. Koga was involved with the blood bank's predecessor in the post-war years. This is his event, not mine."

"So who *are* we sitting with?"

"What is the quote?" He momentarily switched to heavily accented English. "Friends, Romans, countrymen."

She laughed. "I didn't know you read Shakespeare."

"I don't," he said. "I memorized a few lines. Enough to impress the ladies."

"I'm impressed," she said.

"Then it was worth the effort. The gentlemen you're about to meet are friends of mine, from *outside* the biotech industry. I find it gratifying to keep my social life diverse."

I would too, if I had a social life.

"They know your brother," he said. "We're all members of a private club. Shuu worked many of our events. That's where I met him for the first time."

"In retrospect, that didn't turn out so well for him," she said.

He paused to gaze into her eyes. He stroked her cheek and traced the line of her collarbone with his fingers. "I hope you think it turned out well for you."

She tried to ignore the thrill that cascaded through her. "Koga Scientific has been a great place to work."

"Has it, now." He pulled back a dining chair draped with a red cover. She folded the long gown beneath her thighs and sat.

As the other guests arrived, Hiroshi introduced Amika as a brilliant American scientist, Koga's secret weapon in the campaign against bird flu. He avoided using her last name. They seemed impressed, and she loved it. These people weren't scientists. There were some businessmen and their wives, and an aged government official. They didn't know her blemished history. She hadn't felt this much professional respect since she started working at Berkeley.

Hiroshi sat next to her, and with just two seats remaining at the table, a couple approached. Flawless makeup concealed the woman's age, which might have been anywhere from 50 to 75 years. She was the only woman in the entire room not wearing a gown, dressed instead in a pair of wide, sweeping palazzo pants. Unlike her slim, graying escort, she was plump and had not a single silver hair. She moved with a boldness that seemed to leave him in her shadow.

Immediately after greeting others at the table she came straight to Amika. "Dr. Nakamura, it's a pleasure to meet you in person."

Amika glanced at Hiroshi for a clue. "I'm sorry ma'am, do I know you?"

"No, but I know you. Our issue with you on the cover was one of our best sellers ever."

"You're with *Shufu* magazine?"

"I'm editor-in-chief Natsuko, my dear." She dropped heavily into the chair next to Amika and pointed her thumb toward the man. "My husband. His official title is publisher." She leaned in conspiratorially. "He's the money guy."

So this was the person responsible for starting the rape story. The exploitative photographs. The innuendo. Amika's face grew hot, and it wasn't just the alcohol.

Before she found the words to respond, one of the businessmen at the table said, "Nakamura. *The* Nakamura? From the Senkaku Islands?"

Natsuko fanned herself with the evening's program. "She's the one. Shuu Nakamura is her brother."

An embarrassed hush fell at the table as all eyes turned to her. One of the silent wives looked at her with pity.

Not pity. Anything but that.

"I wasn't—"

She stopped herself. No, she wasn't raped, and she hated the stigma. Doubtless these modern people didn't make a moral judgement about her, but they looked at her differently now. The stigma made her weak, fragile, damaged. But hadn't she agreed to play this role for her brother's sake?

Natsuko took a swig of a clear liquid from a shot glass, regarding Amika with deliberate interest.

With discipline, Amika put meekness in her voice and said, "I wasn't sure if I should come tonight." *So much for the brilliant American scientist.*

Hiroshi put his hand on her arm. "You honor us with your presence. You're among friends here."

It was the opening she'd been looking for. She dabbed her eyes with a napkin, then smiled. "Then you know about the danger my brother is in. Is there anything any of you can do for him?"

"Do for him?" exclaimed the businessman. "It's *his fault* I'm here tonight—no offense, Hiroshi."

"None taken," he said.

The angry capitalist continued. "Two days ago I was expelled from Chongquin. Most of my Japanese compatriots were told to get out, or they left in fear for their safety. This affair is costing me a lot of money. The protests against Shuu Nakamura completely shut down one of my factories and blocked deliveries to another."

"And you blame *him*?"

"He's an American. Why is Japan paying the price?"

Meekness forgotten, Amika said, "This is Japan's fight over those stupid pieces of rock. Not Shuu's. Not America's."

Under the table she felt Hiroshi place his hand on her thigh.

Another man, introduced earlier as a retired officer from Japan's Self-Defense Forces, piped in, "The Americans won't intervene because of their summit with China next month."

The businessman said, "By that time, I expect China will impose sanctions against us. They'll make it so hard for Japan to do business that even the Koreans will get contracts."

"The risks are high for all of us," Hiroshi said. "Koga Scientific has lost several accounts. But remember, my friends, this dispute is about more than money."

"National pride," Natsuko said. "Our readers have made it clear they support a strong stand against China."

"We've let Beijing push us around," the retired military officer said. "This isn't the first time they've stirred up trouble in the Senkakus. We need to make sure it's the last. We draw the line here."

A waiter appeared with a bottle of *shochu*. Hiroshi asked him to pour everyone a glass.

The businessman recognized the brand. "*Mori-izou*. How in the world did you get it?"

Hiroshi smiled. "We all have our secrets."

Natsuko was the first to raise her glass. "To Shuu Nakamura, defender of women's honor."

Amika blushed again, her arm frozen with her glass in the air. Ever so slightly, Hiroshi nodded at her. She took the cue and drank.

A quavering voice lifted from an old man on the far side of the table. "Your brother is a fine man."

Hiroshi whispered into her ear. "That's Ichiro. He's a former minister. Still powerful." His breath was warm on her neck.

"Thank you, sir," she said to the man. He was ancient and brittle, his face intricately lined like the glaze of old porcelain. "He deserves better than his current treatment."

"Don't we all," Ichiro said.

"Can anything be done?"

The old man drained his glass and set it down with a thud. "It's difficult."

"If they free him, the Chinese will go ballistic," the businessman said.

"The US wants it to look like Japan is handling this on its own," the officer said.

"He can remain where he is, for a while," Natsuko said. "We won't hand him over."

"What makes you so sure?" Amika said. No one answered.

Old Ichiro gestured for a refill. The businessman's wife swiftly rose, took the bottle to him and poured. "Hiroshi and I have discussed this," Ichiro said. "He asked me if my friends in the current administration could help."

Hiroshi bowed.

"And?" Amika said impatiently.

"It's difficult."

"Of course it's difficult! But a man's life is at stake!"

Applause broke out as a parade of dignitaries entered the room and marched toward the head table.

Ichiro stared at her impassively. She felt like he was judging her, and it stoked within her an irrational rage.

"Your brother is one man," he said finally. "In the life of the nation, his life doesn't matter."

13

The old minister's words were a slap. Aghast, Amika scanned the faces around the table to find others as offended as she was.

No one seemed to care.

The businessman looked at his mobile phone. Natsuko leaned on the table, her chin in her hand, observing with an impartial air. The officer conversed privately with his wife.

Amika propelled her chair back from the table, snagging her silk dress in her haste. *Useless. All of them.* They had money and influence they clearly were *not* going to use to help Shuu. A torrent of fury was loaded on her tongue and ready to fire. She had to get out of here.

"Amika," Hiroshi said.

If she allowed herself to speak a single word, she was going to regret it. The stupid dress slowed her down as she tore it free of the chair's leg. Where were her running shoes when she needed them?

"See you later," Natsuko said.

She wanted to punch the magazine editor. Instead she plunged into the crowd, spiraling around the festive tables and suited men and red-robed women. The din of their chatter isolated her in angry solitude.

Nobody is on my side.

Pressing toward the nearest exit, she collided with someone's arm. A splash of red wine blurred into the silk of her gown. She got to the door and reached for the touch bar to thrust it open. Like magic, it gave way an instant before her hand made contact. Hiroshi had caught up with her.

"Wait." He slipped his body between her and the exit.

"Let me go."

"Of course. Let me come with you."

He held the door open and she plunged into the warm, humid night. The clamor of the banquet hall was silenced, replaced by the soft chirps of frogs hidden somewhere in the lush foliage that unexpectedly surrounded her.

Surprised, Amika stopped with her spiked heels on a flat paving stone bordered by river-smoothed black rocks. Low-voltage lights embedded in a stone lantern cast a glow on the path. The rest of the garden was in darkness.

Hiroshi took a few steps away from the building into deepening shadow. "You didn't know this was here."

"No."

"It's a very famous garden."

She wobbled in her shoes as her agitation collided with the peacefulness of the summer night. She needed a bag to punch, a track to run, or a person to yell at.

"You lied to me." She yanked off her inconvenient footwear. "You told me I'd find friends and allies here tonight."

"Believe me, they *are* your allies." He gently took the shoes from her hand. "Most of them, anyway. They love this country and they're ready to resist China."

"My brother is not 'this country.'"

"No, but in this matter their fates are linked. Those who believe in a strong Japan will fight for Shuu."

"Not according to Ichiro."

"He's an old man who came of age in an uncompromising era. A fatalist by nature. But I know for a fact that he's made inquiries on your brother's behalf."

"Inquiries," she scoffed.

He strolled down the path to an arched stone bridge over a tiny stream. "Don't be so dismissive. Look what happened with you at the embassy. American-style confrontation will get you nowhere in Japan."

"Right. 'It's difficult.' Which basically means 'no.'"

"If we push too hard for a decision on Shuu's case, we might get one. The wrong one. At least until the US-China summit is over, the safest place for your brother is administrative limbo. In Japan. Not China."

Better a Japanese prison than… Her shoulders drooped. "You really think they might hand him over, even without an extradition treaty?"

"Anything is possible, Amika-chan."

She joined him on the bridge. Below, water trickled over mossy rocks. The fragrance of lilies hung in the air. He took her by the hand and steered her toward an ancient willow tree.

Why can't it be simple like this? Just me and a guy, together. Without all the complications. She should've known that going to the banquet would be trouble. Amika Nakamura and social events were oil and water.

Hand in hand they walked in silence, leaving the banquet hall further and further behind. They came to a huge three-story wood pagoda, its straight tower and square, tiled levels radiating order and serenity. Hiroshi set down her shoes, faced her and grasped both her hands.

"You have a lot to learn about the Japanese way of doing things," he said. "You Americans have no appreciation for subtlety. Not every problem can be tackled head-on. Look at this pagoda. You see it and you think, oh, what a beautiful pagoda. You don't know that it's a thousand years old. That it was built five hundred miles away from here, by temple monks who used not a single nail."

She rolled her eyes. "What's your point?"

"Much labor is hidden behind a desirable outcome." He lowered their hands, drawing them closer to each other. "Memories are short. Strong feelings fade. Something else will make news and shift people's focus from what happened on Uotsuri-shima. Slow, quiet efforts in the background—efforts you don't see—stand the best chance of freeing your brother in the end. My family and friends can make things happen in this country. But it takes time. You have to be patient."

Her eyes filled with tears. "That's not easy for me. I need to be *doing* something."

He let go of her and drifted down the path. "There is something you could do. Something you're very good at. I had an idea…"

She slipped her shoes back on and followed him. "What?"

"Never mind, things won't come to that. Don't worry about it."

She scurried to his side. "Tell me."

He turned away and gazed at the sky. "The government won't…they can't possibly…the prime minister would never subject a Japanese citizen to Chinese justice."

"You know Shuu isn't a Japanese citizen."

"That's why…I can hardly fathom…"

She grabbed his arm and pleaded, "Hiroshi, what can I do?"

He caressed the back of her head. "Here's the thing. If, by some slim chance, Tokyo caves in, we need a rescue plan. A way to stop Shuu's transfer to the mainland, even if the government orders it."

"Yes. How?"

"By making the Chinese refuse to take him."

Sure. Why didn't I think of that? "Using what, an ancient Chinese mind trick?"

He ignored her snark. "Contagion. If he was infected with something they were afraid of."

The sarcasm in her tone was not subtle. "Yes, death by smallpox sounds so much better than extradition."

"You asked, so hear me out. There are international rules on quarantine. A prisoner carrying a group three pathogen can't cross a national border. Obviously we wouldn't want to put your brother in actual danger, so we would have to be clever about it. Clever, Amika. With a virus. Get it?"

Her cynical thought-stream froze as her sharp intellect picked up on his idea.

A virus that isn't what it seems. Molecular disguise. Right up my alley.

She put her arms around his waist. "Flu?"

He kissed her forehead. "It's perfect, right? You know more about influenza virus than anyone on the planet. You know all its little switches and functions. Turn some on, turn others off. Make it look deadly even though it's not."

"Maybe." She pondered the possibilities. "It would be risky, for sure. Molecular switches have a way of reverting. You can't always predict how they'll behave when you let them loose in the wild."

"Which is one of many reasons why this is a terrible idea. But it's the best idea I've got."

"It's better than nothing," she said.

"It will take time to do the lab work," he said. "If we wait for the moment of crisis, it will be too late."

"I wouldn't use the virus unless I was absolutely sure it's safe. And I won't know that until I've made it."

"So make it now, and we keep *all* our options open."

Hip to hip they continued along the path. Amika turned the idea over in her mind. *It's perfect.* No, not perfect. The technical challenges were significant but perversely that made it even more attractive to her. Finally, a plan to save Shuu that she understood, one that was in her power to implement. No more Amika as victim. In this scheme, she was the hero.

She had no doubt she could do it. A scientific task. No storytelling, no lying.

The sound of falling water grew louder as they reached a rocky waterfall about as high as a man. Moonbeams made its cascades white and luminous.

Hiroshi looked earnestly into her eyes. "I've never known a woman like you. There have been beautiful women, and smart women. But never both with such a…spark."

Her heart skipped faster. *What should I say?*

His gaze did not waver. She surrendered to it and sputtered, "Thank you."

He pulled her close to him. "It seems that outdoors at night is our time."

Trembling, she remembered that night on the boat, cuddled against him to ward off the chill.

Like magnets their lips drew together and the universe ceased to exist. When she opened her eyes again, all her agendas and goals had burned away except for one.

His fingers traced her neck down to her bare shoulders and passed lightly over her breast. The crisp, stiff support built into the bustier of the dress blunted the feel of his touch.

She wanted more.

He kissed her throat and smelled her skin. "You are the most precious flower in this garden."

She wrapped her arms around his shoulders for balance and coiled one leg around his back side, squeezing his pelvis tighter against hers. When they came up for breath a half minute later, he pointed to a door leading into a different part of the building from where they had originally come.

"What about your party?" she said.

"The party is in my suite. With you."

June 30 (two weeks later)

In movies, a laboratory at night is a sinister place where the schemes of mad scientists go horribly wrong. In Amika's experience, the solitude of the lab after normal working hours was peaceful. Calm. Productive.

Tonight had turned out differently.

"That's a first," Amika said as she zipped up her jeans. "You ever do it at the lab before?"

Hiroshi leaned back on the cushions of the couch, his arms spread wide, making her want to kiss his naked chest again. He didn't answer her question.

"Forget it. I don't want to know," she said.

Amika had been working late into the night (again) when Hiroshi surprised her in the empty Koga building.

"I've barely seen you for three days," he had said.

"I'm working on Shuu's virus," she'd said.

"Not for the next twenty minutes, you're not," he'd said, dangling a set of master keys.

Manami's office had never been put to such good use. Or so Amika assumed.

"Move," she said, shoving Hiroshi off the couch so she could rearrange the throw pillows.

"No one will be here for hours." He pressed himself against her back side as she bent over.

She shook him off. "I have to get back to work. They told me they'll finish sequencing Shuu's DNA tomorrow. I want to wrap up the transmissibility experiments tonight so I'm ready to move forward."

"All work and no play—" He forced his lips against hers.

She indulged him for a moment, returning his kiss with vigor. Then she said, "You know how important it is that I get this right. If it comes to it, I'll be infecting the person I love most in this world with bird flu."

Resigned, he put on his shirt. "How's it going?"

"Great." Her voice brightened. "I've repeated—and advanced—the work I did at Berkeley. I found three critical control switches in the DNA. One controls the virus's ability to infect a particular species or population. Another regulates its transmission from one host to another, and the third influences how much damage the virus will cause."

"You are amazing."

"That's not what my last boss said."

"He's a fool."

She surveyed the office. *I think this is how it looked when we came in.* Anyhow, if Manami noticed something out of place, she'd assume it was the housekeeping staff. "He thought this work was too dangerous. In theory, someone could use my data to make a bioweapon. But I'm using it to design a weaker influenza, one that shouldn't cause more than a little fever, and also can't spread from person to person if Shuu is a carrier."

"Yet your influenza still *looks* dangerous, so we can deceive the Chinese if we have to?"

"Yes. The University forbid me to make my findings public, so the current tests for bird flu can't tell the difference between a potentially catastrophic, pandemic influenza and a weakling like this one."

Hiroshi finished tying his shoes. Then he clicked off the lights and gave her butt one more squeeze before they stepped into the empty hallway.

"I'm ready to do the third modification," she said as they walked back to her lab. Everything was silent except for the vague rumble of the building's ventilation system. "Bird flu, like all viruses, has a molecular 'key' that unlocks the cells it's trying to infect. The bird flu 'key' opens the 'lock' on bird cells. The key generally doesn't work on human cells. My brother might be a bird-brain but he's definitely human. So how to get my bird virus to infect him?" She savored her own cleverness. "By using the DNA sequence of Shuu's 'lock' to design a virus 'key' to match."

"Brilliant," Hiroshi said.

"It was your idea," she replied.

"Maybe, but you're the only person in the world who can actually do it."

"Yay for our team." She went to her desk and pulled out some coins for the vending machine. Late-night munchies had struck.

"I have something for you." He cupped her hand in his and added a flash drive to the coins. "Your brother's DNA sequence data. Finished early."

Awesome! "You didn't tell me when you got here."

"If you had known the data were ready, would you have taken a timeout with me?"

"Smart man." She pecked his cheek and felt absurdly alert for this time of night. *The thrill of the chase.* No one had ever used molecular techniques to change the host specificity of a flu virus in this way. *I am good at this.*

He turned to leave. "I'm sure we won't need to use it," he reassured her. "Shuu will soon be free."

"I know," she said, ignoring the nasty little part of her that wanted a real-life test to prove that her ideas were right. She would find some way to win professional recognition for her accomplishment even if her creation never left the lab.

"You have an appointment to telephone him this afternoon?" Hiroshi asked.

"Yes, and I won't miss it for anything. It's been days since we spoke."

He opened the door. "Remember, they monitor all his communications. You cannot say anything about this, not even a hint."

I don't need to. My baby brother knows I've got his back.

Years in graduate school and post-doctoral fellowship trained Amika to sleep at a desk. After Hiroshi left, she labored another couple of hours at the laboratory bench, and then took a snooze. When her lab mates arrived for work in the morning, she washed her face, drank some coffee, and checked her email.

Jun Taniguchi was back.

She was tempted to delete the journalist's message without looking at it but the subject line hooked her: News about your brother's case. Warily, she clicked.

In the body of the email it said:

> China adopting more aggressive tactics. Boat incident likely to affect handling of Shuu Nakamura's case. I am still here if you want to talk.

She felt her blood pressure rise. What boat incident?

Jun had included links to news stories. At least they did not link to Jun's organization, because that always meant trouble before. Whatever was going on, this time Taniguchi wasn't responsible.

Amika scanned the first article. Last evening, China had captured a Japanese vessel at sea in a remote corner of the Zhoushan Archipelago, which Amika had never heard of. China claimed the fishing boat had entered Chinese territorial waters without permission, and was illegally taking fish. The Japanese crew was under arrest. Some officials were hinting that the fishermen might be tried for espionage.

Isn't this good news for Shuu? Let another flash point between the countries take center stage. Let people forget what happened in the Senkakus.

Her lack of imagination when it came to politics was apparent as she read some more.

A trade.

Several of the Chinese protesters from the Senkaku raid were still in Japanese custody. Commentators suggested that China might use the Japanese fishermen to get them back.

And demand that Shuu be handed over with them.

As Amika counted the hours until her call from Shuu, she redoubled her effort to create the perfect bird flu. Time was running out.

One-fifteen PM. He'd told her he would call at one-fifteen. Now it was almost one-thirty.

Sweat from Amika's hands left prints on her mobile phone. She stared at it, willing it to vibrate but it lay like a stone in her grip. Why wasn't Shuu calling? Had he forgotten? Had something happened at the prison? Her anticipation morphed into worry. Was it the captured fishermen? Had the government made a move on Shuu's case? She set the phone down on her desk and rearranged the test tube racks on her lab bench for the third time.

I can't stand it.

Direct calls to prisoners were impossible, but she had a phone number for the prison's main line, which she dialed now. A recorded male voice offered her a menu of options. None of them applied. She touched 0 to get a live person.

"How may I direct your call?"

At that moment, call waiting announced that Shuu was on the line. She disconnected from the operator and heard her brother's voice over the crackly connection.

"Hey, sis."

She drooped into her chair as the tension left her body. "Hey. You're late, I was worried."

"Well excuuu-se me," Shuu said. "I'm in jail, remember? I don't make my own schedule."

"I know, I know," she said quickly. "I just was worried, that's all. How are you?"

"Frickin' tired. The bed here is shit."

"Do you think they'd let me send you a better pillow?"

"You think that's all it takes? You just mail a package, and everything's fine?"

"No, I—"

"I'm sick of this. I want out."

"That's what we all want. Hiroshi—"

"Don't talk to me about him. That little prick should be in here, not me."

Oh, Shuu. You're right. But you're not the all-powerful Hiroshi Naito. You and I, we're nobody. "He's working hard to get you out."

"The people he *hired* are working. Maybe they're working hard. How would I know?"

"I guess you wouldn't. But he told me it's going well. We just have to be patient."

He paused. "Are you screwing him?"

"What? No. I mean, why would you say that?"

He snorted. "I figured it would happen. You're a babe. He's rich."

"We both care about you very much."

"Yeah, I bet he says a prayer for me every time he bangs you."

"Shuu!"

A moment of silence passed between them. He spoke first. "I can't stand it, 'Mika. I hate this place."

She thought her heart might break. "Do you get to use the gym much?" she asked in a quavering voice.

"Some. Not enough. I do a lot of calisthenics when I'm locked up. Push-ups and stuff."

If she had to deploy the virus and force him into quarantine, he would be locked up all the time. Miserable.

But he would be safe.

"I brought your cricket to my lab," she said. "I think he misses you. Doesn't sing quite as much as I remember."

"He's getting old. For a cricket."

"He likes cabbage."

"Yeah. And corn. Did you ever give him corn?"

"No. I'll try it."

She felt a searing anguish. Her brother didn't deserve this.

"Did you hear about the Japanese fishermen? The ones arrested by China?" she said.

"Yeah."

She was desperate to know if he'd been briefed by someone from Hiroshi's team. Did he have inside information? Delicately she asked, "Has anybody talked to you about it?"

"Nah."

She could tell him what she'd read online. That this incident was yet another excuse for the Chinese to get their claws in him. But why upset him? He couldn't do anything about it. In the end, her work in the lab might be the only thing that could save him.

"When's the last time you had a visit from one of your lawyers?"

"Three days ago. Before that, Koga sent a doctor to check me out."

She knew about the physician's visit. During that medical exam, they took a blood sample. Some of it was used to sequence Shuu's DNA, but her brother didn't know that.

I gave consent. Like I'm his mom, and he's a kid. The way it's always been.

"Pretty quiet, huh."

"Yeah." His voice cracked as he said, "I wish I could see you more."

She choked on tears and turned the phone away so he wouldn't hear her sniffling.

"Amika?"

"Yes?"

"The Chinese jackals won't get me."

"That's right. Hiroshi will work his magic."

"I mean it. Forest hill, you know."

Forest hill? What the hell did that mean?

Forest hill. Foresthill.

Her hand flew to her mouth in shock. What could she say?

"I love you, little bro."

A buzzer rang in the background on Shuu's end. "Time's—" he said as the connection was automatically broken.

She hugged the phone to her chest and closed her eyes. Foresthill was a bridge they'd visited as kids on a trip to Northern California. It was the highest bridge in the state, towering over a steep-walled river canyon. They'd goofed around and made morbid jokes for weeks after.

Jokes about jumping off the Foresthill Bridge.

She understood his meaning. If Japan sent him to China, her brother was going to kill himself.

Preoccupied, she jumped at a rap on the frame of the open door to her lab.

"Dr. Nakamura? Do you have a minute?"

Somehow, rather than releasing a primal scream, she replied politely to the white-coated woman. "Yes, Dr. Hikino. Please come in."

"Are you still on the dead bird project?"

A professional conversation. With a colleague. Nothing about her brother, or captured fishermen, or tall bridges. Just plain old work. *Yes. Good.* She took a deep breath and buried her feelings.

"Not any more. I think Dr. Aizawa is responsible for the viral genome sequencing. You should talk to him."

"I will, but I want to talk to you first. Would you mind looking at something with me?"

"Sure."

Hikino pulled up a chair and set a three-ring binder on the desk. "When a bird carcass or specimen gets sent to Koga, it comes to me. I start a database profile for it. I keep track of whatever information comes in: what kind of bird, when and where it was found, under what circumstances, how long we think it's been dead. That sort of thing. Then someone tests it for influenza virus, and does the DNA sequencing. Aizawa, I guess. The test data get added to the specimen's computer record."

"Of course. I did a lot of the sequencing before I was transferred to another project."

"Did you ever look at the rest of the profile for your specimens?"

"Sometimes. I liked to know where the birds came from. Where the deaths are occurring."

"Me too. I'm a birder. I love to go out to the parks on the weekend. Take my DSLR and telephoto."

Amika had no interest in birdwatching or camera technology. Hikino deflated a little when she didn't encourage her to elaborate on her hobby. "Anyway, there are a couple of sites around Japan that are really special for birders. Lots of birds, lots of species diversity. I wondered if any of them were affected by the outbreak. So instead of looking at each specimen in isolation, I compiled the data and made a disease map."

A standard epidemiology trick. "Smart," Amika said.

"Here's what it looks like." She opened the binder to a map of Honshu, the main island of Japan, speckled with red dots marking the locations where a dead bird had been found. The dots were scattered, seemingly at random, like a rash.

"Widespread," Amika said.

"Which is weird, right?" Hikino said. "No clusters."

Amika wasn't an epidemiologist, but that did seem odd. Infectious disease outbreaks, especially those with a highly infectious agent like bird flu, tended to cluster. One bird catches it and spreads it to others in its flock. A hotspot of death.

"This is only data from specimens that came to Koga?"

"Yes."

"Then you're missing information. Dead birds were sent to other testing centers too."

"That's what I thought. Turns out there are two other labs receiving birds, but they only get about fifteen percent of them. Koga does the majority of the sequencing."

"Could you access their data?"

Hikino turned the page. "This includes all the reported bird deaths from H7N9 influenza for the past forty-five days."

More red dots, but the pattern was unchanged. No clusters.

"What if you look closer?"

"One step ahead of you," Hikino said, revealing additional maps of smaller areas. Even at the local level, the deaths were sporadic, disconnected.

"Huh." Amika said.

"Here's what really gets me," Hikino said. "Two carcasses came from poultry farms. The bodies of wild birds found on the property, not chickens. Two different farms."

"Those farmers must have freaked out. If flu gets into their flocks, they have to slaughter and burn them all."

"That's the weird part. I followed up with the farms. The poultry stayed completely healthy. Not a single case of bird flu."

"Had the flocks been given the Koga vaccine?"

"No. Too expensive."

Avian influenza was notoriously contagious. How could not one, but two vulnerable poultry flocks, jammed into crowded barns, dodge this bullet? Amika drummed her fingers on the desk.

"I came to you because they say you're an expert on virulence factors," Hikino said. "Can you look at the genome sequences and tell whether the viruses we're finding are less infectious than normal?"

"I might be able to."

"If the sequence data support the epidemiology, we'll have good news for the public."

True. If this new virus doesn't spread from bird to bird, then the risk of a bird epidemic is very small, and there's pretty much zero chance of it jumping into humans. That would mean no need for a vaccination campaign.

"I'll look into it," she promised. *After I'm finished with my work on Shuu's virus.*

Hikino gathered up her binder and left. As Amika returned to her labors, one last thought about the epidemiology crossed her mind.

If the new bird flu wasn't infectious, then why were so many birds turning up dead?

14

For the first time in weeks, Amika rewarded herself with a night off. At 4:30 PM, she cleaned her lab bench and walked out of Koga into the steamy July air. The people and cars of Tokyo swirled around her, orderly and vibrant. Near the entrance to the subway she caught a whiff of citrus and stopped at a cart for an icy tea drink blended with fresh fruit juice.

As of today her and Hiroshi's backup plan was ready. If worse came to worst, she could infect Shuu with an engineered influenza virus that would quarantine him in the country. She was satisfied that the genetic modifications she'd made to the bird flu would target it to her brother (based on his DNA) but not make him sick. Of course she had no way to test it directly. Better to find a political solution to his predicament than to deploy this risky stratagem.

Fortunately the news was good on this front. According to what she'd heard today, Japan and China were close to an agreement that did not involve her brother. The Chinese protesters arrested in the Senkaku Islands would be traded for the Japanese fishermen taken in the Zhoushan Archipelago. She'd found no mention of Shuu Nakamura in any of the reports online.

For Shuu, no news is good news.

At her tiny apartment, rays of sun reflected off dust particles floating in the air. With her long hours at work, she hadn't properly cleaned her room in weeks. The refrigerator held nothing fresh to eat or drink. She grabbed a bag of wasabi peas to snack on while picking through her closet for something to wear tonight. To celebrate her triumph at the lab, Hiroshi was taking her out. She chose a miniskirt and mesh tights paired with a sparkly, low-cut top.

Wildly unprofessional. But that was the point. Tonight was going to be fun. Despite the strange and somewhat calculated start to her relationship with her boss, she tingled with anticipation for their evening together. Hiroshi knew how to show her a good time. Originally she had figured she would gradually end the relationship after Shuu's situation got resolved. But the way things were going, she could imagine being his girlfriend for longer.

She took a nap until the sun sank lower in the sky, then got dressed and rideshared to the Tokyo neighborhood where she was meeting Hiroshi. A whirlwind of neon light kept the dusk at bay. Fashionable young Japanese, including adventurous men and women in colored hair, heavy makeup, and boots, thronged around the noodle shops and bookstores. In a few hours, they'd be lined up to get into the clubs and music would spill out into the street.

Some distorted music was already playing nearby. As it grew louder, she recognized the tune and turned toward the source. A black van inched along with the traffic on the congested street while blaring *Kimigayo*, the national anthem of Japan, from speakers attached to its roof. Japanese flags, white with a red circle, drifted from mounts on the rear bumper. They flanked a "rising sun" flag of Imperial Japan, with red rays radiating from the central circle. The van's doors and sides were covered with text. She deciphered nationalist slogans like *Come on Japanese, Stand Up!* and *Koreans, Go Home!* A second van, similarly outfitted, followed the first. Rather than playing the national anthem, megaphones on this car shouted right-wing slogans.

She'd encountered these *gaisensha* around town before. The propaganda vehicles for Japanese ultranationalist sects were not uncommon, or at least, they were hard to miss when nearby. They railed against Communism and pacifism, and they extolled Japanese pride and revisionist history, including the claim that Japan's depredation of its Asian neighbors in the 1920s to 1940s was a noble effort to free them from Western colonialism. To her, the ultra-nationalists were a colorful feature of Tokyo, sort of like the crazy speakers in London's Hyde Park corner or the *desnudas*, painted topless women in Times Square. The cars, vans, and occasional motor coach of the *gaisensha* driving around town were partly spooky, partly embarrassing. Paying too much attention to them felt unseemly. Like most of the people in the crowd around her, she briefly beheld the spectacle and then returned to her own business.

Until she heard the words *Zhoushan* and *fishermen*.

She planted her feet and listened. Why were they using such a crappy sound system? Now that she was actually paying attention, the words seemed garbled. She started walking down the sidewalk to keep up with the van.

The speaker was ranting about China and the Chinese "invasion" of the Senkaku Islands. He criticized the Japanese prime minister and praised the Self-Defense Forces. Amika kept listening for him to repeat what he'd said about the fishermen. Half a block later, he did.

"The Zhousan fishermen were in international waters. The Chinese are kidnappers! We will not pay ransom for the return of our citizens. Bring the fishermen home now! Bring home our naval officer! No trade. No prisoners for citizens!"

Naval officer? What naval officer?

The slogans started over again, exactly the same, with no additional information. She gave up the chase and headed back to her meeting point.

She felt warm breath in her ear an instant before she heard the voice. "Opinionated, aren't they?" Hiroshi said. He'd sidled up to her in the crowd and now placed his hand on her neck.

"Hi," she said, greeting him with a kiss. "They're loud, too."

"If you think that's loud, wait until August fifteenth."

"Why? What's August fifteenth?"

His hand dropped to his side, a look of surprise on his face. "You don't know?"

She shook her head, feeling mildly embarrassed.

"It's the anniversary of the end of the Pacific War," he said. "Japan's surrender at the end of World War Two. After the US used nuclear weapons in Hiroshima and Nagasaki."

"Oh. I never paid much attention in history."

"Maybe you should," he chided. "History does not live only in the past. These groups who drive the vans, the *uyoku dantai,* believe our nation was wronged. So they still fight to restore Japan's glory. On August fifteenth, they'll be everywhere. This will be your first time in Japan on that day. You'll find it interesting."

"I suppose." *Crazy right-wingers. Note to self: work late in the lab that day.*

She threaded her arm around his and they strolled toward the restaurant. "You don't think they'll stop the exchange, do you?" After the warning from Jun Taniguchi, she worried that the fisherman incident would still ensnare her brother.

Hiroshi took another few steps before answering. "No, I don't."

They passed through a door and down a flight of stairs to a small, dark, basement gastropub, an *izakaya* joint. The host greeted Hiroshi by name and gave them a secluded table in a corner. They had barely taken their seats when a waiter delivered a half-full bottle of bourbon.

"On the rocks as usual, sir?"

"Yes. And bring soda for the lady."

Amika realized that the bar stored special liquors for frequent patrons. "I didn't know you liked bourbon."

He took a sip. "Only when it's this good."

Cool towels to wipe their hands and a glass of soda materialized. Hiroshi poured a splash of bourbon into the soda and offered it to her.

"No thanks," she said.

He dug into his pockets and fished out a pack of cigarettes and paper matches. Though smoking was a common habit in Japan, she had never seen him light up before.

He gestured at her drink with his cigarette. "Go ahead. You might need it."

Belatedly she noticed the creases in his forehead, the tension in his shoulders. "What's wrong?"

"Have a drink."

"Not until you tell me."

Their server set a plate of fresh tofu and sauces on the table. Hiroshi rested his cigarette on an ashtray and picked up his chopsticks for a bite. Amika gripped the table. She could not eat until she had an answer. "Is it Shuu?"

He nodded as he slowly chewed. She tried to laser him with her eyes. Finally he glanced around to assure their privacy, and spoke.

"Is your virus ready?" he said in a hushed voice.

Her heart leaped to her throat. "Pretty much."

"We're going to have to use it. Tomorrow."

"No." Not tomorrow, not ever. There were more tests to do before it was ready. *Who am I kidding? There aren't enough tests in the whole world.* Earlier today, the genetic modifications she made to the virus seemed perfect. On paper. But how would the virus behave in real life? How could she do this experiment, take this risk, with her own brother?

Her voice cracked. "I thought everything was fine."

He took a pull on his cigarette. "There's more to the 'fishing boat' story than they're saying in the press," he said. "Top-secret stuff. One of my father's well-placed friends tipped him off. That boat was fishing for more than fish. At least one man on board was an agent with the Defense Intelligence Headquarters."

"A spy?"

"So it seems, though no one is admitting anything."

"Is he a naval officer?"

Hiroshi regarded her with amazement. "Yes. How did you know?"

"The van on the street. They said something about returning a naval officer."

"Then the rumor is spreading. I can tell you, it's true."

"I was on the internet a few hours ago. There wasn't anything about a spy."

"Of course not. I only heard because of my father's connections in the government. I don't have all the details. But what I was told is all we need to know."

"What did you hear?"

"They're going to exchange the Chinese jackals who attacked us on the Senkakus for the legit fishermen on the captured boat."

"That's no secret."

"And they're trading Shuu for the spy."

The smoke in the basement restaurant suddenly felt choking, as if a fire raged instead of a few smoldering cancer sticks. "When did you find out?" she croaked.

"A few hours ago."

"Why didn't you tell me?"

"I'm telling you now."

A boisterous group of four suited salarymen, ending their day at the office with a boozy binge, roared with laughter at a table across the room. Amika felt her soul float to the ceiling, leaving her body hollow and lifeless. Detached, her spirit looked down at Hiroshi and the whorl that formed in his hair at the back of his head, and at the inappropriately festive, sensuous top she had chosen for herself in another time, hours ago, when the world was a happier place.

Hiroshi's hands curled into fists. "If we had known, we could've worked on this. My people had everything under control. We had Shuu's case so gummed up in bureaucracy they couldn't have deported him if he begged them to. But none of us saw this coming. The spooks were flying below our radar."

He failed. My rich, playboy genius boyfriend dropped the ball.

He continued. "I can see why Tokyo is keeping it quiet. With the right spin, this could be turned into a major international incident. What I don't get is why Beijing is going along, not blowing it up. Maybe they realized they'd never get Shuu if the discussion was out in the open. The Japanese people wouldn't stand for it."

She drifted back to herself, her emptiness filling with fear—and anger.

He said, "They'll probably move quickly, for that reason. Do the transfer within a week, I figure. Once word leaks out, the deal might sour. We could try going public with the news—"

"Just shut up for a minute."

He leaned back in his chair and worked on his cigarette. She crossed her arms. The whole situation was his fault. He brought the Nakamura siblings to Uotsuri-shima. He delivered the DGPS device. He'd promised to make things right. He'd claimed he could protect her brother.

But now it was up to her.

"How do we deliver the virus to Shuu?" she said coolly.

He crushed the smoking stub into the ashtray. "We control his medical care. Koga already sent a doctor to visit him once. We can get a nurse in for a follow up."

"A nasal spray would be the most effective delivery system. Can you do that?"

"Yes. Koga manufactures a live flu vaccine that's delivered as a mist into the nostrils. We can make a special one for Shuu."

"Is there any way you can get his consent?"

"Absolutely not. Every word he hears or reads is monitored. We must make this decision for him."

"I don't like it," she said. "There is a risk."

"Don't like it? I hate it. But we're running out of options. If Shuu is moved to a Chinese prison, anything could happen. Even execution."

"Don't say that," she snapped.

It's all on me. In some measure, this was a relief. Other people always let you down. The only question was, what would Shuu want?

Answering that was easy. Her brother was an adventurer, a risk taker. Given the choices before them, she had no doubt he would choose the virus. He would trust her.

Did she trust herself? Was her virus ready?

She silently reviewed her work from memory, each step in the genetic transformation of the flu virus. First: weaken it to cause only mild illness. *Check.* Second: give it an affinity to infect Shuu, based on his DNA. *Check.* Finally: cripple it so it can't spread from him to anyone else. *Check.*

I did everything right. In theory. Yet how many times had she tested a "theory" in live cells or animals and found reality did not match expectation?

Too many times.

Whether she acted or did nothing, her brother's life was at stake.

Do I trust the Chinese not to kill him? Do I trust him not to kill himself? Or do I trust that my virus won't kill him?

She pushed the untouched bourbon cocktail to the side of the table and stood up. "I'll have the specimen ready by midnight."

July 14 (eight days later)

Amika hunched over her desk, trying to stop the J-pop music wafting through the lab from worming its way into her brain. She'd been looking at data from the epidemic of dead birds in Japan, something Dr. Hikino had asked her to do a little more than a week ago, when an email came from her brother. She closed all other windows on her computer so she could savor his every word without distraction.

Two days ago, a health care worker hand-picked by Hiroshi had visited Shuu Nakamura in prison. Amika didn't know what pretext was given for the visit, or what they told Shuu was in the mist they sprayed into his nose. It didn't matter. The bird flu virus she engineered just for him had been delivered straight from her lab to his lungs.

Though he didn't know it, in his email Shuu reported good news. He was right on schedule. The average incubation period for influenza—time from infection to symptoms—was about two days. She'd never been so pleased to hear that her little brother was feeling under the weather. In the message he complained of a headache and sore throat, and he pointed out how unfair it was that he was coming down with a cold in the middle of summer. He blamed the prison environment.

I would too, if I didn't know the truth. Prisons are a great place to spread disease.

Apparently he was in the dark about the threat to trade him for the Japanese spy as he made no mention of it. The existence of the captured naval officer was still an unsubstantiated rumor floating around the ultranationalist fringe. She didn't dare tell him about it because she wasn't supposed to know. When she connected with him for their telephone appointment tomorrow she would have to be careful not to reveal anything.

From the back of her desk, Shuu's cricket made a few chirps. She moved the cage to a sunnier spot to encourage it to sing. "Do you miss him, buddy?"

The rest of Shuu's too-short email offered general complaints but didn't reveal anything new. Good. This was a critical moment. If all went according to plan, his flu symptoms would persist at a low level and the virus would linger in his body. Hiroshi's people would ask for a flu test. The test would reveal that Shuu was infected with H7N9 bird flu, and all hell would break loose.

She'd been in the business long enough to know that when a human catches bird flu, the public health people go nuts. Shuu would be locked down in quarantine, right here in Japan. Not forever, but long enough for the US-China summit to wrap up, and for Hiroshi's allies to put roadblocks in the way of the prisoner exchange.

I'm watching out for you, little bro. We're not going to count on Hiroshi to fix everything.

Her boyfriend's behind-the-scenes political wheeling and dealing had failed. He had connections, but she was re-learning an important life lesson: no one else is going to take care of you. Time to make a backup plan for her backup plan. And Hiroshi didn't need to know about it.

The captured Japanese naval officer was absent from the mainstream media. *The public in Japan and the US will protest this prisoner exchange. I need to make sure they know about it before it's too late.*

But Hiroshi wouldn't reveal his sources to prove it. How could she, an expat American scientist who couldn't even read *kanji* very well, blow the lid off this government conspiracy of silence?

With one phone call, which she had made soon after delivering the virus days ago.

"Jun Taniguchi?"

"My God, is this Dr. Nakamura?"

"Yes," she said, feeling sheepish.

"I think I need to sit down," Jun said.

Amika recalled all the nasty things she'd thought about the investigative journalist, and the things she'd actually said to Jun. "I guess I made it pretty clear how I felt about you."

"I get that a lot in my line of work."

"Well, I kept your number." She had no intention of apologizing. She still blamed Jun for some of her brother's predicament. This call wasn't about reconciliation. It was about business.

"Apparently." Like a good reporter, Jun let Amika do the talking.

"I have a story for you. A big one."

The sound of fluttering papers. "The Naito family?" Jun said hopefully.

There's that vendetta again. "No. But it's something Hiroshi Naito knows and is keeping secret." *A juicy half-truth ought to set the hook.*

"Does he know you're talking to me?"

"Of course not."

"I'm listening."

Amika explained about the Japanese naval intelligence officer captured with the fishermen. That the officer was considered a spy, and the whole thing was hush-hush. That a prisoner exchange with Shuu might be made in secret to avoid controversy. "If you can expose this, the public outcry might stop the trade."

"Maybe. There might be effects you haven't thought about, too. Do you have the officer's name?"

"No."

"Rank?"

"No."

"How about the names of Naito's contacts?"

"No."

"Their departments or affiliations?"

"No." *You're the reporter. Isn't that what you do?*

"Okay. So all you have is a rumor."

"Call it that if you want. The information is coming from pretty high up."

"So you say."

As irritation flared, Amika told herself that someone like Jun was conditioned to question everything. *Trust less, verify more.* "You'll look into it?"

"Yeah."

The tone of Jun's voice was unconvincing. Amika felt a bit of panic. The last thing she'd expected from this call was skepticism. *Does she think I'm messing with her?* "Ms. Taniguchi—"

"You can call me Jun."

"Jun, I know we don't see eye to eye on my brother's case. I'm not saying you were wrong to write the things you did about him. I'm just asking you to help me keep him in Japan. If they send him to China—" Her voice broke. "He could be executed."

"I'd hate to see anyone face the Chinese criminal justice system," Jun said. "I'll ask around."

"This will be a real scoop for your organization."

"I agree," she said. "If it's true."

Now she waited. For Jun to investigate. For Shuu to be tested. In the meantime she could concentrate on her own research again.

The small, familiar movements of Amika's hands had a calming effect. Unscrew a tiny cap. Push the plunger on a micropipette. Swirl a small glass test tube. She finished her "wet" lab work, washed her hands, and turned to her computer, which had just finished processing a set of viral genome sequences.

Dr. Hikino's mystery. For the past six months, an unusual number of birds had been dying across Japan. They carried a new avian influenza virus. Like all new flu viruses, this virus had the potential to evolve and make the "jump" into humans and cause a global pandemic. To prevent this, Koga was managing a nationwide campaign to vaccinate the citizenry.

She'd seen the numbers, and the campaign was going well. She was amazed at how much less prickly the Japanese were about immunizations than the Americans, especially those back in her home state of California. At least forty percent of all the people in Japan had received the Koga vaccine so far. But the campaign was expensive, and not risk-free. Even the safest vaccine causes side effects in a small fraction of the people who receive it. If the virus killing the birds did not pose a threat to humans, then it would be sensible to suspend the vaccination campaign.

Dr. Hikino wondered if this was the case. She had told Amika that the pattern of bird deaths—where the birds were found, what species were involved—did not match what she expected from a normal influenza. The Koga staff scientist had asked Amika if the DNA sequences held any clues.

The DNA always has clues. You just have to be smart enough to find them.

Row after row of letters filled the screen of Amika's computer, As and Gs and Cs and Ts, the nucleotide alphabet of life. The influenza virus had a total of about 14,000 of these nucleotides, packaged in eight segments like books in a series. Fourteen thousand sounded like a lot, but the viral genome was minuscule compared to say, the human genome, with over three billion.

Size doesn't matter. This little bundle of genetic information could invade, outwit, and utterly destroy a bird—or a human.

Computer software helped her organize the data and compare one genome with another, but the influenza genome was small enough that she could recognize certain genes on sight. She scrolled through the letters, telling the program to extract a part here, match with another part there, and to compare the virus found in one dead bird with the virus found in another dead bird.

Her first question for the DNA: did the birds actually die from the infection? Was the virus strong enough to kill?

After scanning the crucial regions, she had her first answer: *yes. Highly pathogenic. These bird flus have what it takes to decimate a flock.*

So why hadn't they? So far, the deaths had been sporadic.

Next question: can one bird easily infect another?

When she engineered the virus for Shuu, she spent a lot of time looking at the gene sequences that controlled this behavior. With an experienced eye, she examined the relevant sites in the genome. *Segment 4, position 328: A; position 553: G; position 558: C.* Dozens of sites, from dozens of isolates. She constructed tables and spreadsheets, looked at probabilities and linkages.

Conclusion: no. The virus wasn't easily spread.

In light of what the DNA was telling her, her colleague's maps made sense. The virus found in the dead birds was lethal. But infected birds had a low risk of infecting other birds. The virus simply was no good at getting out of one bird and into another.

Without a strong chain of transmission, this new avian influenza wouldn't hurt anyone.

Probably.

Should the vaccine campaign be stopped? Well, that was for someone else to decide. She would share her findings with Dr. Hikino, and maybe loop Hiroshi Naito in since he was her boss, after all.

Curious to get a sense of the "personality" of this intriguing new flu, she relaxed back in her chair and clicked through the data, visiting regions of the sequence that she knew well.

What's this?

In a nonessential backwater region of the genome, she found the sequence GAATTC, followed shortly after with its palindrome opposite, CTTAAG.

Those are restriction enzyme sites.

To a scientist who had personally manipulated a lot of DNA, those sequences suggested one thing. Human intervention.

Restriction enzymes let you add artificial DNA sequences. On purpose. In a lab.

Sure, by random chance, any six-nucleotide sequence could turn up in the genome. But twice? In an area where most flu viruses had none?

Did this virus escape from a lab?

For the next half hour, she looked for more evidence of human manipulation of the viral genome. But flu viruses are notoriously diverse. Of the many other sequence variations she found, none was definitively "unnatural."

She clicked her screen back to the GAATTC and pondered what it meant, if anything.

If someone engineered this virus, I can't see what they were trying to do. It looks like a wild type.

And yet, those sequences were like fingerprints suggesting someone had touched it.

Someone who isn't as good at this as I am. The techniques she used were more sophisticated. More subtle. *Maybe this virus originated in a lab many years ago?*

She saved her work and closed the program. *That's science. Questions beget more questions.* This mystery would probably go unsolved. She couldn't reconstruct the virus's history. What mattered was her prediction of where it was headed. And the evidence suggested this bird flu would fizzle out.

15

YASUKUNI SHRINE
CHIYODA, JAPAN (METROPOLITAN TOKYO)

In the shade of cherry trees the old warrior walked toward the famous Shinto shrine, callused feet in orthotic shoes shuffling across the warm concrete tiles. A few months ago, the trees had been in bloom here at Yasukuni.

How many more times will I celebrate hanami, *the festival of the cherry blossoms? Not many. I approach my moment of perfection and then like the petals of the cherry flower I will fall. A life precious, brief, and beautiful, like a samurai cut down in battle.*

Today, in the lull between the big commemorative days of the *obon* holiday and the August fifteenth war memorials, not many people were present to worship the souls of the dead. Many times the old warrior had visited this greatest of all the Shinto shrines in Japan. Yasukuni housed the spirits of Japan's war dead, nearly two and a half million men, women, and children who gave their lives in service to the Emperor. Not only soldiers who died in Japan's wars were recorded in the shrine's Book of Souls, but also relief workers killed on the battlefield, ordinary citizens killed during bombings of Japanese factories, prisoners killed in Soviet labor camps, even schoolchildren killed by an American submarine.

Millions of souls. Countless fathers and mothers and siblings resided eternally in this sacred place. But for the old warrior, only one father, one mother, and in particular one beloved older brother prompted her monthly visit. For over sixty years, once a month, every month, the old warrior had visited Yasukuni, missing only the times she was in the hospital with pneumonia.

Akihiro, I'm back. I have much to tell you today.

The old warrior passed beneath the shrine's enormous steel *daichii torii* gate. Seventy-five feet high, the traditional rectangular arch with two cross beams was the largest such gate in Japan. She appreciated that her visits were quiet affairs. When a Japanese prime minister trod this same path, foreigners and peace-mongers and China-loving traitors shouted their outrage. The international media would call the Japanese leader an aggressor and historical revisionist. As if Japan's head of state had no right to pay his respects to his nation's dead! The meddlers refused to accept that anyone who sacrificed their life for the Japanese nation, whatever their rank or social standing, was the subject of completely equal respect and worship at the shrine.

Anyone, including the souls of alleged "class A war criminals" who were secretly enshrined at Yasukuni in 1978. These martyrs were convicted of war crimes by the victorious Allies in kangaroo courts and executed in 1948. They were leaders like Hideki Tojo, the prime minister who ordered the successful attack on Pearl Harbor, and Iwane Matsui, commanding officer of the Japanese expeditionary force that liberated Nanking in 1937.

Let foreigners fuss about the so-called "rape of Nanking" as long as they're blind to what we accomplished at Pingfan.

In the serene gardens, she caught a whiff of sweet incense. The smell reminded her of the one time anyone paid attention to her visit. Once, when she was still a teenager, she'd come with her uncle Shiro Ishii and the rest of the family, and they'd been given the singular privilege of entering the *honden* building. Unlike the main prayer hall, the *honden* was the shrine's holy of holies, the place where the spirits of the dead actually resided. It was closed to the public. The Shinto priests had invited them in recognition of her uncle's special services to the Emperor during the war. She remembered that inside the *honden*, the incense burned so strongly that she imagined the smoke was the physical presence of the spirits, swirling, surrounding, suffocating. She tried to see her brother in the smoke, the way one might see shapes in the clouds.

Seeing his spirit would have given her closure, certainty that he was dead. The last time she saw Akihiro he was still alive. Bound, maimed, and bleeding, tortured by the Chinese jackals, but alive. It took years for her to accept that his spirit no longer resided in his body, that it could be found at Yasukuni.

After what happened, part of her spirit had left her body, too.

My deafness was a blessing. I couldn't hear his screams.

After the atomic bomb attacks, the Japanese abandoned China, abandoned her and her brother at Pingfan. Her father and mother were dead. She saw them die for the Emperor. Later, her uncle's family had searched for them amid the chaos. They found her, Harumi, alive but in many ways, too late.

The Ishii family brought her home to Japan and adopted her. She never married or started a family of her own. What the Chinese jackals had done to her robbed her of the choice to be a mother.

Harumi passed through several lesser *torii* gates and reached the main prayer hall. Before petitioning the spirits for blessings and good fortune, she performed the ritual water purification. Using a ladle from a wooden fountain, she poured water over the palms of her hands, first the left, then the right. Inside the prayer hall she made a symbolic offering of a few coins into a wooden box. Then she called upon the spirits. She bowed twice, as low as her aged back would allow, and clapped her hands twice at chest level. As she made her final bow, she expressed her heart's desire to the deities.

Success. Mother Koneko, baby Eiko, Aikiko, and beloved brother Akihiro, help me avenge you. Father Masaji, help me finish what you started.

Outside once again under the sparkling sun, she passed a statue honoring the *kamikaze* suicide bomber pilots of the Greater East Asian War. She knew next door in the Yushukan war museum was an exhibit honoring pilots of the less well-known *kaiten* suicide torpedoes, launched from submarines with a man irreversibly sealed inside to steer the torpedo to its target. *Suicide attacks made sense in those days. Now, we are too few in number.*

Fortunately such attacks were not needed. Following where her father and uncle had led, she and those with her had invented a weapon more practical than the atomic bomb, much cheaper to make, and easily delivered not by airplane but by air.

She sat down on a bench near the prayer hall to tell Akihiro the latest news.

Dear brother, we're close now. The data we've been seeking for seventy years is finally ours. Father didn't have a chance; he was born too soon. So much had to be learned, about microbiology, and DNA, and genetics. But with the passage of time and now the skill of a brilliant young scientist, we've done it. Field tests of the Han agent have begun!

Oh, and they say Shuu Nakamura, the soldier who killed those Chinese jackals, has bird flu. They've put him in quarantine at the prison. It's all over the news, everyone is talking about it. It's a huge boost for the vaccination campaign. People are flocking—ha, do you get it? Flocking?—to get their shots. That means we won't have to kill as many birds and plant their bodies around, which should make you happy because I know you don't approve of killing birds. But we had to have some way to motivate people to take the vaccine!

The Chinese jackals who attacked Uotsuri-shima were sent home, which is too bad. But they'll come to a sticky end like the rest of their countrymen. At least we got our fishermen back.

The temperature and humidity were rising, and the old warrior felt the tightness grow in her asthmatic lungs.

I have to go now, Akihiro. I'll be back in a month and I should have big news.

She rose and made her unhurried way back toward the giant entrance gate. Along the route she passed the *omikuji*, or sacred lottery. She usually ignored this bit of fortune-telling found at many Shinto shrines. But with her life's work reaching a climax, she succumbed to the temptation to predict her luck. She walked to the *omikuji* box, pulled out a small scroll of paper and read it.

Han-kichi. The characters said: half-blessing.

It was customary to dispose of bad fortunes by tying them to a pine branch, where the bad luck would then stay. She considered adding this scroll to the hundreds tied to the posts provided at the shrine but chose to keep it.

A half-blessing was better than none. In this venture, if not a billion deaths, a half billion would be enough.

16

July 15 (the next day)

With her brother safely in quarantine for avian influenza, Amika took a break from her sixteen-hour workdays. Catching up on sleep improved her outlook and elevated her mood. Although it was nearly 9 AM, she sprawled across the futon in her tiny studio with no intention of heading to the lab this morning. She was expecting one of the precious calls from Shuu at 10:15. In the meantime, doing laundry seemed like a good idea. She sorted through a pile in the corner of the room and found the low-cut shirt she'd been wearing the night Hiroshi told her about the Japanese spy.

He's not Superman, she thought of Hiroshi's failure to protect Shuu with his political connections, *but we're still a couple and he owes me a date. A night on the town that ends with me at his house, not at the lab.*

To her surprise, the phone rang early, around 9:30.

That's weird. The prison calls are never early.

"Hello?"

"Hey. It's Jun."

She suppressed her instinct to hang up on the detested reporter, reminding herself that Jun Taniguchi was working with her now. "Did you get the scoop on the naval intelligence officer? Can we go public with the information?"

"Those are two separate questions, Doctor," Jun said frostily.

Okay, slow down. Don't offend her. If she has information she thinks is too sensitive to release, you'll have to convince her. "Of course. What did you find?"

"Nothing."

"You mean, like, nothing you can tell me without compromising your sources?"

"No, I mean nothing like, nothing. Your spy doesn't exist."

She fired some sweaty leggings at the floor. "You finding nothing doesn't prove there's no spy. It proves your incompetence." *So much for not giving offense.*

Jun's voice rose an octave in pitch and several notches in volume. "You sent me on a wild goose chase—"

"Or maybe you only report lies, like an autopsy report that frames an innocent man."

"I'm not the liar here, Doctor."

"What is that supposed to mean?"

"I have very good sources. People I know. People I trust. If they tell me there's no missing naval officer, I believe them. You, on the other hand—why should I believe your bullshit about a secret spy exchange?"

"You're calling me a liar?"

"If the shoe fits…"

"How dare you—"

"I dare because it's true. You lost your job in America because you lied about your work. Yes, I know about that. You lied about what happened on Uotsuri-shima. You're probably lying about what your brother did. Now you're trying to use me to spread false rumors about a Japanese spy. The only reason I'm still talking to you is I think it's not your fault. I think you're being played."

"Oh really."

"You're sleeping with Hiroshi Naito. Yeah, I know about that too."

"My private life is none of your business."

"I don't give a damn about your private life. It's Naito I'm after. My group has been trying to pin something on him for years and we can't do it. The guy is a chess master."

"Has it occurred to you that maybe he hasn't done anything wrong?"

"No, it hasn't. He's smart. Maybe even smarter than you. But your book-smarts aren't doing you any good. Open your eyes."

"To what, Miss Know-it-All?"

"To the possibility that your lover is lying to you."

Jun's bold statement struck Amika like a thunderclap. *What if?* Ever since the trip to the Senkakus, she'd felt she was using Hiroshi to get what she wanted: help for her brother, job security, status, sex. What if *he* was manipulating *her?* Could that be? Why would he do that? *I don't have anything he doesn't already have.*

After a moment of silence, Jun continued. "For a smart chick, you're pretty stupid. Why would someone like Hiroshi Naito take such an interest in you?"

"Because I'm prettier and smarter than you?"

"Get over yourself. I'm not talking about sex. Why did he use his foundation to bring you over from America? Why did he take you to the Senkakus with him?"

"Because of my brother. In both cases. And because I'm the best damn virologist in the market."

"Then we agree on one thing."

"What?"

"Your scientific expertise is part of this puzzle."

"What is your problem? Why does it have to be a puzzle? I'm good at what I do. Hiroshi heard about me from my brother. He hired me. He liked what he saw. He decided to take me for a spin on the girlfriend ride."

"Hiroshi Naito doesn't spin on the girlfriend ride. He has casual sex, yes, but he hasn't had a relationship, even one as short and messed up as yours, in over a decade."

"So your news organization hires Peeping Toms, too?"

"We make it our business to know what the big shots in the Naito family are up to. Our dossier on Hiroshi goes back to his first known association with a far-right ultranationalist group, when he was at university."

"Ultranationalist?" Amika said.

"Yes. Didn't you know?"

"We don't discuss *politics,*" Amika said dismissively.

"Then you're one of the few people he doesn't discuss it with. Or more likely, you weren't listening. The overwhelming majority of his associates and friends also dance on the right side. You didn't notice *anything?*"

Amika thought back to the benefit dinner for the Japanese Red Cross. "I dunno. Maybe."

"He keeps it quiet. Doesn't belong to any of the grungy groups, like the ones that drive those propaganda vans. His family is pretty much an elite, private right-wing sect of its own."

His family. His father, the head of Koga Scientific. Grandfather, founder of the global company. Friends with the prime minister of Japan. Rich. Connected. Connected to *her*. Her first reaction to Jun's innuendo was to reject it and yell at the messenger. But she was more rational than that. She turned a skeptical eye to her recent experiences and felt some inexplicable truth resonating with Jun's words. What horse had she tied her cart to? The Asian Center for Investigative Journalism was watching. Why?

Doubt and a vague sense of worry softened Amika's antagonism. She modulated her voice to show she was really asking, not accusing. "Why does your group bother so much about the Naito family?"

"It's not the Naitos per se. It's the Ishiis."

"The Ishiis," Amika repeated, with no clue what that name meant.

Jun sighed. "Do you ever read anything besides science journals?"

"No."

"General Shiro Ishii? Unit 731?" Jun suggested.

Crickets.

"Maybe you've heard of the Nazis?"

"Don't insult me," Amika said.

"How about the Nazi doctors?"

"Yes," Amika said, unease rising as she thought about the unspeakable tortures those men inflicted on concentration camp prisoners.

"Your boyfriend's great-grandfather was worse."

She wanted to plug her ears, to shut down this woman who was hell-bent on making her life more complicated. But as a scientist, she was a truth-seeker at heart. "Tell me."

"What you Americans call World War Two started in Asia a decade before Pearl Harbor. After faking a terrorist attack to give them an excuse, Imperial Japan invaded China in 1931. They stayed until 1945, doing whatever they wanted to the local people in the areas they controlled. One Army doctor, Shiro Ishii, went to China with the idea that germs could be turned into weapons. He commanded a secret Kwantung Army unit—Unit 731—to do the necessary research, and set up a cover that the unit was doing water purification work. In truth, they built a small city at Pingfan in Manchuria, northern China, where the experiments they did on people make some of the Nazi stuff look like health care. They worked on plague, anthrax, gangrene, typhoid, you name it. They liked to do 'autopsies' on live people without anesthesia, and on babies born of raped prisoners. They tested their weapons on whole Chinese cities, poisoning water supplies with cholera and dropping bubonic plague-carrying fleas in the streets."

"I didn't know."

"There's a lot of denial about it in Japan. In America, I suppose you're just ignorant. That's partly your government's fault. They put the Nazis on trial for war crimes but negotiated with the Japanese 'doctors.' Ishii and his highest-ranking associates were given immunity from prosecution in exchange for sharing their data with American scientists, who were developing their own biological warfare program at the time," Jun said. "They managed to convince themselves that it's wrong for Americans to experiment on humans but fine to retroactively outsource it to somebody else."

"So there were no Nuremberg trials for the Japanese doctors," Amika said.

"The Soviets managed to get their hands on a few of them and convict them at Khabarovsk in 1949. Show trials, mostly. Behind the scenes, they probably worked the same deal as the Americans and put them to work, not prison. Shiro Ishii, mastermind of the whole operation, died peacefully at home years after the war. Surrounded by his family, no doubt. Children. Grandchildren." Jun paused. "Some of Ishii's descendants stayed in the family business of science and medicine. One married into another Unit 731 family whose name you *do* know."

"Naito."

"Hiroshi Naito is one of the general's great-grandchildren."

So that explains her obsession with Hiroshi. "You can't blame a person for the crimes of his ancestors."

"No. But the apple doesn't fall far from the tree. Companies have cultures and values. Unit 731 people were involved in the Green Cross tainted blood scandal."

"You know I don't know what that is."

"Thought I'd give you a chance," Jun said. "In the early 1980s, when the AIDS epidemic was new, an American company petitioned the Japanese government for permission to sell a blood product that they heat-treated to kill the AIDS virus. At the time, people who got a lot of blood transfusions, such as hemophiliacs, were catching HIV. This treatment would protect them. Green Cross was a Japanese company that had a lock on the domestic market for blood products, and they weren't prepared to heat-treat theirs. So they collaborated with the Ministry of Health to deny the American petition and instead of publicizing the risk, they told everyone their untreated blood product was safe because their donors were Japanese. Nationalist rubbish. Their actions killed hundreds of people. My point is, when disrespect for human life is part of a company's DNA, it shows in the way that company does business. Green Cross—and the Ministry—were thick with ties to Unit 731 officers."

Both women fell silent as Amika tried to understand what all this meant. Terrible things were done during the war, but that was a long time ago. Members of her own family in the US were forced into the camps for Japanese-Americans, and while Shuu was still steamed about it, she wasn't going to blame anyone alive today for that crime. Did Hiroshi Naito deserve to carry a stigma? How many generations would it take for Jun Taniguchi and her ilk to let it go?

Amika spoke. "You think just because of family history, Koga Scientific is an unethical company?"

"I wouldn't say 'just.' I have my sources and my reasons to think there's something going on. Unfortunately people who work for Koga are unusually loyal. They won't talk to me. And Hiroshi sticks to his close friends. You're the first outsider I know who has genuine access."

"So that's what this is all about," Amika fumed. "You want to use me to dig up dirt on Hiroshi."

"You don't have to dig. There's dirt all over this Senkaku Islands thing. Not the least of which is this fiction about a Japanese spy."

"You can't accept the possibility that you might have missed something? That you might be wrong?"

"No. And what you believe doesn't change reality. There is no naval intelligence officer in Chinese custody."

Their conversation had circled back to the original question. Amika had been counting on Jun to find proof that they could publicize, so everyone would know about the threat to hand her brother over to the Chinese in a trade. But the secret was so deeply buried that even a pro like Jun Taniguchi couldn't expose it.

Or...

Jun spoke. "Amika, he's lying to you. I don't know why. I seriously doubt it's for a good reason."

"He's my—" Amika was about to say, friend, but that didn't feel true. Mentor? Maybe. Lover? Boss? Obviously, but those titles didn't guarantee trust.

What is he? Who is he? Until this moment, she had only considered how he could be useful to her. What about *his* side? What agenda did *he* have?

"We know your brother's life is on the line," Jun said. "He's nothing to the Naito family, except it seems he's part of whatever game they're playing. I can help you, and him, if you help me. I need information."

"Apparently the information I have is false."

"Even lies can reveal truth."

"What do you want to know?"

"Let's talk. Can you meet me this afternoon?"

They made plans to get together after Amika's appointment to talk to Shuu. Jun asked, "How is your brother? Are they keeping him in solitary?"

"Some kind of quarantine. I don't know how their facility is set up, whether he's in a special medical wing or what, but I'm sure they're isolating him from other people. He's doing okay. Some fever, cough. Hiroshi says—" She cringed a little. "Hiroshi says they're taking good care of him." In truth, quarantine wasn't necessary for Shuu. The virus she made wasn't going to infect anyone else. But she wasn't ready to tell Jun that story. Not yet.

The phone call ended. Amika sat on the floor of her room, surrounded by rumpled clothes in piles of disarray that reflected her state of mind. She desperately needed a confidant. She wished she could have a private conversation with Shuu. He'd been Hiroshi's friend for a while. He could help her separate truth from lies.

If Jun was right, she had so many questions. Why would Hiroshi lie? Why this particular lie? If her brother wasn't in imminent danger, why make the virus, why infect him?

In science, "why" questions were her favorite kind. In life, not so much. *How do you design a controlled experiment to test the motives of the human heart?*

The time had reached 10:12. In about three minutes, she would get the comfort of hearing her brother's voice, even if they couldn't talk confidentially.

She folded a pair of pants. Matched some socks. Hung up a shirt that didn't need to be washed. Sorted delicate fabrics. Tried not to think about Hiroshi. And looked at the time.

He's late.

She propped a pillow against the wall at the head of her bed. With phone in hand, she made herself comfortable. And looked at the time.

10:18.

The calls from prison were usually on time.

She stared into space. Thought about Hiroshi. Wondered what she would say to Jun. And looked at the time.

Is it the quarantine? Are they going to let him call me? If not, they should at least have the courtesy to let me know.

She stared at the time and fought the cold, gnawing sensation in her gut.

At 10:32, she dialed the main number for the prison.

Busy signal. Maybe their phone system is down. That would explain the late call.

10:33. Again.

10:34. Again.

She kept her thumb on the dial icon and repeated without pause. At 10:36, she got through. The recorded menu had changed. The gnawing sensation consumed her. A canned male voice directed media representatives to call a special number, which he provided.

Media?

She requested the operator.

"Extension, please," the woman said.

"I don't have—"

"Which department are you trying to reach?"

"I have a question."

"In the current situation, you'll need to leave a message. I'll transfer you—"

"Wait. Just a quick question. I was expecting a call from an inmate, Shuu Nakamura—"

She could practically feel a chill radiate from her smartphone. "Nakamura?" the operator said.

"Yes. He's my brother. We had a 10:15 speaking appointment."

"Would you hold, please?"

Tinny classical pops music—Mozart, maybe—played. The rhythm was slower than her heart. *Situation? What situation?*

Seconds turned into agonizing minutes. One, two, three. She paced a short, winding path through the piles of dirty clothes. *Should I hang up and try again? Should I call that special number?*

After five minutes, a man's voice startled her. "Hello? Is this Shuu Nakamura's sister?"

She sat down on the edge of her bed. "Yes, this is Amika Nakamura. We had an approved phone appointment at 10:15? Is he being allowed to make calls?"

"I'm speaking to Dr. Amika Nakamura, sister of Shuu Nakamura?"

"Yes, I just told you that," she snapped. "Who is this? Can you get my brother to a telephone?"

"Dr. Nakamura, we're dealing with a situation today."

"Your situation is not my problem. I want to talk to my brother."

"I'm afraid those two matters are linked."

Her anxiety ratcheted up to the point she felt physically ill. "What's going on?"

"Infectious disease in a prison is a difficult problem," the man said. "Our health department works hard to keep any outbreaks contained."

Oh no.

"But we have so many men housed together," he continued, "it's a challenge even with ordinary colds or flu."

Not ordinary...

"Are there others sick? With my brother's flu?" she dared to ask, even though she believed it was impossible, desperately hoped it was impossible.

"Not yet," he said, "but we've initiated a lockdown."

"Why?" The word automatically escaped her lips, before she could think, before she could choose not to ask, not to know. Something in her soul sensed she was crossing a Rubicon, that this moment would divide her life into before and after.

"Shuu Nakamura passed away a few hours ago."

17

"Dr. Nakamura?"
No
No
No no no no no no no no no no no no no no no

    Sitting on carpet next to a blue toddler bed shaped like a race car. Shuu belly down on the polyester comforter. Stacks of Pokemon cards with pictures of magical creatures. He wants to trade. Don't take advantage, make a fair deal. He's just a kid.
    Los Angeles back yard. Grass crunchy and brown under bare feet. Water gun fight in hot dry sun. Shuu's molded plastic weapon broken. Give him yours.
    Outdoor breezeway. Chilly gray winter sky. Concrete floor connecting public school classrooms. Picnic tables. Shuu forgot his lunch. You're not that hungry anyway.
    An airport. Suitcase wheels rattling—

"Dr. Nakamura, are you there?"
The disembodied voice over the phone was still talking, miles away yet somehow sucking all the air out of her room. Still talking, like a car radio playing after a wreck. The invisible fist that had punched her, given her visions, thrust her back on to the bed, now lay heavy on her belly, making it impossible to draw a breath. Her throat squeezed painfully.
"He was in isolation in the infirmary during the night."

It's a mistake.

"There's a medical note from the staff, early in the evening."

A different prisoner died. Or didn't die. They don't have a real doctor. Nobody died. There's no body in the infirmary.

"He was doing fine before lights out."

He missed his phone appointment. They're trying to cover for him. It's okay.

"There'll be a full investigation, I assure you, but right now our priority is to protect the people in the facility."

Dear God, I will do anything…

"We're bringing in public health experts as we speak."

Finally the voice shut up, replaced by traffic noise from the street below her apartment. Her tongue felt thick and dry. It hurt to swallow.

"Do you have any questions?"

If she had been close enough to slap the man, she would have. *What a stupid, stupid thing to say.*

"I'm coming over," she said. It would take what, maybe ninety minutes?

"No, no, absolutely not. We have a major situation here. The whole facility is going on quarantine. This virus is a threat—"

"I'm coming over," she repeated, rising to her feet.

"Doctor, you won't be allowed to enter."

"Yes I will," she said, and disconnected the call.

Overcome with nausea, she sank to her knees and touched her forehead to the floor. Her fingers reached out and tightened around a piece of clothing, twisting a blouse into a ball. Through blurry eyes she saw the time. 10:49 AM.

Shuu was late.

She lay prone in a ray of sunlight and waited for his call.

The first time she heard Hiroshi's ring tone, she did not move.

The second time, she sat cross-legged on the floor and cradled her phone, but did not answer. As long as she didn't speak to anyone else, as long as no one confirmed—

It's not true. Shuu is alive.

She pressed her face into the crumpled blouse, already wet with salty tears.

I did not kill my brother.

By the fourth time he called, the sunbeam had migrated to her left, leaving her in shadow.

Someone knocked on the door.

"Amika, it's me."

Hiroshi.

A tsunami of loneliness drove her to the door. Her trembling hand reached for the knob and then recoiled.

His fault. Everything.

"Please let me in," he said.

Her breaths came faster. *The trip to the island. The DGPS unit. His failure over the prisoner exchange.*

"Please." Through the door, she heard his voice break.

Hiroshi Naito is crying?

She opened the door. His eyes were red and his cheeks slightly puffy. In an alternate reality the cause might have been something dull and ordinary, like an allergy or vapors from a cut onion.

If only.

He sniffled and straightened his shirt. They stared at each other across the threshold as she accused him with her eyes.

"It's not your fault," he said.

With that, a dam broke and she wept, deep racking sobs with a river of tears. It *was* her fault. She had made the virus. It was his fault, too. They shared the blame. They shared the grief. To what degree wasn't important. At this moment, sharing was the only thing that mattered. This burden wasn't hers alone, to bear in secret.

His arms enveloped her, drawing her close. Her head pressed against his chest and she was aware of nothing but the steady beating of his heart.

July 17 (two days later)

Hiroshi's people arranged and paid for everything: the spacious hall at the temple, the priests in flowing robes, even the black dress that Amika wore. In keeping with common practice in Japan, they were giving Shuu a Buddhist funeral.

I'm keeping it real for you, little bro. I know religion wasn't your thing.

She was not a person of faith either, but right now she clung to the idea that her brother's spirit lived on in this world. *Are you a resident spirit now? Can you hear me if I visit your grave?*

Will you punish me?

A priest stood before the assembly of men in black suits and women in black dresses and kimonos. He chanted verses from a sacred text. Smoldering sticks of incense held upright by sand in bronze basins filled the air with smoky fragrance. She glanced around and recognized only a few faces in the crowd. Hardly any friends or family from the US had come; the funeral was too soon, the distance and cost too great. Most of the mourners were either friends of the Naito family or Shuu's Japanese friends, plus a couple of her coworkers from Koga.

Mom said she hadn't heard from you in over six months. That's rough, bro. But I know she'll forgive you.

Please forgive me.

Seated at her side, Hiroshi stroked the back of her hand.

Normally the Japanese hosted a wake with the deceased's body the day before the funeral ceremony, after which the remains were cremated under the family's supervision. Her brother's death from bird flu upended all that. Public health authorities had locked down the prison with quarantines inside and out. A hazmat team went in and sealed Shuu's body in complete biohazard containment before releasing it directly to the crematorium. The fear of contagion was so high that Hiroshi had to fight to get permission for her to even be in the room when the body arrived to be burned. She had watched as the plastic-wrapped lump that was once the most important person in her world disappeared into the furnace.

If only I could have hugged you one last time.

Heat incinerated the virus and they gave her Shuu's sterilized ashes and bones. She kept some to take to their parents for a memorial service back in the US. The rest would be interred at the beautiful cemetery at this shrine, courtesy of the Naito family. They had been so good to her the past two days, adopting her as one of their own. Apparently it took a tragedy to break down the walls in this formal, structured society.

Whatever their ancestors might have done in the past, they've been here for me now.

Her conversation with Jun Taniguchi felt like years ago. None of it mattered anymore. Her brother was dead. He couldn't be deported or tried or traded. His persecutors and accusers would have to find another target for their ire. Hiroshi said he'd heard that a new deal was struck to get the Japanese naval officer back. He didn't know the details.

The Chinese jackals can't get you now, brother.

Guilt still poisoned her but over the last forty-eight hours she'd come to recognize that Shuu's blood was on Chinese hands. It was their brazen attack on Japanese sovereign land that led to the shootings and deaths. It was their manipulation and rumormongering that made Shuu's actions look intentional. And it was their attempt to punish Shuu that drove her and Hiroshi to their desperate and misguided decision to deploy the virus.

I had to do it. You understand, don't you?

The priest held the final note of the chant for several seconds. Then the sound echoed against the ceiling for another moment. Respectful silence held until the casual mourners seated at the rear, those who did not personally know the deceased, started to leave.

Amika led a small group forward to scatter flower petals around the urn. Hiroshi stepped away from her side to support an old crippled woman as she laboriously lifted herself up the two stairs to the dais. Amika had met a number of Hiroshi's relatives yesterday and today, but not this one. Hiroshi held the bowl of rose petals for her. The bent old woman took a step, grounded her feet, grasped some petals in a wrinkled hand, and tossed them. Then another careful step, and another toss. Hiroshi attentively kept a hand near her elbow in case she stumbled.

They returned to the chairs. The old woman patted Amika on the shoulder.

"This is my great aunt Harumi," Hiroshi said. "She honors your brother with her presence."

Amika sensed an awe and respect that was rare for Hiroshi. She didn't know this elderly lady's story, but she had to be an important matriarch to the Naito family. Amika bowed deeply from the waist and said, "I am honored to meet you."

The old woman returned her bow but did not speak. Then she spread her arms and wrapped Amika in a grandmotherly hug.

"She's deaf," Hiroshi said.

The warm embrace gave Amika comfort and she squeezed the woman in wordless thanks for her sympathy.

"We're going to get something to eat," Hiroshi said. "Are you ready, Amika?"

"You go without me," she said. "There's something I need to do first."

Hiroshi took his aunt's arm. "Are you sure? Would you like me to come with you?"

"No. I want to be alone."

The Naitos filed out of the hall, leaving the room empty except for an attendant. Solitude settled on her like a lead apron. This was the first time she'd been alone since Hiroshi showed up at her apartment.

Shuu, help me live with myself.

She exited into the cemetery. The air was thick and hot and still. Dark, billowy clouds piled high in the sky. A thunderstorm was brewing.

A storm. A storm killed you.

Shuu's death was so sudden it was hard to believe, but that was the power of influenza. The 1918 Spanish flu pandemic disproportionately killed young and otherwise healthy people. Their healthy immune systems were their undoing. A fast, vigorous immune response spiraled out of control in something called a cytokine storm, blasting not only the flu virus but their own bodies as well. Biochemical scorched earth. A cytokine storm could take a victim from mildly ill to dead in a matter of hours.

That's what happened to you.

She walked among the crowded grave markers in the densely packed urban burial ground. She had hoped to find some greenery near Shuu's grave but it was stone everywhere, the path, the markers. Instead she made for the zone of trees and shrubs that ringed the cemetery. Under the leafy canopy, she opened her purse and took out a small tube.

"Be free, little fella."

As if in mourning, Shuu's cricket had not sung for days. Amika found a grave where a bit of fresh food had been left as an offering. She shook the insect out of its cage. The elderly cricket sat motionless for a minute, then hopped and disappeared into the plants nearby.

18

JULY 27 (TEN DAYS LATER)

Narita International was on high alert, but not for terrorists.

As Amika passed through the Tokyo airport after a week back in Los Angeles, signs of bird flu paranoia were everywhere. Shuu had been Japan's first human death from avian influenza, and people were taking steps to protect themselves. Security personnel wore latex gloves. Quite a few ordinary people wore surgical masks. All arriving passengers walked past thermal imaging machines to screen them for fever. Posters for the Koga vaccination campaign lined a moving walkway to the baggage claim area.

She wanted to shout, *Don't worry. The virus that killed my brother isn't contagious. I made it especially for him.*

Then again, it wasn't supposed to be lethal, either.

The media reported additional bird flu cases in humans. Amika figured they were false positives. No test was perfect. If everybody with a sniffle was running to their doctor to be tested, some tests would come back positive for flu even in people who were not infected.

She trudged through customs and immigration, her feet and heart leaden. The dull, impersonal formality of standing in line suited the flat, formless despair of her mood. The past week at home in LA had been the most exhausting and dispiriting of her life, even worse than the days immediately after Shuu passed. On the Japan side of the Pacific, Hiroshi and his family were bedrock. They dealt with things, did what needed to be done, followed the prescribed customs, kept up appearances. They were people she could lean on.

Her parents in California, on the other hand, were a hot mess on a good day. The death of their son demolished what little connective tissue kept their lives together. By the time Amika arrived, the kitchen was knee-deep in empty whiskey bottles and toxic emotional stew. She found no comfort or consolation in the familial embrace. As the only person capable of doing so, she organized a simple memorial service for Shuu at which she felt more alone than ever. With Hiroshi beside her at the ceremony in Japan she didn't have to bear her terrible guilt alone. In Los Angeles, the weight of her secret shame was crushing.

At the earliest possible moment she had hopped on a plane away from LA. Tokyo was the closest thing she had to a home.

Bleary eyed, she exited the secured area of the airport and to her surprise spotted a man holding a sign with her name on it.

Me?

A warm feeling of welcome washed over her when the driver confirmed he'd been hired to take her home.

Hiroshi!

The black sedan struggled through afternoon rush hour traffic. In the back seat she cried over Hiroshi's thoughtfulness.

July 28 (the next day)

The lab at Koga was quiet except for the hum of the freezers. The J-pop fanboy was somewhere else today, so no music played. Amika sat on a stool and stared at her work bench. Some of her tools were out of place. A coworker must have borrowed her space when she was out of town.

Every object in the room was radioactive with reminders of her work on the virus that killed her brother.

I can't do this.

She was finally free to do the research she wanted to do. She had the funding, the facilities, and the permission, but now she was crippled by doubt. How could she believe in herself when her failure caused her brother's death?

Intellectually she knew that influenza viruses mutate in the wild, that they were as changeable as mountain weather. Shuu's tragedy was a statistical risk, not an error on her part.

Or was it?

If she had been so terribly wrong about this, she could be wrong again, any time, and not know it. Bullheaded certainty had propelled her career. All certainty was gone and without it, she was paralyzed.

"Hey." Hiroshi appeared in the doorway. He glanced around the lab to see who else was there, then motioned for her to join him in the empty hallway. "Are you working late tonight or can I tear you away?"

"I'm not working." She leaned her back against the wall and hung her head.

Hiroshi placed his palms against the wall on either side of her, leaning in close. She smelled the scent of his cologne. "Are you okay?" he asked.

"No," she said.

He touched her chin and raised her face to look at him. "You have to get back to a routine. It's been two weeks since you did any work on our project."

Angrily she pushed his hand away. "I know how long it's been." *Not fourteen days. It's been an eternity.*

"Do you know how important this virulence research is to me? To the people of Japan?"

Old anxieties about losing her job rippled below her grief. "I—I guess."

"While you were out of the country, five people were diagnosed with bird flu. One's been hospitalized."

"It's not…they don't have *our* virus, do they? That's impossible, isn't it?"

"No, your virus died with Shuu. These people were exposed to infected birds."

That was some relief. If the virus she made had actually started an outbreak…

"We're looking at a possible species jump," Hiroshi said. "This could be a critical time. You've got to continue your research. If you can tell us which mutations in the virus make it more deadly, Koga will be able to produce the most effective vaccine."

She nodded. "It's really hard for me to work. Right now. I mean, I'm trying."

He put his fingers under her chin again. "That's not good enough, Amika. As a Japanese woman you have a duty to put service to the nation first. Your feelings about your family must not stand in the way."

A Japanese woman. He was including her in this proud clan that meant so much to him. She wanted to belong.

"I'll do it," she pledged.

"Excellent. But not tonight. I'm taking you to a gathering of some of Shuu's and my friends."

She remembered Koga's charity event for the Red Cross. "A party?"

"No. A meeting."

LATER THAT NIGHT

Amika took a rideshare to the address Hiroshi had given her, an office building whose tenants were mostly law firms in a Tokyo business district that emptied in the evening. There were no signs to announce the gathering.

Private and quiet. Good. She didn't have the energy for anything else. She would've preferred a night alone with Hiroshi to recover from the trauma of Los Angeles, but he insisted that she accompany him here. Maybe she could peel him off from the group in an hour or two. When she'd asked him what was so important about his event, he shrugged. "Nothing, really. But it will be good for you to be among friends who share your beliefs."

"They're not my friends."

"You are part of a larger family. You'll be welcome."

She pressed the buzzer on the door. A young man about her age opened it to let her in.

"Dr. Nakamura," he said. "I've heard so much about you."

He pointed her toward a room down the hall. As she walked down the hushed, elegant corridor she remembered that Hiroshi had said this was a social club with a civic purpose, sort of like the Americans' Kiwanis or Shriners. That didn't sound like something that would interest Shuu. As if through a veil, she also remembered Jun Taniguchi saying Hiroshi belonged to ultranationalist groups. But that didn't sound like her brother either.

Who are these people? She would have to see for herself.

About twenty people occupied a nondescript conference room with rows of chairs for twice that number. Hiroshi, the tallest man in the room, spied her at the entrance. His bow of greeting was disappointingly formal. She was in serious need of a hug.

He placed a glass of Japanese wine in her hand and escorted her around the room. The people were mostly older men but some women and younger guests were also present. Some of them she'd met before at the Red Cross fundraiser. Others were connected to people she knew, such as a staffer from *Shufu* magazine and a Coast Guardsman who had served with Captain Miyashita. As Hiroshi introduced her to each attendee, Amika felt like she was taking a PhD-level practical exam in Japanese etiquette. In her frazzled emotional state, it was exhausting.

Hiroshi left her to prepare a short presentation he was scheduled to make to the group. The young man from the door cornered her to talk about Japanese restaurants in the Bay Area. He'd studied for his master's degree at UC Berkeley and wanted to know if she'd eaten at such-and-such place. And was *this* one still in business?

The air conditioning blew cold upon her. She tried to imagine how Shuu fit in here. This didn't seem like his scene, and no one had mentioned him.

Seconds after she resolved to leave and go home, Hiroshi invited everyone to sit down. Gratefully she escaped the banal conversation. Hiroshi gave a brief, non-technical lecture on the bird flu threat to Japan and the importance of vaccination. He put a lot of emphasis on genetic mapping of the virus showing that it likely originated in mainland China. Then another member spent a few minutes describing a special exhibit on *washi*, Japanese handmade paper, at the Nara National Museum. Finally a woman got up to talk about the history of some Korean island Amika had never heard of, explaining why it was rightfully Japanese even though its meager inhabitants were some obscure ethnic minority.

Her head nodded. *Why did I drink that wine?* Visions of Shuu danced in her thoughts. When he was stationed in South Korea, did he visit that weird little island? She imagined him being exiled there, like Napoleon to Elba. He wasn't dead. He was on the island, still in jail for pissing on the Ahn Memorial in Seoul while Chinese diplomats watched in horror. In her dream, he was still drunk, capering and shouting…

She snapped awake when Hiroshi touched her shoulder. The last speaker was finished, and people were milling about. "Someone wants to talk to you," he said.

A finely dressed old man bowed as she and Hiroshi came to him. She recoiled when she recognized him. He was the former cabinet minister at her table at the Red Cross event. His hateful comments about Shuu had driven her away from the party, and into Hiroshi's bed.

"You remember Ichiro?" Hiroshi said.

"I do." Defying every Japanese social convention, she could not bring herself to bow to him.

"Young lady, I share your grief." To her surprise, the old gentleman grabbed her hand in his bony, cold grip and pulled her further away from the rest of the group. "I know what killed Shuu Nakamura. You are not at fault."

Shocked, she looked at Hiroshi. Had he revealed their secret?

He nodded slightly.

Ichiro squeezed her hand, his eyes afire. "The responsibility lies across the East China Sea. The jackals in Beijing killed your brother. Do not be consumed by guilt. Your anger has a purpose."

"Okay," she said, uncertain, pulling against his skeletal grasp. *Shuu, are you angry? Are you angry at me? Who bears the blame for what happened?*

Ichiro released her. "What do you know of *aikido*?"

Surprised by the change of topic she replied, "It's a Japanese martial art, isn't it?"

He nodded approvingly. "Aikido emphasizes defense. The student of aikido uses the opponent's energy against them. By redirecting the force of an attack, the *aikidoka* neutralizes the threat."

She glanced toward the exit. Most of the people had left already. The young man with a Berkeley degree was straightening the room's empty chairs. "Okay."

"China attacked you, forcing your hand, leading to your brother's death. Your hand yet moves. Do not try to absorb the energy the Chinese jackals released. Direct it back at them."

What the hell is this crazy old man talking about?

"You're not helpless," Hiroshi added. "We're with you."

She had no patience for riddles. "Are you suggesting I take revenge against the Chinese?"

Ichiro cringed at her bluntness, then said, "Not revenge. Redirection of their cowardly attack."

"Whatever." She knew she was being rude. She didn't care. She was tired, so tired, and ready to fly off the handle at the smallest provocation. Ichiro disgusted her. She wanted the silt of her emotions to settle but this cold-hearted old man had clouded the water again with his stirring.

Since I started at Koga, every scheme I've been dragged into has gone sour. The trip to the Senkaku Islands, the Shufu *magazine interview, the virus. Shuu's dead because of the Chinese, but whatever these two are plotting, blame or revenge, I want no part of it. I'm done.*

She took a suggestive half-step toward the door. "Fighting China won't bring Shuu back."

The men exchanged a silent glance. Hiroshi said, "Thank you for coming tonight, Amika. I know you had a long trip yesterday. Ichiro and I would like to honor you with dinner. Will you join us? We still have some things to discuss."

Not with that guy. She wanted to be alone with Hiroshi but she was not going to beg.

"I can't," she said. "I want to go home."

"Please," Ichiro said. "A beautiful young woman rarely adorns my table."

That clinched it. "No. Thank you."

Hiroshi searched her expression to see if her decision was final. "I'll call a cab for you," he said.

Sleep should have come easily.

Amika lay on her bed, wide-awake weary with jet lag. Street light diffusing into the room had never seemed so bright, nor the city's night sounds so loud. Her eyes felt itchy and her ankles felt swollen. She kicked off the sheet and stared at the wall.

The phone rang.

Shuu?

She couldn't help it. An irrational hope that her brother was calling flared every time. As she sat up to reach her mobile, she more realistically wished that maybe it was Hiroshi, that he'd finished his business and was coming over. She couldn't sleep anyway.

It wasn't Hiroshi. It was Jun Taniguchi.

I thought we were done.

She'd had no contact with the journalist since the day Shuu died. They were supposed to have a meeting, she recalled, but of course she had stood Jun up.

Amika didn't care about Jun's innuendo and machinations any more. *What does she want now?*

Agitated and cross, she took the call.

"My deepest sympathies," Jun said. "I have a younger sister. I can only imagine what you're going through."

"It's not good."

"Are they still saying it was avian influenza?"

Amika tried not to cry. "Yeah. It was."

"That's just terrible."

Thanks, Captain Obvious.

"How do you think he caught it?"

Amika choked. "What?"

"You know. How would a guy locked up indoors get exposed to bird flu?"

"What difference does it make?"

"Come on, you're a scientist. Are you telling me you haven't wondered the same thing?"

The woman was terrifyingly clever. *No, I can honestly say I am not wondering how Shuu contracted bird flu.* "I don't care if he had a germ from outer space. The only thing that matters is he's gone."

"I'm so sorry," Jun said. "I know this is incredibly hard. I don't want to be cruel. Really. But there's something you need to know."

"I don't want to know anything. I want to be left in peace."

"I didn't say you'd want to know this information. I said you *need* to know."

Amika rubbed her forehead and felt the smooth tatami mat under her feet. She was too emotionally frail to accept what Jun offered.

Jun broke the silence. "If you turn away for the sake of 'peace,' your brother won't find any."

Why was every interaction with this woman a round of verbal sparring? "What are you saying?"

"Are you alone?"

"Yes."

"Are you sure? If Hiroshi Naito is there, this conversation ends now. You get angry with me and hang up."

"I'm alone!" Amika shouted.

"All right." Jun paused and took an audible breath. "Shuu Nakamura was set up."

For one panicked second Amika thought Jun was referring to the bird flu virus that killed him. That she'd discovered Hiroshi's role in Shuu's infection.

Jun continued. "In the Senkaku Islands. The Chinese attack on Uotsuri-shima was planned."

Planned? "You mean by the Chinese government?"

"No. By someone at the Koga Foundation."

Slowly Amika sat down on the bed, her back straight and rigid. As if a reset button had been pushed in her brain, she felt a flash of white energy inside her head. Her thoughts went blank. Then she stared out at the city lights while her mental processes came back online.

"Are you there, Amika?"

Planned. Attack. Koga. Puzzle pieces that could not fit together in the geometry of the world she knew.

Jun Taniguchi was trying to blow that world up.

"What did you say?"

"The Chinese were lured to the island on purpose. By somebody at Koga."

"Are you high, or schizophrenic?"

"It was the directional GPS unit," Jun continued. "I've been following leads on that ever since the committee hearing."

"Of course you have. Did you find any UFOs along the way?"

"Installing that DGPS on Uotsuri-shima wasn't some innocent attempt to improve navigation. The Senkaku Islands are a tinderbox. Anything that smacks of militarization, or even an attempt to change the facts on the ground and establish *de facto* ownership, is bound to provoke a reaction from Beijing."

"You think Koga was aware of this risk?"

"Someone was more than aware. They were counting on it."

Don't listen. If she's right then we shouldn't have been there and the attack shouldn't have happened and Shuu wouldn't have shot those men and…and…

"From the beginning I thought there was something fishy about government approval of that DGPS," Jun said. "The origin of the request was murky. Who wanted it in the first place? Why? I still haven't sorted that out."

"Then leave me out of it."

"That's not as important as what I *did* discover."

Amika pressed her palm against the wall, physically bracing herself for what was coming next.

"You saw the DGPS unit," Jun said. "It's a small thing, doesn't call attention to itself. It's not like they were constructing an artificial reef or something you can see from miles away. How did the Chinese know about it?"

"I wondered that, too."

"The attack was carried out by civilians but it was certainly authorized, and possibly organized, by the central government. It came the very day the navigation system arrived on Uotsuri-shima. Coincidence? No. According to my sources, information about delivery of the DGPS was quietly, carefully, and *intentionally* leaked to a Chinese radical group. We have evidence tracing that leak back to the Koga Foundation."

"Someone at Koga alerted the Chinese?"

"Yes. In advance. With a date."

"That's imposs–"

Realization exploded in her. *Oh my God. He knew.*

Amika's thoughts cascaded like a thousand dominos falling. Jun's declaration put a filter on reality and she saw her own memories afresh. Mysteries she'd failed to recognize were now solved. Coincidences she'd ignored were now explained.

She remembered that night, fleeing up the cliff, meeting Hiroshi at the tower, the Chinese in pursuit. *Wait*, he'd said, when any sane human being would've sprinted until they ran out of island.

He wasn't brave. That son-of-a-bitch knew!

The timely arrival of the Japanese commandos—how could she not have questioned it before?

Another moment of clarity.

"Hiroshi wasn't the only one," Amika said grimly. "Miyashita—a captain in the Coast Guard—he was in on it, too. I'm sure of it."

Jun whistled softly. "I saw evidence of a Coast Guard connection but it wasn't as strong as the proof I have on Koga."

"They had to know. They had the special security team staged and ready in advance."

Amika was on her feet, prowling, alert, enraged. Cause and effect. Dangle the DGPS. The Chinese attack. Shuu doesn't know the cavalry is coming. He shoots three men and they die needlessly. Cause and effect. Shuu goes to prison. Shuu dies.

You wanted me to blame the Chinese, didn't you Hiroshi? But you're the one who's really responsible. They were just pawns in your game.

Alone in the dark of her room, Amika made no effort to wipe the tears dripping down her cheeks. "What the hell was he trying to do?"

"Force a confrontation with China. Tinderbox, remember?"

China invades Japanese territory and attacks Japanese civilians. That part of the plan sure did stir up diplomatic trouble. But then Shuu fired his dart gun. If those Chinese men hadn't died, global public opinion might have swayed more heavily in Japan's favor.

Especially with a young female victim on Japan's side.

"That's why he brought me to the Senkaku Islands," Amika said aloud. "He needed a victim."

"Quite possibly."

Cause and effect. The greater the victimization, the greater the sympathy.

"Jesus," she said. "Maybe he actually *wanted* them to rape me." What if Shuu's combat reflexes hadn't kicked in? What if the commandos had been late?

And I've been sleeping with that man.

She dropped to her knees and howled, a long, animal cry of pain. Her forehead tapped the floor as she heaved with sobs.

Minutes passed. The heaving subsided and her lungs filled with air. She lifted her head and smeared the back of her hand across her nose. The anguish had steamrolled her grief into a hard, unforgiving road of fury. Her phone lay where it had fallen on the carpet. She picked it up. "Are you still there?"

"I'm here," Jun said gently.

"We go public with this. Expose him."

"I can't prove it was Hiroshi Naito. It might have been someone else associated with Koga."

"Even if he didn't initiate the leak, he was involved."

"No doubt. But the information I have isn't the kind you can use in a legal proceeding."

"We'll try him in the newspapers, then. Court of public opinion."

"Can't do that either. My sources are confidential."

"So what, you want me to kill him in his sleep?" She was at least half serious.

"Don't," Jun said, reflecting the seriousness in Amika's tone. "Hiroshi is one part of a many-headed monster. Maybe not the main head, either. Your access to him is the only access we have to the body."

"You can't possibly expect me to continue my…association with him."

"I don't expect anything. I just know that the path to the truth goes through you. If you want your revenge to do more than superficial damage to the Naito machine, you're going to have to get in deeper."

19

Jun's revelations turned Amika's tiny apartment into a crucible. Amika felt bathed in a paranormal heat.

Sympathetic nervous system.

She paced her hot little cage and opened the blinds, letting the garish nighttime lights of the city illuminate the room.

Damn you, Jun. You're all problems, no solutions.

Still holding the phone with Jun silent on the other end, she stopped in front of her mirror. The ambient street light gave her skin an unhealthy bluish color, worsening her haggard appearance.

Stupid girl. Naive, blind, stupid. I had it all figured out. I thought I was using him.

How many things would she get tragically wrong? The virus that killed Shuu. Her relationship with Hiroshi.

Was it *all* wrong? Her mind played images from recent weeks: Hiroshi at her door, crying. The Naito family, welcoming. Maybe that part was real. The comfort she had felt certainly was. But under it all, a river of betrayal. Even if Hiroshi did not intend for Shuu to be sacrificed, his actions led to her brother's death.

For that, he should pay.

"So you can't prove that Hiroshi gave information to the Chinese?"

"It could've been anybody at Koga, and no, I can't. Even if I could, that's not good enough. Someone at Koga—let's say Hiroshi Naito—through secret intermediaries, told someone in China about the delivery of a DGPS unit to the Senkaku Islands. There's nothing illegal about that. It's not a state secret, not a military operation. Even if we could prove he did it, so what? He's got a lot of friends. He doesn't care about a scolding by the media. He doesn't care if the public doesn't like him."

"Wouldn't he get in trouble for meddling in foreign policy?"

"That's a political question. He might. It's possible that this story could turn into a major scandal. It's equally possible that this government would be sympathetic to what he was trying to do. The prime minister's a family friend, and most of the cabinet leans to the right."

Amika banged a fist against the wall. "Maybe I'll just cut his balls off."

"Always an option," Jun said, "but not what I would recommend. I think he's making a bigger move. You need to find out what it is."

"What do you mean?"

"This whole Senkaku Islands incident was set up for a reason."

"To trigger a war between Japan and China, you said."

"A *confrontation*. First step towards a war, maybe. China's military would crush ours unless the US honored its pledge to stand with Japan."

"Another reason to put me in harm's way," Amika said. "I'm an American citizen."

"True. But I don't think that fully explains his relationship with you. In the broader sense of relationship," Jun hastened to add. "It keeps coming back to, why did Koga hire you?"

No longer could Amika flatter herself that the reason was simply because she was a good scientist. Hiroshi's exploitation of her probably began before the trip to the Senkaku Islands.

"You're an expert on viruses, right?" Jun asked.

"Influenza viruses. Flu."

"That's a rather big coincidence, wouldn't you say?"

Amika's prickly defenses went up. "Don't play games with me."

"You're an expert on flu. There's a bird flu panic in Japan."

"That's not coincidence, that's logic," Amika said. "The outbreak is the reason Koga hired a bunch of virologists."

"Okay, then explain to me the 'logic' that only two people in the whole country have died of bird flu and one of them was the brother of Koga's best flu scientist."

Amika kept silent, smart enough not to walk into a trap and reveal too much. *Does she know?*

"Shuu Nakamura's death solved a messy problem for Koga. By installing the DGPS, Koga was implicated in the murder of three Chinese citizens. The blame got diverted to Shuu. When he died, the scandals mostly died with him. You can't punish a dead man."

Amika snorted. "You think the Naitos murdered my brother."

"Means and motive, my dear."

"You're wrong," Amika said.

"Your judgment in this affair is not to be trusted."

"You can trust me on this," she said. "*I* killed my brother."

Now it was the reporter's turn to be dumbfounded. Amika told the whole story, how she'd designed a virus just to infect Shuu, how it was supposed to cause a mild case of flu, how Hiroshi's people smuggled it into the prison, all to keep him quarantined in Japan.

She didn't mean to tell Jun everything. But once she started talking—confessing—she couldn't stop. Another person knew the truth. She needed another person to judge her, to either condemn or forgive.

"Are you going to turn me in?"

Jun took a moment for the story to sink in. "Listen to me," she said. "It's not your fault. I don't know exactly what happened to your brother, but I am one hundred percent sure his death was not an accident."

Rather than adding to her rage, Jun's conclusion was absolution for her sin. Amika sobbed and could not speak for some time. Like a mother to a baby, Jun uttered soft, consoling nonsense until at last she began the conversation again.

"I told you this before," Jun said. "There was no Japanese officer captured at Zhoushan."

Amika continued to sniffle.

Jun persisted. "The Chinese arrested a bunch of fishermen who were in the wrong place at the wrong time. Fishermen, Amika. Not a spy among them. Whatever you heard about a secret prisoner exchange for your brother was at best a false rumor." Pause. "Do you believe me?"

"Do I have a choice?"

"You can't choose what's true but you can choose to ignore the truth."

Is that what I've been doing? Ignoring the truth? All her life, Amika's strength had been her single-mindedness. She pursued her goals to the exclusion of everything else. That set her up for success in school. It helped her escape the chaos at home. Her eyes had always been fixed on the light at the end of the tunnel.

Tunnel vision. I didn't ignore the truth. I never saw it.

"I believe you." Anger sprouted from the compost of her anguish. "The spy story wasn't a rumor. Hiroshi lied to me."

"Which brings us back once again to the key question: why?"

"You're being gentle," Amika said. "You already have an answer. You think he set me up to murder Shuu."

"What do you think?"

I think the two most important things in my life were my career and my baby brother. I lost one, and I'm going to have to forfeit the other. Forget the Nobel Prize. Hiroshi Naito is going down.

A waft of cool reason penetrated her hot fury. Winning a Nobel might be easier for her than destroying a member of the Naito family.

At least she had an ally.

"I think you're going to get what you wanted from me all along," Amika said. "I will not let him get away with this."

The glee in Jun's voice was unmistakable. "He's not done yet. Getting Shuu out of the way was secondary to some other goal. We have to find out what it is, and stop him. I think what you just told me about your work on the virus is important. Why such an elaborate scheme to commit murder?"

"To implicate me," Amika said. "Or to throw me off, so I wouldn't push for an investigation into my brother's death."

"That's possible," Jun agreed. "But what exactly did Hiroshi ask you to do with the virus? Can you explain it to me?"

"He didn't give me specific instructions. He tossed me this idea, to safely infect Shuu and no one else. I knew how to make that happen."

"Because of your expertise?"

"Yes."

"Do you think anyone else at Koga could have done what you did?"

Amika thought about it. Others had the skills to change the virus but only she knew which changes to make. The work was essentially a *reverse* gain of function, the opposite of what she'd done at Berkeley. Instead of trying to make an influenza virus that was more infectious, she'd made one that was less.

As she explained this out loud to Jun, a sickening suspicion started in her gut.

"Earlier today, he pressured me to speed up my virulence research," she said.

"What does that mean?"

"It means Hiroshi Naito wants to know how to make a killer flu."

JULY 29 (THE NEXT DAY)

After two or three hours of fitful sleep, Amika arrived at the Koga building before dawn. Her stomach churned as she approached the building's security desk. The guard took no notice of her; irregular work hours were nothing unusual at a research facility. The stigma of treason was in her heart, not on her sleeve. Waiting for the elevator she took a deep breath and tried to pretend this was an ordinary day at work.

But nothing about it felt ordinary. A sinister aura surrounded familiar objects. Nameplates on doors listed enemies. A poster about a company picnic was a conspiracy. The laboratory where she used to feel in complete control now resisted her, corrupting her efforts and twisting her aims.

It's not the place that's changed. It's me.

She quickened her steps as she passed Manami's office. How could she speak to any of her coworkers again? Surely even a casual conversation would betray her. No longer was she the ambitious young researcher. She was a foreign spy, a spanner in the works of Koga.

As she'd hoped, the lab was empty. *No one will show up for another two hours. Then I'll move to the biosafety isolation lab.* Her experiment didn't need isolation. She did. It would protect her from her greatest fear for the day: running into Hiroshi. *He won't bother me while I'm in isolation even if he stops by the lab.* She had no plan beyond avoidance. Not yet.

First she needed answers.

Ripping the sterile packaging off a tongue depressor tore the silence in the empty lab. She grasped one end of the flat stick and stuck the other in her mouth, tasting the wood as she scraped the inside of her cheek. The epithelial cells she harvested in this way were a painless source of her own DNA, DNA that she intended to sequence today. Not her entire genome. Just one region of particular interest. She'd have the answer by tonight.

A door slammed somewhere down the hall. She gathered what she needed and hastily retreated to the isolation lab.

She didn't bother wearing all the uncomfortable protective gear; she had nothing hazardous here. The work was familiar and straightforward, much easier than sequencing viral genomes like she'd done many times before. No windows, no people, no sounds except the sounds she and her equipment made. Her mind wandered and déjà vu hit. The room, the paranoia of doing forbidden work under the noses of her superiors—she was back at Berkeley the day they fired her.

For the first time, she regretted what she'd done there, and not only because her actions had led her to this terrible situation. She'd learned she was not the beacon of wisdom and scientific perfection that she thought. *Maybe I was wrong to do the gain-of-function work.* Flu virus was not a thing to be trifled with. The scientific community had put a stop to the research, and she had singlehandedly decided they were all wrong.

Maybe they were right.

Her newfound humility had come at a great price.

Hours passed in her solitary bubble. She slipped out once to use the toilet. The automated sequencer ran her samples. A heavy loneliness weighed on her. *Shuu's gone. Mom and Dad are useless.* She felt a new grief at losing the Naito family. *They were so kind.* She hadn't realized how much she'd embraced being welcomed into the clan.

Lying, two-faced bastards.

Whatever it takes.

She needed a plan. Jun expected to hear from her tonight. Together they would come up with something.

I hope.

As she considered the power and ruthlessness of Hiroshi Naito and his family, it dawned on her that what she was doing was dangerous to more than her scientific career.

She loaded another sample into the machine.

Unlike people, experiments didn't lie. They could be poorly designed or badly executed. They could be misinterpreted or used to deceive. But in the end, facts were facts.

Amika had been told so many lies. What would the truth look like?

Can I handle the truth?

Her stomach grumbled. Food would have to wait.

Then a green light flashed. The sequencer had finished. Her pulse quickened. *This is it.*

As she accessed the sequence data on her laptop, she felt her brother's spirit looking over her shoulder. *Help me. I'm doing this for you.*

Tens of thousands of As, Ts, Gs, and Cs loaded into her genome analyzing software. The vast strings were far too long for a human being to interpret. With fearful anticipation, she carefully programmed the software to compare her DNA sequence with another on file: the sequence Hiroshi Naito gave her to customize the flu virus for Shuu.

He told me it was Shuu's DNA.

The computer aligned the two sequences, one from her, one from "Shuu", matching them where they were identical, and marking where they differed. Her mouth went dry.

Women have been known to lie about these things.

But even with different fathers, half-siblings share a lot of DNA. A lot more than these two did.

I don't need statistics to tell me Shuu is one hundred percent my brother. Line up pictures of us as babies and you can't tell which of us is which. We share a lot of DNA.

This DNA is not his.

The answer was clear. Hiroshi had lied about the DNA sequence. It didn't come from her brother. She was not related to the person she designed the flu to infect.

Whose DNA was it, then?

And why did Hiroshi give it to me?

Before she made any progress on a plan, someone knocked loudly on the door to the isolation lab.

"Amika? Are you in there?"

She felt a physical pain in her chest. The voice was Hiroshi's.

20

Amika immediately closed the DNA sequence analysis on her laptop. *What is he doing here? He never comes to the isolation lab!*

She needed to make up a story that didn't sound like a story. And she needed to do it fast.

If I don't answer, will he go away?

Wishful thinking. *I signed up to use the room. He knows I'm in here.*

"Amika?" Hiroshi repeated.

"Hey," she said in as casual a tone as she could muster. "I'm in the middle of something. Can I talk to you later?"

"Are you all right? I've been trying to reach you all day."

"I've been in here," she said. "I had an idea about the flu virulence project. Needed to do some sequencing." *That could easily be true. As long as he doesn't ask me what my idea is…*

"How does it look?"

She wished he were as far away as his voice sounded through the door. "Promising."

"Well, at least you're back at it. Ichiro and I missed you at dinner last night. Did you get a good night's sleep?"

Neither good nor sleep, you bastard. "Yeah, pretty good. My body clock is still off."

"Can I come in?"

"No! I'm suited up. There's influenza contamination I haven't cleaned up yet." She wasn't actually wearing a protective hood and face shield. If she were, the mask would muffle her words. *Can he tell from my voice that I'm lying?*

"Okay. Listen, sorry I wasn't free to spend last night with you alone. I'll make up for it tonight."

The hell you will. "I don't know. I'm still really tired. When I finish here I think I'll go home."

She jumped as his voice suddenly seemed much closer. The door had not opened. *He must be leaning into the door, speaking into the crack.*

"I need you, Amika. It's been a long time."

The thought of having sex with him made her want to throw up. "I know. Maybe tomorrow?"

Silence. She realized she was holding her breath.

"Call me," he said. Then she heard his footsteps fade away.

To avoid running into him, she waited another forty-five minutes before leaving. She spent the time mulling over how she would handle him going forward. It was easy enough to ignore his texts or calls, but there was no way to avoid him completely. Not if she wanted the information needed to bring him down. She would have to do a damn good job of acting. But how to deter him from sex?

Out of habit she sanitized the isolation lab. After peeking to confirm the hallway was empty, she trotted to the stairwell to make her escape from the building. In the last twenty-four hours she'd grasped that Hiroshi was powerful, deceitful, and dangerous. To work against him she would have to be smart. *No elevator ride with a chatty coworker for me.* She reached the sidewalk outside and blended with the crowd, watching for anyone else exiting Koga at the same time. *I don't want to be followed.*

On her way back to her apartment she bought a prepaid mobile phone with cash. A man who could manipulate national governments could certainly get his hands on her phone and credit card records. She couldn't erase Jun's call from last night, but she sure wouldn't add any more suspicious calls to her log.

That covers my digital trail. But she still had no idea how she was going to stay out of Hiroshi's bed without tipping him off that something was up.

By the time she got home she was famished and boiled water for a package of instant noodles. Standing in her messy little studio with a bowl in her hands, she watched the last of the day's sunlight fade away amid the urban landscape.

A good time for tea, isn't it, brother? She got out the tools to prepare matcha green tea—*just the way you like it, Shuu.* The DNA sequences she'd seen today scrolled through her mind and she wondered: if the virus I made was designed to infect someone other than Shuu, how did he die?

Was it possible I didn't kill my brother after all?

Tea temporarily forgotten, she opened her laptop. Supposedly Shuu tested positive for bird flu. By law, a specimen should've been sent to Japan's National Institute of Infectious Diseases.

I can access the DNA sequence in NIID's online database.

Among hundreds of records, she found one tagged H7N9 avian influenza, from a male, age 23, deceased on the appropriate date. *That's him.*

She swept through the thousands of A/T/C/G letters of the virus that killed Shuu Nakamura to the region she knew best. The answer was clear.

Not my virus!

Her heart felt like it had been freed from a vise. *It's not my fault. His death is not my fault.* She looked around the room, as if she might see her brother's spirit rejoicing with her. *I didn't let you down, bro. It wasn't me.*

We both know who is to blame.

How did Hiroshi do it? She looked at the sequence alignments on her computer screen and gave a bitter laugh. *Of course. They infected him with the flu that's been killing birds. Took it right from the freezer. Makes his death look natural.* She'd studied that virus. She knew it was not infectious, did not readily spread from one bird or person to another. *Perfect for murder. No collateral damage.*

If she had any doubt that her lover was lying to her, this clinched it.

God damn you, Hiroshi. You will pay for this.

She stood and stared out the window, picturing Hiroshi's bedroom, dark and private. *Get him alone, behind closed doors. Naked. Distracted.* But then what? In America it would be simple: she would bring a handgun. Not an option in Japan. A knife? How could she conceal that? And even with the element of surprise, could she really stab him to death?

And then go to prison? I won't give him that. I'll find another way.

Hiroshi's ring tone on her old phone startled her out of her revenge fantasy. The phone's screen blazed like a siren in the dusk light. She did not answer. He did not leave a voice message. Despite the warm room and her bravado, she shivered.

I'm holding a tiger by the tail.

She needed help to avoid getting mauled. Crawling onto her bed, she called Jun Taniguchi on her new burner phone.

"I'm scared, Jun."

"Don't panic," Jun said. "You may not have to keep this up for long. Did you learn anything today?"

"You were right about Shuu. My virus didn't kill him. Hiroshi lied to me about the DNA sequence. The virus I made has a key that fits a different lock, so to speak."

"The DNA he gave you wasn't your brother's?"

"No. It definitely came from someone I'm not related to."

"But the virus you made would attack a person with that DNA in their cells?"

"Yes."

"Do you know who that person is?"

"No. The sequence hasn't been published anywhere."

Jun's garbled voice spoke to someone in the background. Then she returned to the phone. "Could he be planning an assassination? Use the virus to kill a target without anyone knowing it was murder?"

"In theory. It would be risky, though. I weakened the virus to protect my brother. To use it as a murder weapon, it would have to be strengthened. Then you would have to worry about specificity."

"Meaning what?"

"Meaning the virus isn't perfectly specific for only one person. It has the potential to infect more people."

"How many more?"

"I can't give a number without data on the allele frequency. It could infect anyone who shares the same DNA sequence at that place in their genome."

"Like, relatives of this mystery person?"

"Yeah."

"How closely related?"

"Well, at least one parent, of course."

"Sisters and brothers?"

"At least a fifty percent chance."

"What about extended family?"

"Sure."

Jun paused. "What about a bigger pool, like the person's ethnic group?"

"If the people in the group shared a common ancestor, it's possible that many or most of them would carry the same gene."

"So this engineered virus could target an entire race."

Amika gasped. Jun was one smart cookie.

A race. Any member of a particular genetic group. Her heart pounded in horror.

Not assassination. Genocide.

Jun insisted. "Could it? Could the virus pick off people in one ethnic group but not another?"

"In theory. DNA sequencing is a lousy way to identify racial groups, even those we can easily recognize by skin color or facial features. The genetic differences between individuals within a race are greater than the differences between two groups."

"Still, it's possible."

Amika thought for a minute. "Yes. Ethnic groups within a particular race have more DNA in common. But trying to find a gene that was widespread in one group and missing in another would be looking for a needle in a haystack. Even if you found one you'd have to test your theory, and you can't do that."

"Why not?"

"It would require experiments on humans and that's—"

She froze.

Jun finished her thought for her. "Ethical concerns wouldn't stop the Naito clan. They know all about doing experiments on people. Just ask the Chinese."

The recurring slur: "Chinese jackals." My God, is that his plan?

Her thoughts whirled, evidence and conjecture sifting into a pattern. Hiroshi's obvious antipathy toward the Chinese people. His involvement in ultranationalism. His provocation in setting up the Senkaku Islands incident. And most devastating of all, his family history. His ancestors' abominable crimes during World War II. Means and motive, in the words Jun had used the other day.

Last night at the meeting Ichiro suggested I should fight back, take revenge. Is this what he was talking about? A genocidal virus?

Then she was seized with dizziness and a raw churning in her stomach. They were trying to enlist her. *I know why Hiroshi wanted me. Why he brought me to Koga.*

To make his virus for him.

She had just said it herself: *Ethnic groups within a particular race would have more DNA in common.* "Jun...it can't be...but..."

"Tell me."

"If Hiroshi gave me a consensus DNA sequence that's found primarily in Han Chinese, then the bird flu virus I made would specifically target them."

She heard Jun take a deep breath. "Han are more than ninety percent of all the people in China. This virus would be a biological weapon for genocide. Can you prove it?"

"Only with experimental proof."

"Experimental?"

"Yeah. Dead Chinese people."

"Do not make jokes."

"I'm not. I can't find any information about the DNA sequence Hiroshi gave me. If I'm right, it could've taken years for the Naitos to synthesize it. The only direct way to prove who the virus targets is to find its victims."

"So we have to wait until he releases his weapon. That will be too late."

"Unless they test it first, in stages." Amika tried to think like a scientist charged with creating a biological weapon for genocide. There were a number of technical challenges. How to target your hated group was the most difficult, and the Naitos might have overcome this already (*with my help!* she screamed silently). How to protect your own group. How to get the agent to spread. How to get it to kill. *They'll want to test each of these before they deploy it, if they're smart. And God knows, they're smart.* "Shuu isn't the only bird flu victim in Japan, right?"

"Right. There've been other cases. At least one other death. Female, age 36."

"Do we know anything else about that woman?"

"Give me a couple of hours and I will."

"In the meantime I'll see if my virus has popped up in any databases. That would tell us if the Naitos have tested it somewhere."

"Good. Let's talk again tonight."

"Wait," Amika said. "What are we going to do if we're right?"

Jun didn't answer.

Her voice rose. "I'm sleeping with my boss, who happens to be a psychopath who murdered my brother and tricked me into making a genocidal virus. If you don't want me to take the elevator to the roof and jump off, I need you to tell me, right now, *how are we going to stop him?*"

She heard her pulse pounding in her ears as she waited for Jun's reply, which was slow in coming.

"Stay off the roof," Jun said. "If you must, get on a plane and go home to California."

"You don't have a plan, do you?"

"I do, but we need evidence first. My colleagues and I are close to identifying officials we can trust. People who aren't beholden to the Naito family. Believe me, if you can prove Koga is making a genetically modified flu virus, we'll find a way to shut them down."

Believe me. Right. In the meantime, Hiroshi might just show up at my door with a bottle of wine and a condom.

"Can you hang in there?" Jun said.

"With a *billion* lives at risk? What do you think?"

Jun paused. "I think you pick even worse boyfriends than I do."

Her jest cut through the darkness and Amika laughed a little.

"There have to be clues at Koga," she said. "I will find them."

"And I will get back to you as soon as I know anything about the other flu fatality."

They disconnected. Amika finally heated water for that tea she wanted. Even before the caffeine took effect, her thoughts raced. *What if I can't find the evidence she needs? What if she can't get the authorities involved? What if we're too late?* On a personal level, *what if he gets away with it?*

She tried not to worry. Jun was a pro, and she was persistent. She'd never been this close to her quarry. She wouldn't let Hiroshi slip away.

And yet…

Amika held the hot cup and inhaled the tea's steam. *Things go wrong. People fail, systems fail.* She paced the floor. An idea came to her. An audacious, dangerous idea.

She brushed aside any ethical concerns. *I'll only use it if all else fails.* No question it was possible: she'd already been tricked into doing it once before.

I'll design a virus to target a particular person. But this time, the virus will be lethal. And I choose the target.

Hiroshi Naito.

She would need some of his DNA. Sperm would be the ideal source, but no way was she going down that path. Using DNA amplification technology, she could get by with something a lot simpler: a few of his hairs, a bit of fingernail. With luck, even a cigarette butt or a spoon he'd used could be enough.

And then I'll make a weapon of last resort.

Rather than avoiding Hiroshi at all costs, tomorrow she would have to get close to him.

In the meantime, she wanted to know more about Japan's other bird flu death. Was this person a victim of a field test of the Naito family's bioweapon?

Only a few pieces of information about the victim were in the public database: Female. Age 36. Died in a Tokyo hospital five days after Shuu. Like Shuu, she was infected with an H7N9 avian influenza virus.

Which one?

The genome sequence was online. She set up a comparison.

It was one hundred percent identical to the virus that killed Shuu.

I don't believe it. That virus is not infectious. She didn't catch that flu. Either someone gave it to her on purpose, or someone faked the data.

Murder or treachery? Hiroshi's people were capable of both; Koga was connected to many scientists at the National Institute. Until she knew more about the victim's story, she could not guess which.

The answer came sooner than expected when Jun called back.

"Her name was Cynthia Lun," Jun said, mangling the pronunciation of the name *Cynthia*.

Dread crystallized in Amika's chest. "That's not a Japanese name."

"She was Chinese-American. Traveling on business. She was hospitalized soon after arriving in Tokyo from a stay in Hong Kong."

Lun. Chinese-American. No matter what her passport said, the unfortunate woman's DNA was Han.

That can't be a coincidence. Of all the people in Japan, the only one to die of bird flu (other than Shuu) was of Chinese descent.

"I'll bet anything she was killed by a modified version of the virus I made."

"Is that what the NIID record says?"

"No. The entry is a lie. Even if that poor woman toured poultry farms on her trip, she wouldn't have caught the virus listed in the official record. It may be deadly, but it's not infectious."

"What makes you so sure?"

"It's written in the DNA."

"So why hasn't somebody noticed?"

"Because I know more about the genes for virulence factors than any scientist on the planet. My work was never published." Amika set down her phone and put Jun on speaker so she could use her computer while they talked. "She traveled from Hong Kong. If I wanted to test a Han-specific virus, that'd be a good place." She typed and swiped furiously, searching for public health data from Hong Kong. Had there been a spike in influenza cases?

Not according to the official data. "That region of China hasn't reported any human cases of bird flu," Amika said. "But that doesn't mean anything. China has a reputation for either screwing up or covering up their infectious disease reports."

Jun grunted. "Plausible. But still speculation, not evidence."

"I know that!" Her knee bounced and her heel tapped the floor. *I need the sequence of the virus that actually killed Cynthia Lun.*

"Maybe I can get some help from outside," Amika said. "I'll call you back."

Every important biomedical institution in Japan was potentially tainted by the influence of the Naito family. But the US, she hoped, would be clean.

Despite her professional problems back home, she was a legitimate, on-the-record flu researcher for Koga. The US Centers for Disease Control fielded information requests from overseas scientists like her all the time.

She found a contact number for the CDC's global bird flu surveillance program and called Atlanta. It was early on the East Coast. A friendly woman with a comforting drawl took her information and promised a return call from a specialist by the end of the day. Hearing the American accent filled Amika with homesickness. She'd thrown away more than she realized when she squandered her position at Berkeley. Quiet anonymity while working in a lab, something she'd tried so hard to escape in her quest for fame, was now the tantalizing fruit beyond her reach.

Of course if I don't stop Hiroshi, I'll be "famous" beyond my wildest dreams— the architect of genocide. The enormity of it left her numb.

Night had settled on Tokyo and she wearily stretched out on her bed. It might be hours before she heard back from the CDC. She ruminated on what she dared reveal—or not. The conversation would be a dance. How could she ask them to look for a genocidal bird flu without confessing what she'd done, or sounding like a conspiracy nut?

The ring tone startled her awake. Her ruminations had led to sleep, not to answers. The call was coming from Atlanta. She sat up and cleared her throat nervously.

"Dr. Nakamura? Of Koga Scientific?" A man this time, and not a Southerner. From the Midwest, maybe? "Captain Michael Lindstrom. I'm part of the global influenza team here at CDC. How can I help you?"

Captain? What the hell does that mean? She imagined a firm handshake and a steely gaze. "Thank you, I have some questions about…about the human cases of bird flu in Japan."

"Yeah, you're right in the thick of it, aren't you?"

"I'm in Tokyo, yes."

"Japan's National Institute of Infectious Diseases is one of our global partners in the World Health Organization flu network," Lindstrom said. "They're on top of things. Good people there."

"Of course they are. I wasn't saying—" She stopped herself.

Awkward silence hung for a moment. Lindstrom said, "So what can CDC do for you that your local folks can't?"

You can tell me the truth. "I've been sequencing a lot of influenzas isolated from dead birds in Japan. I'm pretty familiar with the local viruses. I didn't think the strains circulating here posed much of a threat."

"Why not?"

I do not want to get into that. "Well, we weren't seeing any local transmission among birds, even poultry flocks on farms. Anyway, when that woman died I had to reconsider my assumptions. I was wondering, though, if maybe the virus that killed her was different from the ones I've seen in the trenches here."

"The Institute posted a sequence. Can I help you access it online?"

"No, that's not it, I have access. I saw the data."

Another awkward pause. "So, what do you want from us, exactly?"

"Did the Institute ship a specimen to you?"

"Yes. That's part of the WHO protocol. We maintain a secure collection of frozen specimens here. A global virus library, if you will."

"Did CDC sequence it?"

"I doubt it. If a specimen already was sequenced at another facility, there's no reason to do it again."

"Right. But is there a protocol, a situation where CDC would do the work independently?"

"In this business, there's a protocol for everything."

"Can a person request re-sequencing of a specimen in the library?"

"Would you be a person making such a request?" Lindstrom asked.

"Yes."

"May I ask why?"

"Well, you can't send it to me to do it myself, can you?"

"Not unless your institution is part of the WHO network, no. But what I meant was, why do you think re-sequencing is necessary?"

"I think a mistake may have been made." *This would be so much easier if I could tell the truth.*

"Go on."

"Like I said, the flu attributed to that woman's death doesn't look infectious."

"And how would you know that, Doctor?"

Because I've done the science. "The epidemiology. And a hunch."

"Really. Did you bring that hunch with you from UC Berkeley?"

The room around her seemed to get brighter and her pulse quickened. She hadn't said anything about her background. *He knows who I am.* This confirmed her fears that the American scientific establishment would neither forgive nor forget—and it made this conversation even more complicated than it already was. "I'm engaged in flu research at another institution now."

Lindstrom chuckled. "Yes, in Japan. Let's see. The message I got says you're a staff scientist at Koga in their vaccine division. Is that true?"

"Yes."

"Funny how the message does *not* mention your expertise on influenza virulence."

"My employment history is not relevant."

"Bull-patooey. You didn't call the CDC on a hunch. You have data."

"Any data I may have had I was obliged to destroy when I left the University."

"I'm aware of the terms of your dismissal," Lindstrom said.

"It sounds like you're aware of a lot but I don't know anything about you."

"Unlike yours, my story hasn't been splashed across the newspapers and TV. So let me fill you in. I'm a US Army officer with a special interest in biological weapons defense. I'm currently working at the CDC. And I'm not the only person who noticed that the first human death from bird flu in Japan was the brother of a controversial influenza expert."

Keep you mouth shut, Amika.

"Heck of a coincidence, wouldn't you say?" When she did not reply, Lindstrom continued. "In fact I've been meaning to contact *you*. Thanks for saving me the trouble of tracking down your number."

"You're welcome." Again she chose to say nothing more.

Lindstrom let the silence linger, then hardened his tone. "There's a reason for the moratorium on gain-of-function work in this country. The work is dangerous. You may have gone overseas to escape the research ban, but the danger doesn't stop at the border. I don't know what you've done but I'm going to assume, based on this phone call, that it's gone out of your control."

Out of my control, yes, but it's Hiroshi Naito's control I'm trying to break. She tried to sound unperturbed. "Assumptions can make a fool out of you, Captain. Are you going to help me or not?"

He didn't let her bait him. "That depends. Frankly I'm scared. If you mucked something up so bad that your brother died—though I don't understand how, since he was in prison—and now you're calling the CDC for help, I'm wondering if I should alert the White House."

It may come to that soon, but for now neither confirm nor deny. "I just have some questions about the virus that killed Cynthia Lun."

"How do you know the patient's name?"

Big mistake. That information wasn't public. "I—it was in the medical report I got at Koga. She died here in Tokyo at one of our affiliate hospitals."

He seemed to buy it. "Why are you asking CDC instead of the Japan Institute?"

Time to bluff. "If I question their work, they'll be insulted. Lose face, you know. It'll hurt my career here. If CDC repeats the sequencing, I can stay out of it." *Give him a reason.* "You're right, my work at Berkeley taught me a few things. I think the Institute screwed up. The virus posted for this fatality wouldn't infect a human being."

"Is that so. Sounds like you got a lot done at Berkeley before you left."

"There are good reasons for a person to defy the research ban."

"No one ever said gain-of-function work wasn't useful. Anyway, I'll see what I can do about getting that specimen re-sequenced. Any particular part of the genome we should focus on?"

She knew exactly which part. *The region I modified when I made the virus. The region that might point it at Chinese people.* She told him, and found a way to make her next request. "That area of the DNA controls the virus's host range."

"It determines whether the virus infects birds, humans, or pigs," Lindstrom said.

"Right." *Or people of a particular race.* "Very important for a pandemic. If CDC finds anything new or unusual there, in any specimens, could you let me know?" *If the genetic modification I made is in the wild, they might stumble on it.*

"Sequences are always posted in the public databases, you know."

"But sometimes it takes a while."

Whatever questions he had about her urgency on this, he kept to himself. "All right. I'll make a note. Anything else?"

"Just wondering about the gap between public reporting and reality. Lun probably picked up the virus in Hong Kong but I don't see any other reported cases there."

"That's the official word. CDC doesn't have any data to contradict it."

"Reporting from China in the past has been unreliable."

"True. We don't really know what's going on in Hong Kong, much less in rural China. Maybe there've been deaths that went undiagnosed. Or it could be the government's covering them up."

"What about deaths outside Japan or China?" she pressed. "Have you found anything in common among the victims?"

"Other than dangerous proximity to Amika Nakamura? No. There's only been a handful of cases. Is there something in particular we should be looking for? Another hunch of yours?"

Her face flushed. Was the time for secrecy past? Lindstrom obviously suspected she was involved in the H7N9 outbreak. What if she came clean, told him to watch for an ethnic bias in the victims? He would have plenty of questions then. Questions she either couldn't or didn't want to answer yet.

He spoke. "It's not my job to judge your mistakes, Doctor. My job is to protect Americans and save lives. If there's a pandemic flu threat out there, you have a moral obligation to share your information."

Don't preach at me. "The Japan Institute is the only one who's made a mistake." Immediately she regretted her defensiveness. *Big picture, Amika. He's right. Remember how much might be at stake.* Meekly she said, "I hear what you're saying. We're on the same side. Losing my brother is the hardest thing that's ever happened to me. I want to know what killed him, and Cynthia Lun. I want to make sure we're not overlooking something important. Something that could hurt other people, too."

After a pause, Lindstrom said, "I'll get the sequencing done. In return, I want you to call me, text me, shoot me an email, any time you feel like sharing one of your hunches. Heck, snail mail 'em to my office postage-due. Just tell me what you know. About Shuu Nakamura, H7N9 viruses, good sushi joints in Tokyo. Anything."

"Deal."

"And a word to the wise? This isn't a good time for you to go off the grid on a beach vacation. If you get a call from the Washington, DC area code, you better answer."

They hung up and she felt pounding in her temples. Lindstrom had been surprisingly diplomatic, considering he knew she was holding back. She wanted to tell him everything. But could she trust him?

I'll discuss it with Jun. Maybe she can get his backstory.

Inviting scrutiny from the outside might illuminate the Naito family/Koga conspiracy. Or it might send the evidence scuttling deeper into the shadows.

Before I bring in Lindstrom, I have to finish my business with Hiroshi.

21

Amika's dark-blue-and-gold US passport beckoned from atop the tiny dresser in her apartment.

I could be on a plane to Los Angeles before noon. Leave all this behind.

She stuffed the leathery booklet into a drawer, along with her fear. There was science to be done today.

So far she had no solid proof that her virus was being tested in the wild, or that Hiroshi was plotting to deploy it to kill Han Chinese. If that was indeed his plan, then Koga had to be growing and stockpiling the agent somewhere. Where?

The Naito family controlled the Koga network of laboratories and vaccine production plants. If they wanted to manufacture a virus to use as a biological weapon, surely they would use a Koga facility, where everything was already in place and the activity would look like business as usual.

Business as usual to the naked eye, that is. The truth couldn't hide from molecular analysis. The Han agent had unnatural gene sequences in it. If she found even a single copy of the unique DNA she'd created, it would prove that Koga was testing or producing the Han agent there.

I am a Koga scientist. An official company insider. I can get inside a factory, and secretly swab the place for DNA while just walking around. Someone—Jun Taniguchi, Captain Lindstrom—would know what to do with that information. Someone more powerful than she would stop the Naitos' genocidal plan, would go to the source and destroy the virus stocks.

But if they failed…

She leaned toward the mirror and streaked a gash of red color across her lips. Today she would begin her plan to customize a killer virus based on Hiroshi's DNA. The project was risky. She could not predict whether her creation would affect Hiroshi alone, or his family too, or other Japanese people like herself, or people all over the world. Her scientific career, already in tatters, would be thoroughly ended if anyone learned what she was doing. Creating a bioweapon was a crime.

But under the right circumstances, she would do it. She would infect him.

Manami's office door was open as Amika walked stiffly down the hall toward her lab. She considered going the long way around to avoid the older woman.

No. I need her. Manami was the closest thing she had to a friend at Koga.

Amika paused in the doorway and swallowed hard on the memories when she glimpsed the office couch. "Hey Manami," she said.

"Dr. Nakamura!" the woman gushed. "I heard you were back from California but I have not seen you." Manami rose from her desk chair and in a very un-Japanese-like gesture, she embraced Amika. "How are you doing? Are you okay? You look terrible. Are you eating?"

Without waiting for an answer, she returned to the area behind her desk and opened a drawer. "This is what you need."

Amika felt a surge of genuine gratitude. "Rice balls. Your famous *onigiri.*"

"Guaranteed to make anyone feel better." She placed the plastic-wrapped package in Amika's hand. "Even people in mourning."

"Thank you."

"So where have you been hiding?"

"I spent a day in the isolation lab," Amika said.

"Needed some time alone, eh?"

"Yes. Well, not exactly. I'm working on a new project."

"Good for you. That's the best way to move forward after what happened."

"That's what people tell me. I'm shifting more into vaccine work."

"That is our specialty. You'll fit right in here."

"Absolutely." Amika's left hand nervously stroked her hair. *Stop. Focus.* "I have an idea. I know Koga makes live virus vaccines. I might be able to increase production at a very low cost. It would be really helpful if I visited the facilities. To see if my method could be integrated into the production system."

Manami lightly clapped her hands together. "That's a good idea. I might be able to arrange that for you. Live vaccine is produced at our Osaka plant. Access is restricted but I happen to know some people."

"Could you contact them? Today?"

Manami sat down and touched her computer mouse. "In a hurry?"

"No, I just, um, my schedule is pretty open this week so it would be a good time before I get much deeper in the work."

Manami typed. "I'm sending an email…now."

"Thanks, Manami." Amika drifted into the hallway, lifting the rice balls for emphasis. "For everything."

As she encountered various coworkers on her way, she relied on their expectation that she would be despondent after traveling to the US for her brother's funeral. She gave terse or single-word responses to their greetings. They left her alone after that.

Where's Hiroshi when you need him?

She set a can of lychee-flavored soda on her desk and surreptitiously wiped the top clean with alcohol and bleach. Then she opened it and dumped a little out to make it look like she was drinking it. If Hiroshi came to visit, she would offer him a sip.

Mouth to rim, DNA to amplifier…

She had other strategies to get his DNA today, but this was the easiest. Especially since she wouldn't have to go out for dinner with him. *I do not want to get cornered into the sperm option.*

Time to look busy. Hiroshi had demanded data on exactly which parts of the viral DNA made it more deadly. Of course she would not give him this. Having already done some of the work at Berkeley, she knew that certain experimental approaches were effective and that others failed.

He wants virulence studies? I'll give him virulence studies: I'll repeat all the experiments that don't work.

It would look like she was working hard, but she wouldn't produce anything he could use.

Next, she needed to justify her request to visit Koga's plant in Osaka. Back in her grad school days, she'd done some work on virus production with a hard-to-find chemical. The work didn't go anywhere, but she could pretend to be doing the experiments for the first time.

She turned on her computer and opened the Koga app that employees used to order lab supplies. The ordering system popped on her screen. Thousands and thousands of chemicals, biologicals, and reagents, everything from table salt to synthetic proteins were listed.

Please be as hard to get as you used to be...

In the exhaustive list, a chemical called L-shikimate was available, but its mirror image, D-shikimate, was nowhere to be found.

Excellent.

Koga company policy permitted employees to order laboratory products from outside suppliers only if the item was not available in their system. Amika switched to an internet browser and hunted for sellers of the D-form. Minutes ticked by as she dug through catalogs and websites and even references in scientific journals, trying to find every possible source of shikimate. She made a point of checking price and shipping details.

Let them think I'm trying to find the best deal.

After three-quarters of an hour on the computer and two phone calls to sales reps, she was satisfied that she'd found every supplier who sold the chemical. There were only two manufacturers of the artificial organic molecule in the whole world. She placed an order for a shipment from one of them.

There's your bait, Hiroshi.

L-shikimate was the starting material for synthesis of Tamiflu, a drug used to treat influenza. If she convinced Hiroshi that D-shikimate, its chemical opposite, made the virus grow faster, he might have the rare substance shipped to his virus production facility.

He'll know that it could be used legitimately in vaccine production—or to enhance a bioweapon.

A stool clattered as one of the scientists working at the other end of the lab room suddenly stood up and bowed. "Good afternoon, Naito-san."

"Good afternoon," Hiroshi said.

Everyone in the room rose and bowed as the boss strode toward Amika's bench.

Her heart skipped. Everything had changed since she last saw him, when he gave his lecture to the strange gathering with Ichiro two nights ago.

She felt a surge of almost blinding hatred and had to swallow a few times to keep her composure. Then he was standing in front of her and she was bowing to him.

"Hello, Dr. Nakamura."

He stayed a few feet away and made no move to touch her.

Why? He can't know I'm trying to get his DNA. Is it because the other employees are here?

"Good afternoon, Naito-san," she replied with the same formality.

"May I speak to you in private?"

"Of course."

Reluctantly she left the soda bottle behind and followed him out of the lab. He held the door for her to a vacant conference room with an oblong table and some chairs. Her fingers tingled with tension. *Hair…if I can snatch a hair from his jacket…*

"I'm setting up—" she began.

He lunged and smashed his lips into hers. Before she even tried to draw a breath, she felt his tongue in her mouth, his hand on the back of her head, pressing her closer.

Repulsed, she instinctively put her palms on his chest to push him away. "Not here," she gasped.

He shoved his knee between her legs and fumbled his free hand under her shirt. "Why not?"

"Someone might walk in."

"I locked the door."

She thought she was prepared for this moment, but the suddenness and totality of his assault, without the usual preamble, left her no room for subtle maneuvering. Every muscle in her body screamed *don't touch me*. But she didn't dare to reject him outright—he would wonder why. And this was her chance to get his DNA.

For Shuu.

Forcibly dissociating her mind from her body, she softened her posture and cuddled her breasts against him.

"Save it for later," she said.

"Amika-chan," he said, "it's been over two weeks."

"So what's a—" she almost said, *a few hours more*, but dared not make that commitment, "a little longer?"

He squeezed her close and kissed her again. "It's torture."

With steely resolve she opened her mouth and raised her arms to fondle his neck. Her eyes focused not on his face, but on the shoulders of his suit jacket. She ran her fingers through his hair, jostling and rubbing as if responding enthusiastically.

I only need one.

Then there it was. She broke off and pretended to brush his jacket with her hand.

"I'm working right now," she said. "And this isn't the time or place."

To her immense relief, he pulled away. "You're on the virulence project like I asked?"

"Yes. And something else, too. A study I started way back in graduate school."

"It better be important."

"It's important for a vaccine manufacturer. A chemical that might increase your yield with live vaccine prep."

She knew the wheels were turning in his brain. Live virus vaccine—or live virus bioweapon.

"Interesting." He straightened his tie. "You'll tell me about it over dinner tonight."

Damn. "How about lunch tomorrow—"

He silenced her with a finger against her lips. "I insist. I'll send a car for you at seven. If you're not in it, you can tell your new employer about your idea."

She forced a quivering smile. "See you tonight."

As she exited the conference room, she had no idea how she would avoid Hiroshi's bed tonight but she knew exactly what she was going to do with the human hair secretly pinched between her fingers.

When she changed trains on her way home from the lab she found an unoccupied corner of a subway station to call Jun on the burner phone.

"I may have something for you after tomorrow," Amika said. "I'm taking the bullet train to Osaka."

"What's in Osaka?" Jun asked.

"The factory where Koga manufactures live virus vaccines. The same equipment could be used to produce a bioweapon. If I pick up any trace of my virus there, it'll prove they're up to something."

"Good. Speaking of vaccines, I've got information."

A train rumbled through the station. Amika pressed the phone tighter to her ear. "About what?"

"About the dead birds that convinced everybody in Japan to run out and get Koga's bird flu shot. "

"I've known for a while there's something fishy about those birds."

"Then you were right. Their deaths probably weren't from natural causes."

Amika gasped. "How do you know?"

"A Koga affiliate has been making payments to a bird dealer in Tamba, not far from Kyoto. The bird guy primarily deals in specialized poultry for research and other non-agricultural applications. But in the past year, he's filled unusual orders for wild birds. Not exotics. Ordinary local birds, trapped and delivered live."

Puzzle pieces clicked together in Amika's mind. "If Koga artificially infected those birds and then released them, or planted their dead bodies, it would explain why they carried bird flu that wasn't contagious."

"Exactly. Why do you think they did it?" Jun asked.

"I don't know. To cause panic? Or maybe it was some kind of field test. If you want to spread a genocidal bird flu, birds would be a good way to do it."

"I don't like it," Jun said. "I'll keep digging. I get the feeling we need to move fast. If you find virus DNA at the factory tomorrow, we'll go straight to the authorities. By then I'll have identified a person we can safely contact. As long as you're willing to testify about the genetic manipulation you did, they'll have to investigate—at the very least, the presence of your virus at the factory would be a safety hazard."

"The sooner we go public, the better." Amika made light of the situation. "I don't think Hiroshi's going to be very happy when he doesn't get laid tonight."

Jun did not laugh. "The Naitos are dangerous people. Be careful."

"You too."

The subway train's door opened with a gentle whoosh and the rush hour crowd swept Amika into the car. She looked at the sea of faces around her and imagined the effect of a flu epidemic in the megacities of China. What if the Naito family's crimes of the 1940s were just a prelude? What if they were on the verge of unleashing a genocide?

What if they silenced her before she could expose them?

A heavily pierced Japanese teen rose for the door, vacating a seat on the train. Amika claimed it, pulled a sheet of paper from her bag and started to write.

Dear Captain Lindstrom:

She didn't want to telephone him; he would have too many questions she wasn't ready to answer. But someone needed to know the exact DNA sequence she'd put in that virus. Someone other than Jun needed to know her suspicions about what the virus did—just in case. And because she would need help tracking any shipments of D-shikimate, she told him about that too.

A few stops later she exited, walked to a Japan Post office, and mailed the letter to Atlanta. It would arrive in a couple of days. *Perfect timing.*

She left the post office with the grim satisfaction of someone who's just purchased her own tombstone.

At seven o'clock Amika had *not* changed her clothes or freshened up; the last thing she wanted was to make herself more attractive. Now that she had some of Hiroshi's cells and had put the DNA into the amplifier and sequencer, she again wanted to stay as far away from him as possible. The car he had dispatched arrived on time. She looked at it warily as the driver opened the rear door. Black and sophisticated, the European sedan looked sinister. She climbed in anyway. *I have to see this through or he'll get suspicious.*

They drove in silence through the endless traffic, neighborhoods blending one into another. Upscale shops started to appear and the car rolled past the clock tower of Tokyo's famous Wako department store. Amika squirmed in her seat. If Hiroshi was springing for dinner in the ultra-fancy Ginza district, he was going to expect a happy ending to the evening.

Too bad chastity belts went out of style.

The driver let her out and pointed to an ornate, oversized wooden door that had no markings except the number 8, sandwiched between glossy storefronts for designer clothing.

What is this?

The door was not locked. Uncertainly, she pushed it open.

An Oriental carpet lined a softly lit hallway decorated with Impressionist paintings of ballerinas and odalisque nudes. The aroma of roasted meat and rosemary was in the air.

Hmm. A French restaurant.

At the end of the hall, an antique wooden podium, like something from a church. Attending there, a Japanese woman, beautiful, subtle, impeccably dressed in understated elegance. If Amika's slovenly appearance troubled her, she didn't let on.

"Welcome, Dr. Nakamura. Your party is waiting."

Amika followed her through a hushed dining room that seated no more than twelve and then into a private chamber off to one side. The hostess slid a pocket door closed behind Amika as she left.

Amika's chest tightened. Hiroshi lounged on a plush sofa with oversized throw pillows. He wore a slim, dark suit with no tie. His white dress shirt was unbuttoned suggestively low.

He patted the cushion next to him. "You found it."

You disgust me.

With a fake smile, she slinked to the table and filled his glass with the French wine chilling at the table. "I did. Very exclusive place, huh?"

He patted the cushion again. "Very."

She sat down next to him. "Sorry I've been such a wreck."

"Understandable," he said, offering her a glass.

"To the conquest of flu," she said as they clinked their drinks. She took a sip and felt the warmth flow down her throat. He stretched his arm over her shoulders. She could smell his scent.

The pocket door slid open and a waiter presented the *amuse-bouche*, small bites of a salmon mousse.

"So what's this new project you said you're working on?" Hiroshi asked.

She arranged a pillow behind her back. "It's something I started years ago, in graduate school. The data were promising. I gave it up because we were having trouble getting the supplies."

"What were you trying to do?"

"I was studying a chemical that seems to boost the growth of influenza virus. If I'm right, it could make Koga's industrial production of live virus vaccines much more efficient."

"That could save us money."

"And save lives if there's a pandemic when you need to make a lot of vaccine, fast."

"What is this chemical?"

Gotcha.

"Shikimic acid."

He frowned. "That doesn't make sense. Shikimate is used to make a drug that *kills* the virus."

"The naturally occurring form, yes. But the D-form—its mirror image—seems to have the opposite effect."

"Really."

"I did some preliminary studies years ago. I started running the experiments again today."

He leaned over and kissed her throat. She tried not to cringe. *How am I going to get out of this?*

She poured him more wine. *Maybe if he gets drunk...*

Never happen. He's too disciplined.

Unobtrusively, a server placed the first course on the table and exited in silence. Hiroshi turned his attention to the food. With studied effort, Amika made small gestures of discomfort: touching her belly, adjusting her posture, not eating.

Her portion was cleared away undiminished. "Would you like them to make you something special?" Hiroshi said.

"No. I'm not hungry." She pretended to burp.

"I see." He gave a penetrating stare. "I am."

A minute later, steaming plates of *wagyu* beef were set before them. She moved it around and then set down her fork. "I'm not feeling so good and I have to get up very early in the morning."

"You're going to Osaka."

Unwittingly she froze for an instant. "Yes. I only just made plans. How did you know?"

"I speak often with Manami. You think this trip will help your research?"

Shaken by his omniscience, she tried to say something intelligent. "I think so. At least, it'll help me think about how the shikimate process might be scaled up, if it works."

"You could do that without wasting a day. I can get you on the phone with the plant engineers."

Her fake stomach upset was becoming real. "I'd like to see it for myself."

"I hope this isn't a distraction from your primary task. I've told you we need data on virulence."

"Not at all. I've launched that work, too. You know how it is. Best to have two projects going. Otherwise there's a lot of down time in the lab."

He nodded. "I've been meaning to visit the Osaka facility myself."

She felt her eyes widen.

"A surprise visit is always best if the boss wants to see how things are really done on a typical day. I'll join you."

If she'd had food in her mouth, she might've choked. "I plan to leave very early," was her first, lame protest.

"Of course. Even on the *shinkansen*, it's a long trip."

Her mind was spinning. *Can I convince him not to go? Should I even try? Can I get my samples while he's around? He won't follow me around the plant, will he? He'll have his own corporate business to attend to?*

"Don't be so excited about my company," he said sarcastically.

"No, sorry, that's great," she said and shifted her position. "Honestly, I feel kind of sick. Would you excuse me for a minute?"

He waved her away and tackled the beef.

Hunched over, she fled the table and left the private room. She longed to run out into the street and hail a cab, but instead she visited the restroom to regroup. She leaned over the sink and splashed water on her face. Her hands were trembling.

Does he know?

If he wasn't spying on her, he would be by the time the day was over tomorrow. How could she keep up the girlfriend façade for all those hours seated next to him on the train? How could she explain herself if he caught her taking samples at the factory?

I can cancel the trip. Plead sickness tonight and into tomorrow.

But she had a sinking feeling he would change his plans to match hers.

I've got to get into that factory.

Slowly she plodded back to her enemy. His eyes stayed on his plate when she entered the room.

"I have to go home," she said. "I think I might be sick."

He raised his head, jaw grinding as he chewed. A moment of hostility flashed across his face. "I'll have you picked up at 5:30 AM. I expect you'll have recovered by then?"

"I hope so."

He plucked another morsel off his plate. She turned to walk away.

"We won't spend the night in Osaka," he said to her backside, "since that seems to be a problem."

She slid the door closed behind her.

22

Soothed by the serenity of the *karesansui* garden she'd commissioned years ago, the old warrior paused in the moonlight to admire her favorite bonsai tree. The dwarf pine was old, even older than Harumi herself. Like her, the tree was gnarled and misshapen, sculpted into its present form by the slow work of larger forces. It was one of several exquisite specimens in this private outdoor space within the Koga Foundation complex, carved like a tiny, perfect diamond out of the urban mountain of Tokyo.

She had always detested the city and yearned for spaces of nature, places without people. *When we reclaim Manchuria, I will visit the windy plains around Pingfan.* After the Han pandemic, the vast reaches of China would be largely purged of the Han hordes. Vacant cities would beckon the Japanese people who now crowded into Tokyo and Yokohama. They could stretch out, build gardens and parks, create livable environments where young people would *want* to have children.

The Germans called it Lebensraum. *It's time for Japan to take it.*

She settled onto a wooden bench near a massive stone, two meters tall and naturally carved with intricate crevices and ridges. She reached out and touched the rock. Parts of it still radiated heat from the day's sunlight. Deaf and partially blind in the darkness, she took conscious breaths of the humid night air.

Too bad the girl couldn't be turned.

They had certainly tried to stoke a hatred of the Han in Amika Nakamura. First, the unprovoked attack on her and her brother at Uotsuri-shima. Then Shuu's arrest, entirely China's fault. And finally, his death. All the while, Hiroshi and his patriotic friends whispered in her ear. Why the seed of racism hadn't taken root was a mystery to Harumi. During their time together around Shuu's funeral, she thought the Naito family had finally done it, had made Amika a true believer in their cause.

Then the girl had drifted away. Harumi believed the journalist poisoned her. Her great-nephew was more philosophical about it. "Amika thinks too much like an American," he'd said. "Everything is about *her*, her career, her life, her brother. Always the individual. Never a vision for the group." Was that the problem? The girl's ingrained individualism made her blind to collective responsibility? Or was she just too selfish and ambitious to adopt a cause greater than herself?

Maybe. Regardless, it was too late.

From the base of the giant rock, smooth black pebbles were perfectly raked in a pattern like water. *Everything flows. Time, history. We cannot stop the flow, but we can direct it.* Her father and uncle had started dredging the channel that led here. With the help of her nephew and great-nephew, she had dug the rest. The flow of history would wash over the Han.

A light flickered on the other side of the garden. Harumi's heart swelled with affection. *My loyal great-nephew.* The boy was smart, her favorite. He'd mastered sign language at a young age, giving them a special, secret way of communicating that cemented the bond between them. As head of the Koga Foundation, she had persuaded the family to put him in charge of the research institute ahead of his older relatives. He had continued to make her proud ever since.

The lantern bobbed closer until Hiroshi set it down on a stone slab. He grasped the old woman's hands and bowed low.

"*Obaasan,*" he said respectfully out loud. Then he sat next to her and they spoke in sign.

"Did you plant the listening device on her?" the old warrior asked.

"Earlier today. In her undergarments."

A wrinkled grin on her lined face. "You had your hands in her bra."

Hiroshi chuckled. "It was my duty, *obaasan.* You were right. She was using a second mobile phone, not the one I was monitoring."

"And she is still talking to the reporter?"

He nodded. "I heard their conversation this afternoon. They've been conspiring against us. Today Jun Taniguchi revealed that she knows about our bird supplier in Tamba."

"The bird man!" She felt a surge of respect for her young adversary. The investigative journalist was very good at her job. Too bad it would cost her her life. "Does she know why we faked a bird flu outbreak in the home islands?"

"No, and Amika did not guess either that getting the Koga vaccine into as many Japanese as possible protects our people against accidents with the virus. But if Jun Taniguchi has tracked down our bird supplier, she may know a lot more."

"My thoughts exactly," Harumi said. "She's been a thorn in my side for too long. Time to get rid of her."

Hiroshi bowed. "A tragic accident before the sun sets tomorrow."

"And the other weasel in our henhouse?"

"She thinks we're blind, and tries to betray us from her position inside Koga. Stupid bitch."

"She will discover that once you are on a tiger's back, it is hard to get off."

The old woman struggled to her feet. Hiroshi gently took her arm and they tottered around the garden, pausing to sign their conversation.

"She may be a fool but she is a genius in the laboratory," Harumi said. "I have the latest data from our field tests for specificity. *All* the victims have been Han."

"Incredible," he murmured aloud, then signed, "She engineered that virus in a week. We might've struggled for years to evolve an influenza that does that."

"Years? Your forefathers and I have struggled with this challenge since the 1930s. No one knows better than I what a breakthrough Nakamura has made."

"The pintail ducks are flocking at the site," Hiroshi said. "Is the rest of the timeline intact?"

"My agents are on their way to the vaccine factories in Europe and the US. And those dimwitted mandarins running Hong Kong have intentionally silenced any alarms over the human cases. We will be ready for August fifteenth as planned." She gave him a hard look. "The last modification to the virus is your responsibility. We have a virus that preferentially strikes the Han and spares nobler races. It spreads among birds but does not harm them. Now we must guarantee that it kills as many of its susceptible human hosts as possible. This must be the deadliest influenza of all time."

"Of course, *obaasan*. Our virus will make smallpox look benign."

"Do you still think you can get the virulence data from the girl?"

Hiroshi helped the old woman seat herself on a stone platform. "She lies and says she has more experiments to do, but she already knows the DNA sequence we need. Don't worry. I have looked into her heart. I know how to persuade her. Amika Nakamura *will* give us the secret."

"Excellent. With her help we won't need as many logs for testing. Which is good, because *maruta* are not as easy to come by as in the old days."

23

Amika's wake-up alarm served no purpose. Sleepless, she rolled out of bed with a tremor that a cup of coffee did nothing to relieve. She tried calling Jun, again, to get her advice about the Osaka trip, but her friend still wasn't answering. Why? The sick feeling she'd faked at the restaurant had become more real with each passing hour. Like a robot she showered and dressed with no real conviction that she was going to leave the house. Then the burner phone buzzed. Finally, a text message from Jun.

"Can't talk. If you find what you're looking for today we can move. Call me in an hour."

A lot of good that would do. An hour from now, Amika would be with Hiroshi, about to board the bullet train.

It doesn't matter what Jun would say. I have to do this. Shuu, watch over me.

She packed the sterile swabs and other small supplies she would need for testing the factory into a cosmetic bag and hid them under a maxi pad, then stuffed it into her shoulder bag. Then she logged into her Koga account on her laptop to see if the sequencing of Hiroshi's DNA had been finished yet.

The file list gave her cheer. The numerical code for the DNA extracted from his hair follicle was marked "complete."

I've got you now.

She could make a virus to kill him—if she lived long enough.

In the back seat of the hired car, Amika shut her eyes against the morning sun and tried to calm herself for the day ahead. It was hopeless. She was too agitated to even keep her eyes closed. Instead of meditating she stared out the window, letting the tumult of the city hypnotize her.

Wait a sec, where are we?

She didn't know the sprawling metropolis well but she was familiar with the area near the shinkansen station, and this was not it. They passed a sign for the airport.

"Driver, is this the way to Tokyo Station?"

"Not Tokyo Station, Miss. Haneda Airport."

"The airport?" She glanced at the time, suddenly concerned she would miss the train she didn't want to ride. "No—"

"I'm sorry, Miss, I thought you knew. Naito-san changed your destination this morning."

"Are you sure?"

"Yes, Miss. He'll be there to meet you."

She fantasized about a fortunate miscommunication. *I don't show up at the station, he gets on the train without me. I go to Osaka tomorrow, alone, with an iron-clad excuse.*

They bypassed the bustling international travel zone at Haneda and pulled up to the general aviation terminal. Only a couple of people stood on the walkway. The tallest one was Hiroshi.

No mistake, then. We're flying. The knot in her stomach somehow tightened even further. *I have a bad feeling about this.*

Hiroshi, on the other hand, was weirdly bright and cheerful. She was barely out of the car before he forced a kiss on her lips. "Amika-chan, so glad you're feeling better this morning. I hope you don't mind I decided against the bullet train. My time is extremely limited this week. A private jet charter will save us an hour each way."

"A private jet?"

He had the excitement of a little kid showing off. "Yes. Trust me, you'll love it."

She wasn't loving it yet. As much as she'd been dreading the shinkansen ride, the train was a public place. The train would go where it was supposed to. Hiroshi couldn't demand sex on the way there. But a private jet?

What if he suspects?

Determined to keep up appearances, she pecked his cheek. "Sounds like fun. I've never been in a private jet before."

As he squeezed her buttocks, she wondered nervously how "private" it was.

The terminal was cool and and smelled of pine-scented cleansers. Light classical music played from somewhere above. The crowds and chaos of commercial aviation terminals were notably missing.

A growing sense of warning told her she was making a mistake.

I have to talk to Jun. She could call her from a restroom. Almost an hour had passed since the text.

"Potty break?" she said to Hiroshi as he hurried her toward the plane.

"You can go on board. We don't want to miss our takeoff slot. You must've kept your driver waiting while you were making yourself so beautiful this morning."

With that, he escorted her out to the runway where a movable staircase led to the door of a stylish mid-sized Gulfstream jet. Sweat dampened her skin as she climbed the stairs, and she knew it wasn't just the oppressive summer humidity.

A hush descended when the pretty flight attendant closed the aircraft door behind them. The plane's interior was spacious and smartly decorated, with seating for eight people. With the first relief she'd felt all day, she noted they were not alone. In addition to the flight attendant, two suited Japanese men were seated at the rear. Strangers sharing the ride, she thought, as they looked up but did not acknowledge her or Hiroshi.

Hiroshi steered her into a seat next to him at the front. Moments later, the jet was taxiing and within ten minutes they were in the air. Hiroshi was engrossed in reading a stack of papers so she didn't have to grapple with conversation. Everything seemed normal. She relaxed a little, sinking into the luxurious leather chair.

"Tea?" the flight attendant offered.

"Please," Amika said.

"Green, black, or oolong?"

"Green."

"I'll have black," Hiroshi said.

The tea was surprisingly poor quality but was served in a beautiful porcelain cup that felt comfortable in the hand. She gazed out at the clouds and thought about her brother. The weight of her worries lifted but her eyelids drooped as the sleepless night caught up with her. Tea spilled warm on her fingers, and her brain started to feel as cottony as the clouds outside.

Louder and louder, squawking pierced the veil of Amika's sleep. Just as quickly, the sound receded away from her.

Geese. Flying past.

Although she perceived the light of day, she kept her eyes squeezed shut, desperate for a few more minutes in bed. Her mouth felt like she'd rinsed with glue, and her body ached. With a soft spinning sensation she sighed and settled into the pillow.

Aiiii!

Panic hit like a bucket of ice water and she bolted upright. Pain hammered her skull and she collapsed again, rubbing her temples.

The private jet…Hiroshi…

Fragments of thoughts slithered through her mind. She struggled to corral them into cohesion but they were so slippery…

Heart pounding, she lay motionless and tried to get her bearings. She was, indeed, in a bed, double size with a homey patchwork quilt spread over it. Above her, an ordinary ceiling. Four walls painted pale blue. A generic painting of a sunset over the ocean on one wall. An open window with white muslin curtains fluttering in a gentle breeze. Soft light as of morning.

Where? How?

The air was cool and carried a smell of damp earth. Hesitant to trigger the pain in her head again, she stayed horizontal and listened. Songbirds outside. Honking of geese coming closer. The birds' shadows crossed the window as they flew by. Missing: the sound of traffic. No car noise at all, not a single motor passing. No voices. She rubbed crust from her eyes and felt more aware of her own confusion. Her last memory became clear. The flight to Osaka. Sitting next to Hiroshi. Drinking tea.

What did he do to me?

This time she sat up gradually, bracing herself against the headache. She swung her feet to the floor. They were bare and she was dressed in unfamiliar, thin cotton pajamas, faded from too many cycles through the wash. With alarm she noticed she was naked under this light garment; someone had removed both her bra and underwear. Acid burned her stomach, whether from hunger or nausea she couldn't tell, and she had no idea when she last ate. Her shoulders and back felt like she'd been folded in a box.

A bruise on the inside of her left forearm caught her attention. She shivered in horror. There was a needle mark. *An IV. I've been hooked up to an IV.*

Defying the aches and dizziness, she stood up. On a battered oak dresser she found her own shoes and clothes, neatly folded and smelling of a laundry detergent she didn't recognize. None of her other possessions were anywhere in the room.

Surely they went through my purse. They'll have found my virus sampling equipment!

It hardly mattered, though. He already knew. Why else would she be here—wherever here was— rather than Osaka?

As she got dressed, a tremor ran through her. *What does the Naito clan do with traitors?*

There had to be a way out. *Jun Taniguchi knows I was traveling with Hiroshi. When she realizes I've gone missing, she'll contact the authorities. They'll figure it out. There must be a record of where the plane went?*

Problem was, she could've been taken anywhere after the plane landed. But Jun was still her best hope.

Taking deep breaths to try to clear any drugs from her system, she went to the window. Gauzy curtains billowed in her face. She pulled them aside and tied them back. A few mosquitoes clung to the other side of the screen, two stories above some muddy grass. A whiff of manure in the air. Beyond the window, an expanse of meadow with a few cattle grazing, bordered by a pine forest. She was on a farm. In the further distance, a white-capped mountain range.

Where?

She had traveled little in Japan, and this landscape was wholly unfamiliar. The mountains seemed very high, and the population of humans very low. Maybe she was somewhere in the central mountains, or even on the northern island of Hokkaido?

The farm had several other structures. A modern-looking windmill stood nearby, its turbine blades rotating lazily. Far off to the right, a small airplane backed into the wide doors of a hangar building. To the left stood a huge corrugated metal barn with a peaked roof and no windows. The building extended beyond her line of sight to the other side of the house. A short smokestack rose from the barn. White smoke curled from its top.

A jump from the window looked survivable, but she'd never escape with a broken leg.

Abandoning the window, she turned to the small, worn bathroom attached to her room. There was a pedestal sink with rust stains around the faucet, and a shower stall with black mildew in the corners. An old-looking porcelain toilet…

A water-guzzling, oversized, non-electrified toilet.

Not very Japanese.

Could this be a Western-style room designed for tourists? Everything about the style of the bedroom, from the furnishings to the fabrics, was sort of American. On a hunch she lifted the cover off the toilet's tank and turned it over. There was a sticker with a chart of the toilet's features and working parts.

In English.

Bewildered, she replaced the cover.

The door leading out of the bedroom was closed. Gently she tested the knob and was surprised to find the door unlocked. After listening for a moment and hearing nothing, she warily exited into a carpeted hallway. The aroma of fried eggs and miso soup drifted up some stairs at the end of the hall. She gripped the handrail and descended on tottering legs.

When she reached the lower flight, the voice she feared and expected greeted her.

"Ah, Dr. Nakamura. Glad to see you on your feet. You're just in time." Hiroshi stood in a worn but tidy 1970s-era kitchen with scratched Formica countertops and garish lime green cupboards. He held a steaming cup of tea and wore a track suit, looking rested and relaxed. "We're enjoying eggs from hens right here on the farm. Have a seat."

He gestured to a chrome-legged table where a shriveled old woman sat. The woman squinted at her with a severe, judgmental expression that made Amika's throat tighten.

"You remember my great-aunt Harumi?" Hiroshi pulled out a chair with a plastic-covered seat and motioned her to take it. "She remembers you."

Amika wanted to refuse, wanted to make a dash for the door and run, but queasiness forced her to comply. She sat down, avoiding the old woman's predatory gaze. An Asian girl, not more than eighteen years old, scurried to the table. With a bowed head she placed a dish in front of Hiroshi's aunt, then scuttled back to the stove.

Hiroshi said, "Have some rice. It'll help. I recommend the eggs, too. Linqin is generally useless but she does know how to prepare an egg."

With a chill Amika heard the girl's name, Linqin. *She's Han Chinese.* "What the hell is going on? Where are we? You can't—"

"Shh." He put his finger against her lips. She recoiled so he couldn't touch her.

"You don't remember anything?" he said.

"Don't give me that."

He threw a meaningful glance at his great-aunt, who went on chewing. "It's the concussion," he said. "Memory loss immediately before and after is common."

"What concussion?"

"So is hostility and anger, so I'll forgive you."

"*What concussion?*"

"On the flight. We hit turbulence. Severe. Like nothing I've ever seen. Plane dropped like a stone. Your seatbelt failed. You hit the ceiling, hard. We landed at the nearest airport."

Instinctively she touched her head, feeling for a point source for her headache.

"You were in the hospital for a while. When you woke up I convinced them you'd recover better here than there. You asked to be discharged."

"I just woke up now."

"That's what you remember. But it's not what happened."

She stared at him, hatred smoldering in her heart. "Where's my purse?"

"I'm sorry," he said. "Apparently it got left at the hospital. I'll send someone to pick it up tomorrow."

Their eyes locked. The old woman slurped her broth.

Hiroshi sat down and picked up chopsticks. "You don't remember, but I explained to you this charming farm is actually a Koga applied research facility not far from where we landed. Agricultural biotech. We field-test livestock vaccines. On the side, we're experimenting with converting ag waste into electricity. Maybe you saw the smokestack for our cogeneration plant from your window?"

She was willing to believe this was a Koga property, but not the rubbish about an in-flight accident. *Where's my cell phone, you lying piece of crap?*

The Chinese girl set down a bowl of white rice with an egg and a bowl of miso soup. Amika saw no point in refusing to eat and indeed, the food made her stomach feel better. She said nothing; she was deep in Hiroshi's web and would have to wait for his next move. The old woman didn't speak either but made a few hand signs to her nephew, reminding Amika that she was deaf.

I suppose I'm lucky to be alive. If they haven't killed me yet, what do they want?

She didn't really want the answer.

Hiroshi pushed his chair back from the table. "Are you able to walk? I'll give you a tour of the property."

"Let's get on with it," she replied. She needed to know as much as possible about this place. She rose and felt Harumi's eyes track her as she followed Hiroshi out the front door.

They exited to the front porch of a weather-beaten, wood-frame farmhouse. As she'd seen from the bedroom window, they were in beautiful country, expansive and green, framed by distant snowy peaks. A rusted tractor swallowed by weeds stood lonely to one side of a gravel driveway, where two black BMW sedans and a van were parked. A couple of boxy, modular buildings looked like temporary bunkhouses or offices.

The corrugated metal building that dominated the property was now fully in view. This barn was very large, maybe a hundred yards long. A stink emanated from it, a foul but healthy farm stink quite unlike the Skunk she'd encountered on the island.

"Watch your step," Hiroshi said as he pulled the handle on the barn's huge steel door. It moved ponderously until he opened a gap wide enough to step through. "After you."

The smell of manure dominated her impression of the cavernous space. Suspended particles of dust and hay sparkled in sunlight beaming through rooftop skylights. A breeze from giant ceiling fans blew malodorous air across her face. A boardwalk of wood slats ran down the center of the barn. Steel-fenced pens flanked it on both sides, occupied by about twenty large, pink hogs.

"A fine batch of bacon, wouldn't you agree?" Hiroshi said.

"I'm not one to judge," she said.

Pigs, birds, and humans: the three major hosts for influenza viruses. Is it a coincidence that he's keeping pigs here?

She moved gingerly down the boardwalk, wondering if the animals were part of an experiment. The pigs, most of which were sleeping, made soft grunting sounds.

"As you can see," Hiroshi said, "this area has no airborne infection control systems. Some of the work we do requires a higher level of containment."

I bet it does.

They came to a wall. Amika estimated this wall was roughly in the middle, dividing the barn in half. A flashing green LED drew her attention to a security camera staring down at them above a windowless steel door. Hiroshi put his finger on a tiny scanner and typed an alphanumeric code into a key pad. The door unlocked with a click.

"My secret of secrets," he said.

They entered an elevator foyer, with another door opening to the other side of the barn. Not for the first time she wondered what she was being lured into. "What's over there?" she asked.

He pressed the elevator's call button. "The incinerator and power plant. We convert biowaste into electricity." The elevator door opened. "Our laboratories are one level down."

"Underground? Why?"

"Earthquake protection," he said.

I can't believe he said that with a straight face. They're hiding something.

As the elevator slowly descended, her heart beat faster and the dizziness returned. Unlike the second-story bedroom, here there was no way out.

"How do you feel?" Hiroshi asked.

"I've felt better."

"This is a good place to heal. Much quieter than in the city."

"I'd prefer my own apartment."

"As you're about to see, you can experience natural serenity here and still do your work."

Based on the buttons inside the oversized elevator car, the facility had two underground levels. At the first level, the elevator emptied into a single large, low-ceilinged room that bustled with activity.

"Welcome to Koga Scientific's satellite lab," Hiroshi said.

The room was brightly lit, spotlessly clean, and full of high-tech equipment. She recognized much of the apparatus: thermal cycler for PCR, automated DNA sequencer, cell culture hood, liquid nitrogen storage tanks, microarray analyzer. A fully equipped molecular virology lab.

"Our staff here is small but well-chosen." He gestured at four Japanese men in white coats moving around the laboratory. They cast quick glances her way but didn't acknowledge her. "Like I said, you can continue your work here, on both projects. Find the sequences that make influenza more virulent. And figure out how we can use shikimic acid in our vaccine production process."

Her fingers clenched. *So that's why I'm here, and still alive. He wants my data, and he wants to control me while I'm getting it.* She wondered if he thought she believed his cover story about the accident. *Should I play along? Or should I confront him?*

He strolled across the room, pausing to examine what each scientist was doing. She noticed a ripple of anxiety in each of the workers as they endured his evaluation. As she trailed along, they passed an open doorway into a smaller adjacent room. Warm, humid air and a low mechanical rumble poured out. She looked inside. A stainless steel tank, resembling a very large beer keg, stood upright in the center of the room. An assortment of pipes and tubes connected the tank to a console with an LCD screen, then to a floor centrifuge that looked like a top-load washing machine. The apparatus ended with a huge plastic box that held a tank of liquid nutrition for cells.

She recognized the setup. *That's a stirred perfusion bioreactor. Probably a thousand liters of capacity.* It was a completely automated system for feeding and growing cells, and then using the cells to grow virus.

In other words, a production facility for influenza.

She took a sharp breath. Even though she never reached Osaka, she'd found what she was looking for.

They're not using a Koga factory. They're manufacturing the Han agent here. Wherever "here" is.

Underground. In secret.

I have to tell Jun. She pictured the landscape above. How far would she have to go to find a town, if she fled? Which direction?

"Amika, come look at this," Hiroshi said.

With slow steps she joined him and peered at a graph on a computer screen.

"Dr. Juro here ordered the shikimic acid—D form, correct?—and started experiments on boosting virus production. As you can see, it's not working."

"I see."

Hiroshi straightened to his full height. "You must fine-tune the process. I want a protocol in seven days."

"Seven days! That's impossible."

He fixed her in a cold stare. She felt naked as he seemed to probe her thoughts. *He knows I don't believe him, that I betrayed him. He's known for a while.* And in that moment she realized how badly she'd underestimated him. How thoroughly he controlled this situation, and every situation they'd been in together.

Just like that, the game was over. He said, "At the same time, you will provide me with a modified viral DNA sequence. One that makes the flu more lethal in humans."

"Over my dead body," she snarled.

He snapped his fingers. A burly Japanese man who'd been loitering around the lab immediately came and clamped a steely grip on her upper arm. She twisted to pull away. He seized her other arm, too.

Hiroshi strolled to the elevator and the man steered her in his wake. "Dr. Nakamura, I think it's time for us to be honest. For the sake of clarity."

The pain in her head flared and her legs buckled. *Kill me, then. I won't do any more of your dirty work.*

Hiroshi pressed the button for the second level down. "I have a deadline to meet. Do you remember what I told you about August fifteenth?"

August fifteenth. The end of the Second World War. Japan's surrender in 1945. "If it's your birthday, don't expect a present," she said.

"Funny you should say that. It's a very important day for my great-aunt. I promised *her* a present. It's nearly finished. You already contributed the most important part." He waved his hand dismissively. "The rest is—how do you Americans say—'icing in the cake'?"

One level down, the elevator opened with an outward rush of air. Instead of a big, bright room, they faced a gloomy, sterile corridor with doors on each side, like a dormitory. Digital locks fronted each. An antiseptic smell was in the air.

The goon pushed her into the corridor. She wriggled. Her hands tingled, the circulation cut off by his squeeze.

"I'm quite serious about my deadline," Hiroshi said. "You *will* do the science for me, in time."

She tried to condense as much hatred into her voice as possible. "You murdered my brother. And now you want to kill millions of people. I won't help you."

They came to the first door. "You may rethink some of that," he said, peering in a small window at eye level. "I want to show you something."

Amika shook her head but the goon pushed her to the door. Apprehensively she looked through the slit.

An austere room, no windows, no color, no decoration. Harsh unnatural light. A sleeping cot with rumpled blanket. A free-standing toilet next to a steel wash basin. A drain in the center of the concrete floor.

Two Asian girls sitting listless on the floor.

Instantly Amika was reminded of the Chinese girl who worked in the kitchen. These two appeared to be about the same age—under twenty, for sure. Their downcast gazes did not change while she stared at them like animals in a zoo. She wanted to ask but didn't dare. In her heart she knew why those girls were here.

"In some ways, they're lucky," Hiroshi said. "Most girls in their situation end up as sex slaves."

Amika was herded to the next door, on the other side of the hall. Same kind of room. An Asian woman, somewhat older, pale-faced and twisted on the bed. Coughing.

"Don't worry," Hiroshi said. "We use negative pressure to keep the contaminated air inside. And as a Japanese woman, you can't catch it anyway."

More doors, more Chinese test subjects, a couple of them male. Amika's head throbbed. *This is my handiwork. I made the virus.* If Hiroshi thought this callous display would somehow persuade her, he was terribly wrong. *I'll do whatever it takes to slow or stop the Naito family's plan.*

But as she remembered what she'd read about the gruesome horrors of Unit 731 back at Pingfan in China during the war, under the command of Hiroshi's forefathers, she quailed. Would her resolve survive torture?

At least if they brutalize me, I won't be able to work.

They neared the final doors at the end of the hallway. "It's quite simple," Hiroshi said. "Starting tomorrow, every day you do not give me what I want, I will infect another room. The *maruta* you see alive today will be dead within seventy-two hours."

"You're going to kill those people anyway."

"Perhaps."

Of course you are. And even if I could save the Han in your clutches here, they're nothing compared to the number of people who will die in a pandemic.

"Time passing, with each door," Hiroshi said, dramatically pointing from one door to the next until he reached the one before them. "In the unfortunate circumstance that we get this far with no data from you, I'll have to try something different. As you'll soon understand, I cannot use the Han flu on the maruta in this room." This was the first door where he reached to open the digital lock. "That's okay. My aunt has a nice bubonic plague experiment she's been wanting to try."

He typed in a code that Amika tried but failed to see. She held her breath in dread. What was different about this room?

His hand moved to the door handle. He pressed it down and as air whooshed into the negative-pressure room, she heard a sound that she sorely missed.

Cricket song.

The goon shoved her into the room. She stumbled and would've hit the floor except someone caught her.

A whistle momentarily drowned out the cricket as the door squeezed shut and the air pressure stabilized. Trembling, she looked up at the prisoner who held her.

Her knees collapsed in shock. He clung to her so she did not fall.

"'Mika," Shuu said. "Not like this."

24

Body and soul, Amika dissolved in an acid bath of emotion. Her brother guided her to the cell's solitary bed. Blubbering, she sank into his lap, every muscle stunned into weakness.

He's alive. He's alive.

His death was a trick, a cruel and marvelous deception. She touched him and smelled him to prove he was real. He was saying something. All she heard was the sound of his voice. Shuu's voice. Alive.

"Shuu," Amika sobbed.

Her little brother stroked her head. "I'm here."

"I buried you," she said. "You were dead."

"That's what they wanted you to believe," he said.

I believed it. I can't believe this. Am I dead, too?

They hugged and cried. Amika's mind was transported away from Koga and the Naitos and was overloaded with chaotic emotion.

"I'm sorry I dragged you into this," Shuu said.

She cupped his face in her hands. "It's not your fault."

"I told Hiroshi about you, when you needed a job. I should've seen he was a bad man."

"He fooled us both."

"Why do I always screw things up?"

"You don't *always*."

Shuu jumped to his feet. "I do! And then you—"

Over an intercom, Hiroshi's voice interrupted their reunion. "How much do you know about bubonic plague, Doctor?"

Her eyes didn't leave her brother. "It's going to be okay, Shuu. You're alive. That's all that matters."

"I'll tell you," Hiroshi said. "Bubonic plague begins two to six days after infection. The start seems gentle. Chills and fever. Some muscle cramps. Swellings in the groin and armpits follow. They grow and become exquisitely painful."

"I'll take care of you," she whispered.

"If the disease is not treated, black boils will cover the body. Blood and pus will seep out."

Shuu raised his middle finger at the intercom speaker next to the door.

Hiroshi's voice was tight with malice. "Gradually, gangrene turns the skin black. It rots while the victim is still alive, driving him to delirium from the pain. There's vomiting of blood. Lots of diarrhea. It's a mercy if coma precedes death."

"What is he talking about?" Shuu said.

Hiroshi finished. "Unlike flu, plague is a bacterial infection. It's curable if antibiotic treatment is started in time."

The cricket caged in Shuu's pocket cried out in song. Amika wrapped her arms around him and squeezed like she would never let go.

A rush of air as the door reopened. The heavyset goon filled the doorway.

From out in the hallway, Hiroshi's voice dripped with contempt. "Yes, your baby brother's alive. If you expect him to stay that way, come back to the lab."

Shuu gave him a dirty look. "What's going on?"

"He's plotting genocide against the Chinese," Amika said.

"Genocide?"

"Your sister doesn't want to protect you," Hiroshi said.

"That's not true," she said. "He wants me to help him murder millions of people."

"What does that have to do with me?" Shuu said.

Hiroshi sneered. "In four days we will inject you with bubonic plague if she does not produce the data we need."

Shuu shoved Amika away. "WHAT?"

"Please," she said, "you have to understand. We can't do this."

"We?" Shuu said. "Do what he tells you!"

She struggled to her feet. "I can't."

He grabbed her by the shoulders. "I don't want to die!"

"Shuu, I—"

"Just do it, okay?"

The goon grasped her arm and tugged her into the hall. Hiroshi's arms were crossed behind his back. "If you do not finish before we infect your brother, you'll have another day or two at the most as we will give him appropriate antibiotic treatment as soon as your job is done."

"Don't do this," she pleaded.

"If you perform your duties in a timely manner, he should survive. The longer you delay…"

The door to Shuu's cell locked with a click. She twisted to see him through the window one more time but could not. Seeing him, touching him, already felt like a dream. Was there anything from her memory or senses she could trust? She'd walked this hallway only minutes before but now everything had changed. Those Chinese prisoners were strangers, aliens. She cared about them in the abstract, as human widgets. Shuu wasn't an abstraction. He was real. He was alive. And she cared about him more than her own life.

If only I'd taken a dive from that window when I had the chance. If I were dead, Hiroshi would have no reason to torture my brother.

The elevator lifted them back to the laboratory level.

"Your choice," Hiroshi said. "Will you watch your own brother die slowly?"

"Shut up," she said.

He smirked. "Feisty. Like your friend, the journalist. What was her name?"

She flinched. Did he know about Jun?

"Jun Taniguchi, wasn't it?"

"What have you done?" Amika said.

"I didn't do anything. The reports said she committed suicide."

No! Jun!

The tears in her eyes distorted the bright lights of the laboratory. She stepped into the room like a zombie. Hiroshi's enforcer planted himself adjacent to the elevator and crossed his arms.

Hiroshi waved his arm in a gesture encompassing the whole room. "Everything you need is here. The computer has no connections outside this room but you'll find I had your files loaded from your Koga account. You've got eleven hours until lockdown tonight. Make good use of them." He strolled back to the elevator and turned to look at her with an expression so frigid she barely recognized him. "You have one chance at this, Doctor. Don't be clever and give me bogus data. If your data are fake, we'll know within a week. Keep in mind my great-grandfather left a lot of experiments unfinished. My dear aunt is particularly intrigued by his vivisection studies. Performed without anesthesia, of course."

The elevator door closed and Amika collapsed onto a stool. Two other scientists were working at stations around the perimeter, ignoring her. The rhythmic clinking of glass test tubes in a rotating shaker bath was a ticking countdown to her doom. She dropped her head to the countertop and tried to pull herself together.

The dead were living, and the living were dead. No way did Jun kill herself, but if Hiroshi knew about her connection to Jun, then she didn't doubt that Jun had perished. *They probably murdered her before I ever got on the plane.* That would explain why Jun didn't answer her calls.

And if Jun was dead, that meant no one was looking for her.

I'm on my own.

Her options were grim. Escape from this subterranean prison was highly unlikely. She could give Hiroshi fake data to waste time, but that would only increase the eventual punishment. Cooperation was out of the question. What was she to do? Hiroshi knew everything, was controlling everything…

Wait a minute.

She turned to the computer. First she verified that she could not communicate with the outside world. If there was some way to connect or send a signal, it was beyond her technical ability to find it. Then she found her Koga files, clearly labeled. She glanced at the other men in the room. The guard was the only one looking at her. As far as he knew, she was doing exactly what she was supposed to.

Oh please be there.

Heart racing, she opened the appropriate folder and scanned the file names.

You made a mistake, Hiroshi. One, fatal mistake.

The last thing she'd done in the lab before getting on the plane was sequence Hiroshi's genomic DNA.

The sequence information was there.

A cruel sense of purpose calmed her. He had unwittingly given her one more option. A final option, for both of them.

Kill him. Then kill yourself.

For the next eleven hours she worked to, and past, the point of exhaustion. Every hour was critical. She would construct a virus that targeted Hiroshi before they infected Shuu with plague. She would release it—several ways were possible—and then she would commit suicide. Poisons and hazards for that purpose were plentiful in the lab. No one would suspect trouble while she worked; the experiments would be virtually identical to what she would do if she were actually cooperating.

I'll even enhance the virulence of this flu for you, you bastard. It will find you. And it will kill you.

After that, her brother's fate would be out of her hands. At least if she was dead, they would have nothing to gain from torturing him.

By the time a guard escorted her into the elevator she was so tired and hungry she could barely function. As they descended to the prison level she prayed, *please put me with Shuu. If I only have days left to live, let me spend part of them with him.*

They passed the cells of Hiroshi's condemned *maruta*. Her modest wish came true when the guard unlocked the door to Shuu's room.

He was sitting cross-legged on the floor eating dinner from a tray. She dropped to her knees and hugged him.

"All right, all right, I'm fine," he said as she fussed over him, patting his back and touching his hair. "Your dinner's over there."

She sat down with a second tray, still in disbelief that her brother was alive. "They told me you died of influenza, in the prison."

Shuu shook his head. "Never had more than a little fever. The prison doc was in on it. Told everybody I was dying. Then they got their hands on another guy who died. Made him into me. I got out. They incinerated him."

"I saw the body. I can't believe it wasn't you."

"Hiroshi set it all up. Told me I was going to be turned over to the Chinese jackals and the only way to avoid a firing squad was to 'die' first."

She had suffered so much—needlessly. "You couldn't tell me?"

"Had to be convincing. You had to believe it was real. Hiroshi promised me I'd get to see you again, eventually." He circled the small room. "Didn't expect it to be like this."

She reached for his hand. "What is *this*? Do you know where we are?"

"You won't believe it." He shook off her touch and rubbed the bangs from his forehead. "Welcome to Alaska."

Her mouth dropped open. "Alaska?"

How did they get me here? And good God, how long was I unconscious? Most of all she wondered, *what the hell is the Naito family doing in Alaska?*

Shuu pushed his empty tray toward the door and stretched out on the bed. "Since I was dead, they had to smuggle me in. Set me up in a shipping container with enough amenities to get by. I was so damn glad to be getting out of Japan I never asked Hiroshi how he knew how to run a human smuggling operation like that." He slapped a wall that they shared with another cell of *maruta*. "Now I know. He's in the business."

She imagined her unconscious body packed somehow for the trans-Pacific trip. *I'm lucky I survived.*

"Everything was fine when I first got here," Shuu continued. "It kind of made me feel good, not to have an identity. A fresh start. Hiroshi was still back in Japan. The farm was being run by a couple Koga guys. Nice guys. Showed me the ropes, had me doing farm work. I fed the incinerator. I even hauled pig shit and thought it was fun. Can you believe that?"

Amika smiled. "No, I can't."

"They've got a crop duster aircraft here. And chickens. Lots of free-range chickens."

"Why are they here, Shuu? Why Alaska?"

He shrugged.

She chewed on some rice, thinking. Back in Japan the Naito family controlled all the levers of power. Surely they could operate a modest research facility like this in secret somewhere there. Why take the risk in the US?

"I didn't know about this lower level until they locked me up in it," Shuu said. "One day I was part of the crew. The next, I'm in the stockade. They didn't tell me why. Now I get it. Hiroshi's using me to get to you."

"I'm sorry."

"Yeah, well, as long as you do the stuff he asked for it should be okay. You started on it today, right?"

What do I tell him? That I refuse to cooperate and I condemn him to a painful death? She loved her brother but she knew he had a few character flaws. To her, sacrificing their two lives to save millions of Han Chinese was an obvious decision. Shuu might disagree. He had a hard time seeing the big picture. How many times had he done something without considering the consequences beyond himself?

I'm not strong enough to tell him. Let him live in hope. I will carry this burden for both of us. And maybe he will survive.

"Right," she said.

"Good. 'Cause earlier it sounded like you were gonna put those Chinese jackals ahead of your own brother."

She dropped her chopsticks. "Stop calling them that."

"Fine. Just tell me you won't let that plague shit happen to me."

For no discernible reason, Shuu's pet cricket started to sing again.

Her voice cracked. "Of course not."

He stood up. "You take the bed. We need you rested." He kept the pillow and one blanket for himself and settled on the floor.

The mattress was hard and squeaky, and her body ached, but exhaustion drove her swiftly to sleep. In her dreams, cranes spread their wide wings and soared through a stormy sky. Wind-driven rain pelted her upturned face, and a cricket called out in warning.

Hiroshi was not with the men who came for her in the morning. But the old woman was.

It felt like the middle of the night when the door rudely opened. Shuu's cricket chirped and her brother covered his head against the sudden light.

"Back to work," one of the men said as he held the door for her.

The old woman scowled and stared.

"I'll work hard," Amika said to Shuu. "I promise." She wondered if he heard the lack of conviction in her voice.

They led her down the hallway. She shivered when they stopped at the first door. The old woman caught her eye and nodded. The men opened the door, and they all went in.

The two girls she'd glimpsed the day before were huddled together on the bed. They squinted and sat up. One seemed to ask a question, in Chinese.

The old woman opened an insulated bag she carried over her shoulder. Then she snapped her fingers.

Amika's heart beat faster. *Don't make me watch.*

The Japanese men lifted the slight Han teenagers to their feet and wrapped one arm across each girl's chest. The girls shrieked and struggled but the men held them in an iron grip. They tilted the girls' heads back slightly. The old woman produced a small syringe (without a needle) and inserted it into the first girl's nostril. In a swift motion she depressed the plunger, misting perhaps a half teaspoon of liquid into the girl's respiratory system.

Flu. Hiroshi was keeping his word. Each day, another room.

The old woman repeated the action, infecting the second victim.

Stop it! Amika strained against her captor. The Naitos had perverted her own work to make this happen.

The old woman locked her gaze on Amika and held up three fingers. "Three days," she said in garbled speech.

Three days until they come for Shuu.

They released her into the lab.

She put her emotions in a box and focused on the science. The pieces were coming together. Her virus against Hiroshi could be ready tomorrow night. To keep up appearances, she also ran experiments with the shikimic acid. And as she worked, she evaluated every object and chemical in the lab for its potential use as a means of escape or suicide. Methods for self-harm abounded, but nothing offered a way to overpower armed guards and operate the encrypted elevator to get her and her brother out of the building.

Hours later they came to take her back to her cell. As they passed the first door in the hallway she heard a hacking cough.

Even without the enhanced virulence that Hiroshi wanted her to add, the Han agent was claiming a victim.

The grim routine repeated the next day. Shuu pleaded with Amika to save his life. The men came for her in the morning. Harumi infected a Chinese prisoner in another cell. In the lab Amika applied all her experience to hasten the work. She cut corners and skipped steps, rushing to produce a tiny bit of the virus by tonight. The endgame was nigh. The day after tomorrow that horrible old woman would infect her brother with bubonic plague. Amika had to take herself out of the picture before then.

I'll leave you, Shuu. You'll be safer without me. Two more days.

She had never compressed so much work into so brief a span. Despite the rushed and sometimes sloppy technique, she succeeded. Minutes before closing time, she filled a tiny plastic tube with a clear, innocuous-looking liquid. In case she was being watched, she filled several and pretended to put them all in a freezer. One, however, she hid in her sleeve.

How to get it to Hiroshi? She hadn't seen him in days.

If he doesn't turn up, I'll infect the old woman. The virus was designed for Hiroshi's DNA, but quite probably other people shared the same DNA. His great-aunt, for example. *I give it to her, and she gives it to him.*

Unfortunately the virus might affect people outside his family, too. For all she knew, it would kill her and her brother. For herself, it didn't matter. For Shuu, it was a risk she had to take.

"Did you finish?" Shuu demanded when she returned to their cell.

"Not yet."

"Aren't you cutting it a little close?"

"I have one more day."

Shuu's hair was greasy and he'd grown a few scrubby whiskers on his face. He paced the small room, rubbing his temples. "Mika, Mika, I don't want to die."

"Don't worry." She draped an arm around his back. "I'll have the data Hiroshi wants by tomorrow night."

"Promise?"

She swallowed hard. "I promise."

I promise that Hiroshi won't have a reason to hurt you anymore.

The automatic lights in the cell were still off when Amika woke. She felt weirdly rested, as if she'd slept a long time. How long? Underground and deprived of a clock, she couldn't tell. For a while she lay in the dark, listening to the blood rush through her ears. Shuu rustled and sighed. *He's awake, too. It must almost be time.*

In the sensory deprivation of the room, she imagined that time had stopped. That she could stay in this suspended state forever. That her future did not include wrenching choices or personal agony.

"It's late," Shuu's voice said in the dark. "Where are they?"

She, too, felt she'd been getting up earlier the previous days. "I don't know." Was the delay a good thing? Or a problem?

Her stomach churned and she fingered the tiny tube of death in her sleeve. She heard Shuu use the toilet.

Finally the lights came on and the door opened. She blinked and sat up. A different, larger crew came today. Four muscular toughs entered first. Their eyes were all fixed on Shuu.

Her brother backed away with clenched fists.

Hiroshi Naito and his elderly great aunt strolled in behind them. Amika felt a wave of loathing and delight.

"Good morning, Dr. Nakamura."

Pretending to cross her arms in defiance, Amika reached into her sleeve and softly popped open the tube. Hidden from view she smeared the drops of liquid over her fingers like hand lotion.

I must touch them. Aim for the face, but their hands would be good enough.

Hiroshi planted himself directly in front of her, so close that their bodies nearly touched.

Come and get it, baby.

He stroked the side of her head and dragged his fingers down her neck. Using her contaminated hand, she swatted his hand away.

"Don't touch me," she said.

"Where's my little temptress now?" His breath was hot in her face. "You might be clever in the lab but you make love like a dead tree."

Slowly, lovingly, she caressed his face, making a point to touch his eyelid, his nose, his lips. "Yeah, you're right. I'm not very good at *faking* it."

A twitch and slight twist of his mouth told her she'd touched his ego. But this small victory was nothing. She allowed herself a cold smile. Her victim still walked the earth, but he had just become a dead man.

On August fifteenth you can celebrate with your ancestors, you son of a bitch.

He put his hands on her breasts and pushed her. She dropped to a seat on the bed.

"So eager to play the game when you thought you were in charge," he said. "Stupid girl. Such an American. All you see is today and tomorrow, and yourself and your 'dreams'. You want to do everything for yourself. By yourself. You have no idea of the power in community. In family. In *history*."

Shuu had retreated as far as the room allowed. His jaw was clenched and his torso hunched in tension, muscles bulging.

"Your history is your shame," she said.

"The victor writes the villain," Hiroshi said. "The history you've read denies Japan's glory."

"There's nothing glorious about torture."

"How many animals have died for your influenza research?"

"Mice and ferrets aren't people. There's a difference."

"And there is a difference between the Chinese jackals, and the people of Japan." He turned to his great aunt, and his hands fluttered as he spoke to her in sign. She responded and opened a small pouch she was carrying.

"We're running a bit late today," Hiroshi said. "I hope you enjoyed sleeping in. Unfortunately you're going to miss the hours lost in the lab, as our schedule has changed overall."

The old woman pulled out a clear plastic device, about the size of a thick, stubby pen. A spring mechanism was visible inside. Amika recognized it. *An intradermal microinjection device. Tiny automatic needle for injections just under the skin.*

Rather like a flea bite.

Plague!

"Wait—you said four days—"

The big men who'd come in with Hiroshi moved in unison, swooping on Shuu. They grabbed his arms before he got more than half a swing at them.

"Stop!" Amika shrieked. She rushed the old woman. Her contaminated hand swiped Harumi's wiry gray hair before Hiroshi tackled her. Pain seared her elbow when she hit the concrete. Hiroshi straddled her hips. Shuu howled like a caged beast. She struggled, tried to rotate her body to see what was happening. Hiroshi pinned her wrists against the cold floor.

"Sure you don't want some action, for old time's sake?"

"You wish!"

"My aunt has *Yersinia pestis* in there. We've found the intradermal route to be highly effective for establishing disease that mimics a natural infection."

"You're a monster!"

Shuu was cursing. The old woman hobbled toward the exit, her work already finished.

Hiroshi released her arms and peeled himself off her. "In the next day or two at most, your little brother will get sick. Very sick. If you want him to get antibiotics, you'll give me what I asked for."

Ashes, ashes, we all fall down. You, me, her, him. "I need more time!"

"Then let's hope your brother has a vigorous immune system."

"Hiroshi, wait—"

He put his hand on the lock panel next to the door and held the door open for his elderly aunt. After the old woman was safely clear of the room, he turned to his men and said, "Bring her to the lab."

Three of them continued to hold Shuu, sprawled on the floor and struggling. The fourth herded Amika to the door.

"This is your fault!" Shuu's scream disintegrated into sobs. "Just give him what he wants."

She walked out, weighted with grief but resolute.

I know what I have to do.

The final act began.

Upon arriving in the lab Amika washed and disinfected her hands. Then with great mental effort she continued to perform meaningless experiments to cover her true intentions.

Set the stage. Bring down the curtain.

She couldn't let her brother die a slow, horrible death. She couldn't let Hiroshi use her expertise to commit crimes. She couldn't escape from his clutches. She couldn't put a complete stop to his family's plan.

So many things she couldn't do. But one thing she could.

Destruction is easier than creation.

She wished for just ten minutes on the internet. Surely the lab had chemicals she could use to build a bomb of some kind. But she didn't know how.

A poor man's bomb, then.

She was going down and she would take Shuu with her, and as much of the Naito project as she could. Thanks to her handiwork, Hiroshi and Harumi would probably die of bird flu. One of them might survive or other members of the Naito clan might continue the project, but she wouldn't be around to see it. She would destroy as much of the lab and influenza production facility as possible. That would at least slow them down.

I'm going to die in Alaska. I've never even been to Alaska. What a shame. I've heard it's a beautiful state.

Her funereal thoughts led her to wonder once again, why Alaska? Why did the Naitos leave Japan?

I guess I'll never know.

The hours ticked by. She wondered if her parents would learn of her death, or if she would just go missing forever.

She wondered if in the afterlife Shuu would forgive her for killing him a second time.

More immediately, she wondered if her plan would work. Timing—and some luck—were critical. As long as her captors followed their evening routine, which had been clockwork regular so far…

Quitting time approached. She feigned urgency and assembled a packet of fake data to give to Hiroshi. Hidden among her other movements in the lab, she surreptitiously set up a natural gas explosion.

Six gas spigots in the room fueled Bunsen burners and other tools. She went to each of them and turned the handle slightly, ever so slightly, toward the open position. The gas leak had to be so slow that no one would smell it before leaving. Over several hours, the gas would build up. In the dry air, static alone could trigger an explosion. To encourage that, she sidled up to a tank of liquid oxygen and started a tiny leak from that as well.

An explosion or fire would damage the facility but what she really needed was smoke. Within the confines of the underground prison, smoke would quickly overwhelm the air filtration. The cells where the prisoners were kept—where she and Shuu were sleeping—had negative pressure systems for infection control. They sucked in air from the hallway. Even in the absence of catastrophic fire, smoke would concentrate in the cells—and suffocate the occupants.

Better than bubonic plague, Shuu. Believe me.

She wanted to tell him. Wanted his permission. His forgiveness.

Hiroshi took the choice away from him. He's already dead.

The guards escorted her out of the lab and down the hall one more time.

She mothered him and spoke tenderly to him. When the lights were extinguished she put him in the bed and kneeled beside him. She touched his forehead to check for fever. None yet.

A thousand things she wanted to say.

"Do you remember those games we used to play in the dark when we were kids?" Shuu asked.

"I remember making shadow puppets with our hands. But you need a flashlight to do that."

"Yeah. Too bad."

"We could tell ghost stories."

"Right."

Silence, with a conspicuous absence of ghost stories, followed. Eventually Shuu's breathing settled into a regular rhythm with a light snore. Amika curled up on the floor next to the bed. With every breath she wondered if it might be her last. But still there was no smell of gas. Her heart beat as if she were running a race. As hours passed and she couldn't stop imagining what breathing smoke would feel like, she tried to picture Hiroshi's infected lungs swelling with fluid. *I hope you figure out it was me that did it to you.*

Suddenly red light flashed into the room from the hallway. She leaped to her feet. Would Shuu sleep through it? Then a blaring alarm sounded. Her brother sat up, casting the blanket aside.

"What the hell?" he said.

Clang—clang—clang

The undeniable smell of smoke reached her nostrils at last. She sat down on the bed and wrapped Shuu in a hug, trying to be brave for both of them. *At least we're together.*

In the sinister red light she saw smoke seep in around the door. It spiraled to the ceiling, filling the room like an upside-down swimming pool.

"Shit!" Shuu pushed her away and dashed to the door. Smoke streamed in an outline of the door's shape, a giant smoke ring scrambled by the turbulence of his approach.

She expected him to pound on the door, on the electronic keypad. To shout for rescue in the minute or two they had left to draw breath.

Instead he typed in a code and laid his palm against the biometric lock.

The door clicked open.

25

*H*ow...

Amika sat paralyzed on the bed. *What the hell just happened?*

Shuu dashed over and shoved the pillow into her lap while grabbing the sheet with his other hand. He shouted over the alarm, "Cover your face!"

She was coughing now, her sinuses and chest irritated by the billowing cloud. The primitive drive to survive silenced the questions in her mind. She stooped low and moved to the door.

He pushed the door open, unleashing a torrent of smoke that burned her lungs, stung her eyes and blurred her vision. The siren was now exponentially louder. "Follow me," he yelled.

He dropped to the floor and crawled out.

Move! Move!

Out here the smoke was thinner and her eyes cleared a little. As she'd predicted, the negative pressure rooms were sucking in the smoke, leaving the hallway relatively safe for another minute. Shuu scurried to a windowless door just a few yards away.

He unlocked the door. The system recognized him!

She pressed the pillow against her nose and mouth. *It can't be.*

Another digital lock. Another code. Another door opened to her brother's touch.

The last illusion shattered.

He's one of them.

For the first time she saw her little brother as he really was. No more excuses. No more lies to herself. He was, and had always been, a selfish, mean-spirited human being. He didn't have a hard time seeing the big picture.

He saw, and he didn't care. He used people. And now he had brutally used even her, who loved him more than anyone else in the world loved him.

Baby brother, what have you done?

In those few seconds, the smoke thickened. The hallway was a death-trap. Shuu plunged through the doorway, fleeing the suffocating air. Amika followed, gasping and coughing, into a stairwell. Shuu pulled the door shut and sealed the worst of the smoke on the other side. *No negative pressure in here. It's a fire escape.*

Shuu leaped upward two steps at a time.

She hesitated. What about the other prisoners? Soon they would be dead.

Only Shuu could open the doors—and he wasn't going to do it. *I can't help them. But...*

Escape.

If he led her outside, maybe she could get away in the chaos. Tell the world what was happening here. She had given up hope of escape. Now she latched on to it like a bulldog.

She sprinted up the stairs.

No one else was using the stairwell. Two stories up, some smoke collected at the exit. She held her breath until Shuu got the door open. Then they tumbled out together at ground level.

Got to move fast. She spun around, scanning for a way out. They were inside the hog barn above the secret lab, but there were no hogs. Instead an enormous black box the size of a one-car garage dominated the space. They were on the other side, at the incinerator Hiroshi talked about. The fire alarm continued to sound, but not as loud in the huge space.

She spotted only one exit, a door adjacent to the one she'd just emerged from. Unfortunately it probably led to the elevator lobby, not the outdoors. No choice. She lunged for the door.

"Where do you think you're going?" Shuu seized her wrist. She twisted, trying to break free. In the blink of an eye, she was on her knees with her arm bent behind her back.

"It takes more than that to get past a soldier," he said.

"You're not a soldier," she panted. "You're one of *them*."

"Different war. Still a soldier."

"What they're doing isn't war. It's genocide. An American soldier would never—"

He let go of her arm and pushed her to a seat on the floor. "This isn't about America. America doesn't know who its friends are any more."

With every passing second, her hope for escape receded. By now Hiroshi's men would be gathering on the pig side of the barn, to deal with the fire. Was there another way out on this side?

"Politics isn't an excuse for genocide."

"Got all the answers, don't you?" He affected a woman's voice. "Amika Nakamura, such a brilliant young woman. Not like her stupid, screw-up brother."

"I never thought you were stupid."

"Like hell you didn't. You think I'm so dumb I kill people by accident." He pulled a little harder on her arm. "Like I can't even tell the difference between a bottle of tranq and a bottle of antidote."

Oh God. The island. The pathologist was right. It wasn't an accident. "You murdered those Chinese men."

"Don't you see? They aren't men. They're jackals! They attacked the Japanese nation. They deserved to die."

Her eyes searched the room. Wisps of smoke leaking from the fire escape drifted around pipes and cylinders that connected the incinerator to a huge chimney. "Okay, so those three were asking for it. But Shuu, do you realize what the Naitos are planning? They want to kill *a billion* people!"

"They're all the same."

Where did it come from, this casual violence, this hatred of the Chinese? "Whatever Hiroshi told you—"

"He didn't have to tell me. I can figure some things out for myself. It's us or them. They're the sworn enemies of the Japanese people. Their Communist filth runs all over Asia. Them and the Koreans—"

Korea. It must have started while he was serving in Korea. "It's not the Koreans' fault you had a bad conduct discharge. No one forced you to vandalize that memorial in Seoul."

"A memorial to a man who murdered the prime minister of Japan." His voice rose. "Those fancy diplomats from China, crawling around, drinking. Plotting with the Koreans! It made me sick to look at it."

Finally she spotted the exit. She tried to stand up. He shoved her to the floor again. Her brother. A murderer.

It's not too late for him. She reached up and grasped his hands. "You can get your honor back. Help me stop this."

"No. *You* help *me.* Then we can claim victory together. You, me, Hiroshi." His voice took on a wistful, pleading tone. "Why didn't you just give him what he asked for? We should've been such a good team."

She heard voices on the other side of the wall. Coming closer. She gathered her feet beneath her in a squat. "He's using you."

"Yeah? At least he thinks I'm worth the effort. Even if I'm not Miss Doctor Perfect."

"He doesn't care about you. He used you to get to *me.*"

Rage flashed across his face and Shuu's right arm pulled back, winding up to strike her. But he stopped himself, cupping his left hand over his fist.

She sprang from her coiled legs, passing under his arm, struggling to get upright, to run—

His reflexes were faster. Her cheek and ear smashed painfully into the floor. Shuu gripped one ankle, then swiftly pinned both. She sat up, bending at the waist. Blood trickled down her neck.

She'd traveled only a few feet from where she started but the view had changed. Her eyes fell on a misshapen pile, stacked like logs, near the incinerator's feeding hatch.

Three body bags. With person-sized contents.

"Let me go," she pleaded.

The door to the elevator foyer opened. In strode Hiroshi with two of his guards.

Gasping, she kicked with all her might to escape her brother's grip. One leg came free. Arms out across the floor, she tried to drag herself away. Shuu let go of her other leg. She staggered to her feet, lurching forward, desperate for escape. But once more he was too quick. Shuu expertly snared her shoulders, then pinned her arms behind her back.

Her brother's treason was complete. *I wish he had died back in Japan. I wish I never knew the truth about him.*

"The system recorded that you opened the lock," Hiroshi said. "There was no other way?"

"The other way was to die," Shuu replied.

Hiroshi nodded. "Well, there's nothing to be done about it now. Our little game is up." He gave Amika a scornful look. "Not that there was much more to be gained, at this point. You made some very dangerous choices, my dear. I did warn you."

She felt breathless and sick to her stomach. No witty retort came to her lips. Heat radiated from the incinerator. *What will he do to me?*

"The fire suppression system worked. Sensors indicate the laboratory fire is out. Shuu, I want a report on damage. We'll take it from here." Hiroshi motioned to his henchmen to assume custody of Amika.

Shuu looked from Amika to Hiroshi, and to the guard, and back. Was he hesitating?

"All right." Shuu stepped back as the other man grasped her wrists. "I'll see what I can find out."

Shuu left. The guard twisted Amika's arms and significantly tightened his hold, sending pain through her shoulders. Hiroshi crossed his arms and glared at her in silence. She felt her lung capacity shrink with each breath as the backward pull on her arms ratcheted up. What about his lungs? Was her virus there, silently multiplying?

"Here we are." Hiroshi slowly paced back and forth in front of her. "Your brother didn't think it would end like this. He thought you could be turned. I suppose people of weak character can't understand people like you and me."

"Don't put me in the same category with you."

"You're right. Although you do have strong opinions, you're quite easily manipulated."

"You poisoned my brother's mind."

"Not poisoned. Fertilized. The seed was there already. By itself that ridiculous stunt he pulled in Seoul was enough to bring him to my aunt's attention. But when I learned about his sister, the reckless virologist…well, that sealed the deal. We had to have him on our team."

It was as she'd suspected. His manipulation of her went back to the beginning. Before their sex affair. Before the trip to the Senkakus. Before she even left Berkeley.

She spit at him. The saliva landed on the front of his shirt.

He lashed out, striking her across the nose with the back of his hand. Her face exploded in pain and the air left her lungs. Unwittingly her eyes closed and she fell forward, but her captor did not let go. Searing shoulder pain forced her back upright. Warm blood dripped into her open mouth as she tried to breathe.

"You arrogant, stupid, American bitch. I gave you every chance to join us willingly. But you had to make it hard. I surrounded you with my friends. People like Miyashita. Manami. I put out the bait for those Chinese jackals on Uotsuri-shima, to make trouble for your brother. Shuu said you'd come around if we could blame the jackals. You didn't. Fortunately I anticipated that and had a trick planned to get you to make the virus for me." He laughed. "You are genius in that regard. A bird flu that preferentially attacks the Han."

"I want no part in your race war."

"Too late. You're a big part of it already." He reached for her chin and let a drop of blood fall on his finger. Then he streaked it across her neck. "This attempt at sabotage might slow us down but it doesn't change the outcome. I still want the virulence sequence from you."

The only virulence sequence you're going to get from me is the one incubating inside you right now.

Shuu re-entered the room. He saw his sister's bloody face and gave a start. "What happened?"

Hiroshi ignored the question. "What did you learn?"

For a moment Shuu stood frozen. Then he tore his eyes away from Amika and said, "Most of the freezers are still operational. About a quarter of the lab instruments won't power up at all. The rest have burns or smoke and probably will malfunction. Especially in the production room. Looks like we lost the bioreactor. Worse," he paused, "all the maruta are dead."

Hiroshi's face tensed and his fingers clenched. "That will set us back months."

"Can't we still launch on the fifteenth, using the stuff we've got? The boys and I filled and moved virus storage tanks to the hangar yesterday."

"That virus is Han-specific but not as deadly as it could be."

"It'll still take out a good chunk of them, won't it?" Shuu said. "Just load up the crop duster and let nature do the rest."

"I would expect about twelve percent mortality," Hiroshi replied, "but we can do much better. Can't we, Amika?"

"I can't work without a lab."

"I don't think you need a lab," Hiroshi said. "I think you already know the sequence I'm looking for."

She tried not to let her face show he was right. "That's ridiculous. And besides, you can't threaten me anymore."

"You might change your mind when the first buboes appear. I hear the pain is beyond intolerable."

Her lip quivered but she boasted nevertheless. "I can take a lot of pain."

"But can your brother?" Hiroshi made a small flicking gesture with his wrist.

The man at Hiroshi's side took a step behind Shuu, drew a weapon and fired.

Amika cried out as Shuu tumbled to the floor, his limbs stiff and twitching. A crackling buzz came from the Taser in the man's hand. Two wires connected Shuu's lower back to the weapon. He made a soft, animal squeak. Hiroshi dropped swiftly and secured Shuu's hands behind his back with a zip tie.

She strained against her captor, flaring the pain in her shoulders that was probably nothing compared to the electric shock running through her brother.

"Let him go," Hiroshi said.

The Taser went silent and the awkward spasms in Shuu's legs stopped. He groaned and rolled over on his back. "What the hell are you doing?" he said.

"Feeling a little off today? A bit feverish, perhaps?" Hiroshi said.

Shuu pulled on his bound wrists. "You son of a bitch. You told me the injection was fake."

"I may have forgotten to mention that to Aunt Harumi when she prepped the device."

"You're full of shit," Amika said. "You didn't give him bubonic plague."

Hiroshi shrugged. "I was pretty sure you wouldn't surrender the virulence data without a fight. It's easy to ignore the abstract idea of your brother dying. You'd gotten quite used to the idea of him being dead already. But it's something else entirely to be locked in a room with him while he slowly rots to death before your eyes. The *threat* of plague didn't seem sufficient. Obviously I was right."

Shuu got up on one knee. Hiroshi's henchman gave him a roundhouse kick in the head. Shuu collapsed back to the floor.

The lies on top of lies had thrown Amika into an emotional vortex. Fear, anger, worry, shame, regret. Love? Hate? She didn't know what to feel. The only thing certain: She would not help them. No matter what.

"Take her back to the house," Hiroshi said. "I'll be there in a few minutes."

The man steered Amika away from her last glimpse of Shuu on the ground. They passed the incinerator and exited into the cool air, leaving a drip-drip-drip trail of blood from her nose. The light was dim and the sun was low in the sky, as if sunset though it was the middle of the night. The midnight sun of Alaskan summer.

A flock of perhaps fifty ducks roosted on the soggy ground between her and the house. As they approached the front porch, the birds scattered and took flight, a dizzy cloud of squawking and fluttering.

Birds. Crop duster. Finally she figured it out.

Alaska. That's why the Naitos came to Alaska!

One of the biggest hurdles to successfully deploying a biological weapon was dispersal. How do you deliver a disease-causing agent to its target? It was a surprisingly difficult challenge if you wanted to affect a lot of people over a wide area at once.

The crop duster wasn't for spraying people with a mist of virus. It was for spraying birds.

Alaska in late summer was the last stop on the Pacific Flyway. Millions and millions of migratory waterfowl gathered for the final days of food and rest before flying thousands of miles back to their winter homes in North America and Asia.

That's their plan. The Naitos would infect wild flocks with the Han agent. The virus was designed to harm Chinese people, not birds, but the birds could be carriers. They would spread the virus to one another and carry the Han agent virtually everywhere in China (and other countries too). The virus would selectively infect humans of Han Chinese descent, wherever they were.

Undetected, unstoppable, striking everywhere at once. The perfect, nature-designed dispersal system for global genocide.

And no one knew it was coming.

The porch steps and her next prison were a few strides away.

She kicked the man's legs as hard as she could, and wrenched her whole body down and around to break free. He stumbled and lost his grip on her. She shifted her weight, squirmed to one side—tripped, and fell to the wet grass. His knee dug into her back and her arm was once again wrenched harshly backward.

"Get inside," he said.

The sitting room was empty and quiet. The guard turned on a light and pointed at a wingback chair with torn upholstery. "Sit down."

She sat. He held a Taser in his hand.

Upstairs, someone coughed. Perhaps it was the Chinese servant girl. *Perhaps not.* She dared to hope it was the old woman, that flu death was coming to them all.

Minutes later, she heard the screen door creak open and Hiroshi entered the house.

He spoke to the guard first. "Someone's going to have to take the truck into town—"

Then the door flew open again. Two men dashed inside.

"What is it?" Hiroshi said.

"The aerial perimeter sensors are going off. Multiple locations."

He stiffened. "Drones?"

"Looks like it. They're small. Probable surveillance, not attack."

Hiroshi was already moving for the door. "Lock her in the upstairs bedroom," he ordered. "Then get out here with me." As the door closed she heard him say, "Did someone get out the drone guns?"

The guard's face betrayed concern. Amika's heart leaped. Surveillance? *Does someone know we're here?*

She obeyed as he directed her up the stairs. They approached the first open door in the upstairs hall.

The coughing sound was coming from there. Feeble, wet coughs. Raspy, shallow breaths in between.

Amika glanced inside as they passed. An antique four-poster bed. Harumi, the old great-aunt, ashen-faced. Withered body buried under blankets.

Dying of bird flu. My flu.

With grim satisfaction she continued to the room where she'd woken up earlier in the week. The man hastily pushed her in and locked the door behind her. She heard his footsteps as he rushed down the stairs.

As soon as he was gone, she went to work on the door. Tried to jimmy the lock. Tried to break it down with her best imitation of a flying karate kick. The only damage she inflicted was to her knee.

To the window, then. She lifted the pane and looked out in the strange light. Scattered birds flew in the sky. If there were drones among them, she couldn't tell. Pastoral quiet covered the land. The fire alarm had stopped, but smoke still rose from the barn to her left. A few dark-clad men moved about the grounds, carrying bulky, boxy-looking gun things.

One man broke away, running toward the house. He passed the window close enough that she could see who it was.

Hiroshi. Heading for the airplane hangar to her right.

A faint sound began. She cocked her head to listen as it grew in intensity. A distant, deep-throated, choppy rumble. A weird feeling of déjà vu washed over her.

Military helicopters.

Could it be? An attack, a rescue?

Does someone know I'm here?

She leaned out the window as far as she could, craning to see what was happening—

Wait. Why was Hiroshi going by himself into the airplane hangar?

She remembered what he'd said.

Crop duster. Virus storage tanks. Twelve percent mortality.

A distant flock of birds, perhaps disturbed by the approaching aircraft, spiraled into the air. Her stomach knotted. Shuu had said there was virus in the hangar. All Hiroshi had to do was fill a sprayer tank on the airplane and get outside. By spraying or even spilling his cargo on a flock, on a few stray ducks, or even on the ground, the highly infectious virus would spread like wildfire among the huge gathering of birds.

Quickly she made a last-ditch effort to break down the door with her shoulder and a kick. No more success than last time. She looked at the ground below her second-story window. Grassy, somewhat muddy. *Could be worse.*

She yanked up the window sash. Kicked out the screen. Backed her legs out the window. Her belly rested on the sill while she gathered her courage. *One—two—three—*

A mere instant of free fall. A dull thump as she hit the earth. Searing pain in her left ankle and elbow. A fresh flow of blood down her chin.

Breathless for several heartbeats, she planted her right foot and leaped up. The first stride brought her back to the ground. Cursing, she reached for her ankle and probed it with her fingers. Something broken? How would she know? Twisted or sprained, for sure. It hurt to touch it. Then she gently raised herself and applied some weight.

That was pain.

About fifty yards between her and the hangar.

The rapid thump-thump-thump of helicopters was coming closer.

She kneeled in the cold, damp grass. The soldiers could take care of it—if they knew.

If they didn't know and they shot down the plane, aerosolized influenza would go everywhere.

A billion people at risk.

She rose on her uninjured leg and hopped forward, immensely grateful for the strength she'd built up from running. Her bad ankle, suspended in the air, throbbed.

Halfway there, a metallic clang came from the hangar. The broad sliding door started to open.

She stumbled and fell, twisting to protect her injured side. Rose again with a one-legged squat. Lactic acid in her thigh muscle burned. She panted to keep hopping.

The door was fully open.

An engine thundered to life inside.

Too slow. She turned her hops into an excruciating, uneven run. Pain seared her ankle like a knife. If she was making the injury worse, so be it. *That plane must not leave the building.*

A helicopter rumbled on the other side of the property. Over by the barn. She did not waste time to look.

She hobbled along the edge of the hangar building. Bales of hay stacked at the corner. An ancient plow and some rusty gardening tools. She grabbed a spade and a couple of long-handled hoes. Using one as a walking stick, she struggled into the hangar, centering the open doorway behind her.

Hiroshi locked eyes with her from the cockpit of a small single-engine aircraft. The propeller on the nose was about as high as her forehead.

The propeller made one slow rotation. Then it turned faster, and faster, until it was invisible in a whirl of motion.

Time had run out. Only one person stood between the Han agent and the flocks outside.

But how could she stop a plane?

The tools.

Wind whipped her hair. The plane taxied forward. Screaming a battle cry, she threw the spade at the spinning blades with all her might.

With a clang the spade was batted away. Did it damage the rotor? She could not tell. Hiroshi neither veered nor slowed. In seconds the plane would run her over on its way to freedom.

She could see him yelling but the roar of the engine drowned out all sounds.

She planted her feet, raised the two remaining tools and pointed them like lances at the propeller.

I'll see you in the spirit realm, you bastard.

26

"NO!"

Another voice. Something collided with her. Not the plane. The hoe went flying. She fell. Hit the concrete elbow first. Daggers of pain stabbed her twisted ankle.

The propeller passed over.

She had to stop it, somehow. But a heavy weight pinned her down. Pushing herself up, her hand slipped on the floor of the hangar.

Blood.

An airplane wing now overhead. She reached as if to snag it and hold it in place.

Her hand touched hair instead. Someone's head. A body on top of her.

Shuu!

In one panic-primed instant, she took it all in. Somehow he'd come to the hangar. Then he knocked her out of the way of the propeller.

Saving her life.

The price: a hefty chunk of his right chest where the propeller tip must have caught him.

And Hiroshi's plane headed for the door.

Desperately she struggled to untangle herself and pick up one of the hoes, to toss it at the plane in a last-ditch effort.

Then she uncovered the handgun.

Shuu had arrived armed.

The grip was slick with his blood. Still sitting on the floor, she held the gun awkwardly with both hands and pointed it in the general direction of the crop duster.

At least it was obvious where and how to work the trigger.

She squeezed it. The weapon's recoil threw her back. Her elbow struck the hard floor again. She sat up and braced herself this time. Squeezed. Again. Again. Again.

Twelve times. Then the gun fired no more.

The shield over the cockpit was splintered. The plane drifted right as its engine sputtered. The propeller slashed into the edge of the corrugated steel door. It all came to a halt at the threshold. Jarring silence settled over the hangar.

A whisper. "Mika."

She dropped the gun. Her legs were still pinned under her brother's mangled body. His head lay at an awkward angle in her lap.

"Shuu." His chest was ripped open, the broken ends of ribs sticking out above the bloody tissue of his torn lung. What could she do? "Hang on. They're coming."

He blinked. "Sorry."

"No…it's okay." She stroked his hair. "I—"

She meant to say, *I understand*. But she didn't. How her beloved little brother had become this person was beyond comprehension.

Outside, the sound of gunfire drew nearer. Even if it was US military, they weren't going to be able to save him. As the blood pooled beneath them, she doubted Shuu would survive longer than another minute.

I may never understand. But that's not what matters now.

She leaned over and kissed him. "I forgive you."

His eyes no longer blinked. Her eyes went blind with tears.

I love you, little bro.

Oblivious to the gore, she wrapped her arms around him and whispered, "I'll protect you." *No more Hiroshi Naito, no more conniving ultranationalists to lead you astray.*

You helped me stop him in the end.

She raised her head to look upon the wreckage of the crop duster.

The cockpit window burst into pieces that went flying and crackled as they hit the floor.

A leg appeared, then hips. Hiroshi clambered out and stood on the hangar floor.

He saw her.

Her former lover's face was speckled with bloody cuts and bore an expression of raw hatred. "I'll kill you both."

How many times could she die today? With her brother dead in her arms, she laughed at Hiroshi's threat.

"Go ahead. I already killed *you*."

He marched toward her, not hampered by any apparent injury. Adrenaline surged in her veins. She dragged herself out from Shuu and got up on one leg.

"You think I wasted my time here?" she taunted.

Hiroshi bent over and picked up the spade.

She hopped toward the rear of the hangar. "A special flu, just for you."

The rhythm of his steps broke.

"But I see it likes your precious aunt, too."

He raised the spade like a baseball bat. "YOU!" he roared.

She reached the wall. Nowhere left to hop or run. She fell into a crouch and pointlessly covered her head with her arms. *Let it end, then. We all die.*

More gunfire. Closer still.

She waited for Hiroshi's blow to fall.

Then the spade clattered on the floor. She looked up and gasped. Only a few feet away, Hiroshi sprawled face down in a deepening puddle of blood.

Beyond, silhouetted against the light of the midnight sun, a group of humanoid figures clumsily hastened into the hangar. They were covered head to toe in camo-green suits and their faces were concealed by respirators.

They also carried rifles. She raised her hands above her head, recognizing American soldiers in full biohazard protection gear. They fanned out around the hangar.

"There's a virus," she sputtered. "In the plane. Don't let any birds—"

One of the soldiers rushed to her and dropped to one knee. "We know, Dr. Nakamura. You warned us what we were getting into."

The voice was distorted by protective gear but it sounded familiar. She tried to see the face behind the plastic face shield. "Captain Lindstrom? From the CDC?"

He gently laid a fat rubber glove on her arm. "From the US Army," he said proudly. "Temporarily on loan to the CDC. Thanks for the letter."

The old warrior had much experience with death. She knew it was coming for her.

The fever had taken hold of her that afternoon. How many times had she experienced fever in her long and painful life? It was nothing. But the cough was a problem. Her scarred lungs had no capacity to spare.

Last evening after a very small dinner for which she had no appetite, she had retired to bed. Hiroshi, dear boy that he was, had made sure she was well taken care of. He offered to drive her the many miles to the nearest hospital, but they both knew their presence would create a security risk. Let me rest, she'd said. In the morning we can decide whether I should return to Japan at once.

Hiroshi promised to have the jet ready.

Long before morning, a rumble interrupted her fitful sleep. As she struggled to sit up in bed, even in her deafness she felt it in her core. Helicopters. Her shallow breaths came faster and she wobbled to her feet.

The Naito family did not have any helicopters in Alaska.

She prayed her great-nephew would live out what she had taught him. *Do not seek first to save yourself. Think of the mission. Achieve honor through sacrifice. The way of my father.*

Shivering, she stumbled into the hallway and to the stairs.

The rumble changed. Now there were explosions, strong enough she sensed them with both belly and ears.

Gunfire.

In her fevered mind she saw her family, her mother, her dear brother Akihiro. She felt the explosions at Pingfan and saw the dust and rats—she remembered the rats—and gunfire. Mother's brains blown out, scattered on the dirt. The baby...

Akihiro, I have always served the Emperor. I will join you at Yasukuni.

Downstairs in the sitting room, one of the Koga men crouched at the door. His head turned as something sailed into the room.

A flash of light as bright as a uranium bomb blinded her. And a bang so loud the old deaf warrior heard it clearly.

Then Harumi heard and saw no more.

Amika quickly summarized everything she knew about the site: the underground lab, the Chinese captives, the old woman, the fire, and of course the Han agent in the sprayer tanks of the damaged aircraft nearby. She kept one detail to herself. The soldiers were implementing a containment protocol to avoid accidentally sparking a pandemic from the heavily contaminated site. Every person at the farm, alive or dead, would be treated as a biohazard.

They didn't need to know what she'd done to Harumi and Hiroshi Naito. Her custom-made virus would die here along with the Han agent.

Lindstrom supported and half-carried her outside the hangar into the early dawn, passing Shuu's body on the way. Shadows from a flying flock of cranes chased and then overtook them. More soldiers delivered a plastic-sheathed isolation stretcher, designed to transport contagious patients. She slipped inside. It was like being trapped in a Ziploc bag. But it felt warm, and safe. She closed her eyes as the stretcher bobbed up and down on its way to the helicopters. A long stay in quarantine was in her future. She would have plenty of time for regret, and to think about how to start anew from the shattered remnants of her life and career.

Now was the time to mourn.

She wept as the stretcher slid into one of the helicopters, which soon lifted off and carried her away.

THREE MONTHS LATER
ATLANTA, GEORGIA

On her first day at the Centers for Disease Control, Amika's new boss Ed North said he hired her because he liked to keep his friends close and his enemies closer.

Admittedly she wasn't very good at reading people, but she thought he said it with a mischievous grin.

I can work with this guy. Which was lucky, because she didn't have a lot of options. If she was toxic to employers before going to Japan, she was positively radioactive now. She didn't know why Lindstrom had gone to bat for her. Sure, he'd successfully argued that nobody on the planet understood the molecular details of pandemic influenza better than she did. But he'd also advocated for her character.

Maybe he just believed in second chances.

I won't throw it away.

The micropipette tool felt comfortable in her hand as she measured and mixed chemicals for her experiment. It was good to be back at the bench.

With a laugh that echoed down the hall, Michael Lindstrom entered the lab. He shook hands with a coworker, then came to Amika and handed her a small bottle. "Special delivery."

The label on the bottle read *D-shikimic acid.*

"You know I don't actually have any use for this," she said. "I tricked Hiroshi into ordering it only because it's such an unusual reagent."

"That's what you said in your letter. We didn't purchase this. After you disappeared, we were trying to find the Koga facility. I was working with the people at the company that sells this stuff. Somehow, in the process of helping us track the shipment to Alaska, they mistakenly shipped some to us, too." He tapped the bottle on the bench top. "It's been sitting on a shelf ever since. Keep it as a souvenir."

"I will."

With a smile, he touched her shoulder and left the room. Like a brother, she thought wistfully.

The Koga facility in Alaska had been neutralized and decontaminated. Fortunately influenza viruses weren't particularly hardy in the environment. By now, any infectious threat in the soil or structures was long gone. She closely watched the global influenza reporting networks. No one detected new cases of the Han virus.

Hiroshi Naito and his great-aunt Harumi were beyond the reach of the criminal justice system. Hiroshi, of course, had perished in the hangar. The old woman died of influenza the day after the Alaska raid. Amika heard that Hiroshi's father had denied any knowledge of the Han plot or the murder of Jun Taniguchi, but an investigation in Japan might yet lead to charges against members of the Naito family and others. Captain Miyashita of the Japan Coast Guard had fled the country.

She sighed and turned back to the solace of work. During the two weeks she spent isolated in biohazard quarantine she'd thought a lot about science and the role of scientists. For her, science had always been about winning personal acclaim. But the quest for glory had blinded her to ethics. Now she knew that some knowledge was dangerous, that science did not exist in a moral vacuum. Could she find another reason to do what she did?

I'll never reveal what I learned about flu virulence.

But another scientist might follow the same path she did. The world needed to be prepared.

A universal flu vaccine. Effective not only for one season against one flu virus, but giving immunity to all influenzas. That's what we need.

That's what I'm going to do. As part of a team.

As she rebooted her career she vowed no more selfish, solo science with an eye on the Nobel. What mattered was to do work that contributed to the common good, like the universal flu vaccine. If the project succeeded, no single researcher would get the credit, and all of humanity would benefit.

Because the power to create a Han agent, or something similar, was still out there.

THE END

Technical notes from Professor Rogers

As with all my novels, science in *The Han Agent* is based in reality.

Influenza Virus and Gain-of-Function Studies

The influenza virus, or flu, is one of the two deadliest viruses in human history—and we've eradicated the other one, smallpox. Why can't we get rid of flu? The virus keeps changing, and unlike smallpox, influenza isn't limited to humans. Pigs and birds also get the flu. Inside these animal reservoirs, influenza viruses can shuffle their genes and emerge with a fresh disguise that our immune systems don't recognize. Such an "antigenic shift" causes a global outbreak (a pandemic) which can kill tens or even hundreds of millions of people.

Smaller genetic changes happen in flu viruses on a regular basis. That's why a new flu vaccine has to be made every year, and why you can get sick from influenza more than once in your life. Scientists are constantly monitoring flu viruses around the world, watching for genetic changes that might herald the birth of a pandemic virus. But how do they know which genetic changes to look for?

In 2011, two groups of scientists performed experiments on what it takes for a bird flu virus to "learn" how to spread through the air from one mammal (ferret) to another. This "gain-of-function" research sparked a global controversy. What if the newly empowered virus escaped the lab? Were these scientists providing a blueprint for a terrorist to create a bioweapon? For sixty days, all work was halted, and the scientists were forbidden to publish their data.

After much discussion and media attention, the papers were published later in 2012. By January 2013 regulatory agencies had put appropriate guidelines in place and the moratorium on gain-of-function studies ended.

But perhaps it should not have…

If you're interested in influenza, I highly recommend *Flu: The Story Of The Great Influenza Pandemic of 1918 and the Search for the Virus that Caused It* by Gina Kolata.

Molecular detail: In *The Han Agent*, for the sake of simplicity I refer to flu virus DNA. In reality, influenza has a genome made entirely of RNA.

Can a virus be used to commit genocide?

I'm not the first novelist to use the idea of a targeted bioweapon in a plot. For example, Frank Herbert of *Dune* fame wrote *The White Plague* in which a renegade scientist creates a deadly pathogen that kills women. Is it merely imagination to think a virus could be designed to selectively kill a particular person or group?

Unfortunately, no. Advances in genome science and gene editing make it increasingly likely that a microorganism could be designed to assassinate an individual. A November 2012 article in *The Atlantic* by Andrew Hessel, Marc Goodman, and Steven Kotler called "Hacking the President's DNA" explores this possibility in depth.

Creating a genocidal virus like the Han agent would be a bigger challenge. In order to target a particular ethnic group, members of that group would all have to share a unique genetic feature that could be exploited. Such a feature might not exist, and even if it did, it's unlikely the feature would be limited to one group. Humans have interbred so widely that although ethnic groups may be enriched for particular DNA markers, such markers are typically neither universal nor unique to that group. If the perpetrators were willing to accept these limitations, an imperfect ethnic bioweapon could be made.

https://www.theatlantic.com/magazine/archive/2012/11/hacking-the-presidents-dna/309147/

Other notes

Contraceptive vaccines for wildlife; Skunk; Yasukuni Shrine and contemporary Japanese ultranationalism; the Green Cross blood scandal and its connection to Unit 731 officers; the Ahn Memorial Hall in Seoul; and the Sino-Japanese conflict over the Senkaku Islands are all completely real.

Unit 731's wartime crimes against humanity and the aftermath are chronicled in nightmarish detail in *Factories of Death: Japanese Biological Warfare 1932-1945 and the American Cover-up* by Sheldon H. Harris.

Acknowledgments

I would be lost without the Warp Spacers critique group: Judy Prey, Stephen Prey, Lee Garrett, Dennis Grayson, Christian Riley, Jane O'Riva, James Czajkowski (aka James Rollins), Chris Smith, Caroline Williams, Chris Crowe, Leonard Little, Sally Ann Barnes, Jesse Cox, and Tod Todd. Thank you, Spacers, for shepherding me through the many, many iterations of this novel.

In memory of Scott Smith

Educator, writer, and Christmas decorator *extraordinaire*

A good book speaks to you, but it can't talk.

Spread the word about author Amy Rogers and her smart, science-filled thrillers. Tell a friend, share on social media, post a rating at GoodReads or your favorite online bookseller.

Book reviews are solid gold for authors! You don't have to say anything fancy for your online review to help another reader discover *The Han Agent*.

Learn more about the author at AmyRogers.com

To invite Dr. Rogers to speak at your book club or other event: Amy@AmyRogers.com

If you enjoyed *The Han Agent*, you might like other titles published by ScienceThrillers Media.

ScienceThrillers Media specializes in page-turning stories, both fiction and popular nonfiction, that have real science, technology, engineering, mathematics, or medicine in the plot.

Visit our website and join the STM mailing list to learn about new releases.

ScienceThrillersMedia.com
publisher@ScienceThrillersMedia.com

About the Author

Amy Rogers, MD, PhD, is a Harvard-educated scientist, novelist, journalist, educator, critic, and publisher who specializes in all things science-y. Her novels use real science and medicine to create plausible, frightening scenarios in the style of Michael Crichton. Formerly a microbiology professor, she is the founder of ScienceThrillers Media and runs the ScienceThrillers.com book review website.

Learn more at AmyRogers.com

Twitter: @ScienceThriller
Facebook.com/ScienceThrillers